Love and Lust

L.R. Claude

I felt sick to my stomach, like a herd of wild bison had trampled me and if I had eaten anything, I would have vomited it all up on the freshly mopped floor. I let the tears stream down my face as I encouraged Roger to keep telling me everything. I already had the pieces and it was clear that James was waiting to leave me for this other girl and was making arrangements with a lawyer to do it. Roger showed me some images of a young pretty redhead, I didn't recognize her but she looked to be in her mid-twenties at best.

I was destroyed. It was obvious that my marriage was over and there was nothing I could about it. I wanted to know how long it had been going on, how long he had been sleeping with this slut; I wanted to know more about her but all Roger could do was raise his hands that he didn't know many answers. Roger agreed to following James for two more days and that he'd let me know what he found on Friday. I did my best to swallow down the lump in my throat and not let the kids see me upset as I tried to ready them to leave. I was furious, how could he cheat on me? Roger told me that James was leaving work mid-day and then meeting up with the girl for lunch, disappearing for the rest of the afternoon together. I was beside myself, the man that stood across from me and vowed to love me and only me forever had been screwing someone else.

I couldn't stop thinking about James screwing some twat. I imagined going down on Ben right after he screwed Lisa to taste her on him but the fact that I let James into me and he might have had the slime of some strange snatch on him made me feel dirty. How many times had James wasted all of his sex energy on some ho and passed up on making love to his wife, or worse, had he perhaps been flirty texting this chick all night and when he was finally aroused enough was he sliding into me while thinking about her? That son of a bitch was boinking some bimbo while I was at work and our children were at school, maybe it meant he wasn't tagging Kaylie but there was no way to be sure.

My rage was immense, I couldn't deal with the tight chest and I felt ill about everything. I thanked Roger for his diligence and looked forward to catching up with him again on Friday for the final payment and report before the weekend hit. I spent half of the afternoon chasing the kids around the park. My legs shook and I couldn't keep anything down that I tried to eat but I kept a brave face for them. I was miserable. I should never have met up with Ben, or maybe I should have kept him if James was doing to divorce him, now I was without both of them and feeling like the biggest ass in the world for having hurt him. It was nice to watch the kids play until I had to drop them off and go to work.

It helped to go to work to not be home when James arrived, I don't know if I could have kept my calm and not killed him right away. I just pictured him smelling of that whore and coming into our home where our kids sleep. Gretchen could tell there were problems as my hands trembled and I couldn't focus enough to keep a conversation going most of the afternoon. I felt faded and oblivious to just about everything going on around me both that night and a majority of the next night as well, they both passed painfully as I tried to keep my focus on waiting to hear about what was happening with my husband while he was skipping out on work.

I got a text from James around midday Friday as I was making plans to meet up with Roger that he was working late that night, he never worked late and if anything, lately he was hardly working at all. I texted Roger in a hurry, he needed to try to find out where the hell James was and to hurry up and find him. I couldn't help my rage, I was finally in love with my husband and I wasn't the only one. I feverishly texted Roger to find James because I was done with everything and wanted to have enough proof to call my own lawyer and keep from getting blindsided. My head was spinning, my world was crashing down around me and it was taking my breath away.

Erin called me while I was trying to keep tabs with Roger, I was frazzled and tried to listen to her but my mind was somewhere else. I tried my best to be sympathetic to my friend but I was also insanely distracted with everything that was going on and it was dizzying. Erin was having a hard time and asked if I could meet her at the Arsenal Hotel bar where our kids could play at the guest playground in the fenced in area and we could sit and talk or maybe even have a drink. I was a nervous wreck; pacing and sweating, I even thought about buying a pack of cigarettes hoping that maybe it would help to calm me down, but I decided that I didn't want my kids having that memory of me.

I packed up the kids and made the twenty minute trek to the hotel. Out of courtesy I texted James that I was headed out for the afternoon and we'd catch up later sometime. I knew that James wasn't at work and now he knew I was out driving around. I wanted James' ass to pucker and maybe the interrupting text would ruin his pathetic cheating time. The hotel is just a few stories and is usually used for conferences or weddings so it wasn't hard to spout a bogus room number to get passed the front desk and take the kids to the playground they had for the families.

Erin looked like she hadn't been sleeping very well but she was dressed nicely and even had her makeup lightly done to help hide her puffy eyes. I tried to keep my head on my shoulders as I began to tell Erin about Ben and about James. Erin sat with her mouth hanging open and her eyes mostly fixed on me with the occasional glance at the kids, I needed her to listen. I knew she called me so that she could vent to me and cry about missing Charlie but she sat there with her mouth hung open as I described Ben and the things we had done. I went into a fury over James and his cheating ways when I was tapped on the shoulder.

"Ally" I heard a voice from behind me. I spun wildly to lock eyes with, Roger. Everything in my vision began to blur with a white hot rage that could set the Spanish Flu loose in New York and not think twice. "James has him a hotel room, here" Roger spoke. I jumped up to leave the kids to play with Erin's and I stormed inside to find a clerk to give me directions to his room. As I stormed Roger kept up with my brisk pace while telling me that James had spent the morning getting a massage and running around through appointments, including to the lawyer once again.

I pieced it all together that he was at the hotel with the whore, he was having his good time and was going to start the divorce next week so we'd have all summer to finagle living arrangements before the kids started school again. I left Erin behind with the kids before she had a chance to talk and I was ready to turn that hotel inside out. The clerk looked up the room because I was the wife and I demanded to have my key. I was too impatient to wait for the elevator so I stormed up the stairs to find the room on the second floor. I nearly kicked the door in when I barged through.

The bed was covered in rose pedals and there was a bottle of champagne on ice in the corner. I glanced through the dimly lit room, the bathroom light was on and illuminating the long wall of the room and making small shadows glare off the bent petals spread out on the bed. I quickly stormed through the bathroom door hoping to catch James. I kicked the door as tears flooded down my cheeks; I held my breath as my lungs burned from rage coursing through my body. The door slammed open to reveal an empty bathroom with bright white lighting overhead. James' absence baffled me.

"He's downstairs" Roger spoke up, he stayed hot on my heels until I got the room number from the clerk and began running and left him behind, that was when he noticed James sneak in through a door off the lobby, just barely missing me. There is no real way to measure how hard someone cries, to say I was balling was an understatement, I was frantic and out of control, there was no stopping me either. To say buckets of tears were streaming from my face is also an understatement, the top of my shirt was wet from crying and my sinuses hurt from snorting in hard to keep from snotting all over while charging up the stairs. I was huffing and puffing trying to keep some breath in my chest as I turned back around and charged back down the stairs.

I charged into the door Roger pointed towards and I readied for blood. I was enraged, my heart beat like bombs exploding and it would take the building falling down around me to stop me from killing James. There were people in the room as I scanned looking for James, it was hard to find him through the rage and tears at first. I found him standing and talking to a few people, including the fiery red-head I saw a picture of. I lunged to tackle James. My fury was out of control, I screamed and shouted and spat and kicked and flung my hands as crazy as I could to make sure that he would never get up again. I was done, all of my futile attempts to force myself to fall back in love with my husband, or my fighting to stay away from Ben and even the heartache of leaving Ben was all for nothing, I was getting divorced and my family ruined anyways.

I felt people pull me off immediately once we landed on the ground. I swung thinking that the red-head dared to touch me; I was going to kill that bitch too, first. I was ripped from the floor to come face to face with Laura, James's mom. My head spun even more as my heart pounded in my ears, blocking out all other sounds. I was dizzy and couldn't in the world figure out what the hell was going on. I ran out of breath from screaming and crying to catch on that Tom, James' dad, had a hold of me around the waist as I was sitting on him, sitting on a chair. Erin came rushing in with all of the kids in tow while Roger was putting his hands up trying to calm the situation down.

Tom pulled me back a bit to sit on a chair at a table, my chest heaved up and down with mighty breaths as I chewed on my cheeks and struggled to fix my blurry eyesight. We were in a smaller conference room but a room nonetheless. I couldn't figure out what the hell was going on. I was feeling overwhelmed and with everything rushing I couldn't stop the room from spinning around me. Erin ran to hug me and as I continued to feel sick her beginning to cry made me take stake of what was going on around me. I saw Laura and Tom, Erin, our kids, her kids, and even Kaylie our babysitter, was he plugging her too? Did James sleep with Erin, why is everyone here and how can I get them all to stop staring at me while I still cry harder than I ever have in my life.

Erin hugged me tightly until I calmed down enough to begin to hear things going on in the room around me. "Honey, your folks are on the way, just keep your mouth shut and listen." I wanted to begin vomiting, I wanted to spew questions because I was so lost and I couldn't understand anything going on. James pulled up a chair next to me and nodded for Kaylie to take the kids out to the playground to play some more. Tom and Laura pulled up chairs and Erin sat behind me to wrap her arms around me. Roger was still saying "whoa whoa" and was trying to also get a handle on everything going on.

James introduced himself and then it was Rogers' turn to explain why he was there. I couldn't see the red head so she must have been behind me. "I have cancer" James spoke up. Laura began crying and Erin began sniffling again. I couldn't understand what I was hearing, none of it made sense, I still couldn't figure out who was saying what as the room still spun around me. "But the cheating, the ducking work, the steroids, the the he" I began to ramble. Erin kissed me on the cheek and hugged me tightly, "he's dying." I couldn't piece everything together. I didn't understand what the cheating had to do with him dying or if he was even going to die or what the hell he was talking about.

"The woman you are asking about is named Yvonne, she is a dance instructor that has been teaching me to dance so I can dance with you for our last wedding anniversary, tonight." James began to talk. Everything just blurred to more white noise for a moment while I tried to process. James told me that my parents were on the way as was Gretchen from work. James had spent weeks trying to figure out

True love should be a right to anyone, it cannot be forced or faked and I truly feel sad for those that have lived without it.

.

Love and Lust

Every girl dreams of that love that takes a twinkle from your eye and places it into the heavens for the entire world to see for a thousand lifetimes, this is nowhere near that kind of story. This is hardly a story, more of a memoir so I can relive it all again and again. When the lonely nights call I want to be able to slide my fingers between the pages and take myself right back to where I was, the bed, the couch, the porch, anywhere where he had me and we had each other. I know that anyone that knows me would surely die if they knew this was what I kept hidden but my shame has given way to skin flushing lust and a need for the animalistic things I have done.

Growing up I was always told that lust gave way to love, that the deep carnal cravings for a boy would lead to marriage and within marriage my lusts would turn to love, to have children and through kids, mortgage, car payments, and time, that our love would compound. Here I am, forty-one and a stranger to myself. *BRRRRP* (farting noise) it's hard to confidently say my lust turned to engulfing love for my husband; he's the one farting in his sleep right next to me. I know I agreed for better or worse when I said my vows but his latest apnea test suggests a c-pap machine is on the way, it's one of those Darth Vader contraptions that make a sucking noise all night, if that thing shows up in my room I'm done.

My husband James and I married eighteen years ago, jeez I can't believe it's been that long already. Together we have a ten year old little boy, he was the light of my life and now he's my tough little hockey player even though he still cries for me when he gets checked too hard. James and I also have a six year old little girl, we are the perfect family, a boy, a girl, big house, new cars, and a dog all packed neatly into the tighty-whities of suburbia. I jog most mornings as the sun comes up; it's tranquil and pretty for those forty-five minutes of bliss before I return home.

I run passed the gladiolas lining the drive way and up to my slate blue home with black shutters, it looks peaceful from the street. My gold handle opens with my push and just beyond the door is my daily routine of hell covered in chaos and sprinkled in monotony. I jog to fight off gravity and age, my ass sags, my hips have spread, and my once full B-cups are now soft A's while my nipples no longer point straight ahead to the horizon; the price of having two kids. James is usually dressed and hurrying out the door to get to the gym before his work days while I pull the pin on my morning with the waking of the kids.

James is a business kind of guy, he works out before work to try to keep some bulge in his arms but the bulge in his pants is the one he should be working on. James has been a supportive husband; he attends to as much as he can but on his quiet time he reads about stocks and trading (kill me) not something rugged like chainsaw reviews or anything. Once I get back home after my morning jog Bruno (our Irish setter) goes bezerk, he knows to be quiet when I leave to jog but once I return he explodes in energy with barks and jumping. James is ready to bail for the day the moment I touch the door handle, ready to flee from the molten mess, leaving it for me to deal with.

A colloquial kiss on the cheek as we pass and James is out the door. Bruno won't shut the hell up until I feed him and only kicking him outside will get his relentless barking to quiet down enough to be able to see straight while I work. Bruno is a good dog but it's tempting to give him an Ambien at night so he'd stay asleep till at least 8 a.m. When I let Bruno out he barks, they all bark, but his barking is often a focal point to my next door neighbor; Joy, to nag about. Joy is a decade older than I am, she's up at 5a.m. and yet, Bruno's barking is always brought up with a crooked sneer when she greets me through her yellow coffee stained teeth when we pass.

Lately I daydreamed about socking Joy in the mouth and watching her choke to death on her stained teeth and laughing as she gasps and gags on the ground. James tries to stay awake at night while we lay in bed next to each other reading but once he gets some of his daily jargon out about Bill or Bob or whatever overweight middle-aged guys he showers with in the gym, he's asleep. Most nights it's me, just me, sitting up in bed under my reading light wondering how I became who I am. I'm Ally by the way.

My real name isn't Ally but with a pen name I can splurge out all of my indiscretions and enjoy them. Oscar Wilde once said: "If you give a man a mask he will show you his true face" so with that in mind I can hide behind Ally and not filter any of the incredible things I have done and I wouldn't have to feel guilty while I can still smell the sweat and taste him on my lips because it all really did happen to me. My life with James was mostly rewarding in the grandest term, someone I could grow old (and boring) with and have all the milestones that you could typically find in every reprint of life, the cars, the retirement and so on. If you truly think about it; there is no such thing as a happily ever after, someone in the perfect marriage dies first and that shits all over the last person standing so maybe being raised with the Barbie fairytales is just a mean thing to keep a girls hopes up with.

So forty was really hard for me, no girl ever wants to pass another decade milestone, men become endearing when they get older but no so much for women I'd say. When I first met James I was sure that he and I would age gracefully and that he would be a handsome old man to walk around the park with. I remember before kids when my feet pointed straight ahead as I walked, now that two kids have spread my hips I watch myself walk and see that I am a bit pigeon toed in my stride and there is no turning the clock back. Aging sucks, your body slowly breaks down and you have to spend longer and longer thinking back to the last time you got all pretzel twisted up with your lover in a romantic session rather than counting the minutes until your next one.

The kids are up at seven after my jog, I awake my son and let him have fifteen minutes to get dressed and his bathroom stuff done before I awake my daughter. I was so excited to have a little girl to dress up and play with; every mom wants a son like his daddy and a daughter just like them. My little girl takes much more effort in the morning so I blast through making lunches and help to brush the snarls out of the bed head as both kids eat and then argue their way to the bus stop. The mornings are exhausting and just the half hour of man maniacal shouting orders and frantically moving around leaves me spinning and spent, more so than my jog does.

So the week of my fortieth birthday James planned a week for he and I to go to a cabin in the Smoky Mountains, we were going to have a small party with family then his parents were going to stay at the house with the kids so he and I could go and be away, just us because we needed our adult time. I was depressed about turning forty but maybe spending a week walking around naked and humping like teenagers would have helped all of that. James was giddy and looking forward to some adventurous sex with me and it was nice to feel wanted and attractive again. James had plans for a few wilder trysts, he even blushed when he talked about maybe standing behind me in the front porch overlooking the deep stretching valley and slipping into me first thing in the morning before the fog lifts from the valley below.

After eighteen years of marriage it was hard to get excited about sleeping with my husband, it was usually numbing to think about him sexually. Don't get me wrong, my buttons like being pushed but his once a month wink and smile that lead to ten minutes of "hold right there" or "I won't fall asleep, I'm just catching my breath" isn't much to get riled up over, which now a days leads to me pushing my own buttons in the shower after he starts snoring. Sometimes I'll watch James' sex face, his eyes all squinty and his cheeks red as he hold his breath and focuses on what he's doing, never mind that I hardly bother to even take my shirt off anymore, why bother to get cold when it'll be over quickly anyways right?

I don't know exactly when but some of my desires and interests have changed a little as well, some days I find myself revved up watching some movie that wouldn't have caught my attention before. In my younger years the notion of my husband and I taking turns pleasing one another was more than enough to prime the pump but now I find that some of the more taboo subjects keep my attention while I take care of things. Subjects that the young girls can hardly fake an interest in or get squeal about are now things I think about just to get myself in the mood, and I am not sure why, is it boredom or the need for something new? I feel conflicted that I should be able to express my desires to try some new things with my husband but doing so would rile strange suspicions rather than entice his will to join me.

James occasionally brings up that I used to go down on him regularly when we were first married and that we had an insatiable appetite for each other, well he used to go down on me too, ships in the night I suppose. Every other month after a date night movie James might hint that he'd like me to take him into my mouth and he might even try to proposition me with a hip thrust and a wide smile, but frankly what am I getting out of it? I would have to spend twenty minutes to try to even just think of the year he last went down on me, and it was as phoned in as it could be if I remember correctly. James used to be ambitious when he headed south, he'd even warn me he was going to "razz matazz" meaning he'd let his tongue wander all around and tickle areas during play. I wonder if watching a child come from my lady parts is what turned him off to lapping me up; perhaps it's like seeing a rat at your favorite restaurant, either way you never want to eat there again.

My grandma once told me that love should be extraordinary; his touch should always make you quiver and want to dance even when there was no music in the background. My grandpa never returned from Germany so the few years she had with him before were probably spent in some pre-electricity missionary style nights of passion. My grandma did have a point, she may have been naïve because the love of her life never came back and when you don't have closure you kind of stay stuck in that mind frame but there is enough mediocrity in life, love shouldn't be another one. I used to flip channels on the TV and sometimes I would stop for an extra second when I caught a glimpse of skin and I would wait to see if there was a hot body to go along with it, those days are long gone now too. I find myself bored with many things, young hot bodied young men working around the neighborhood landscaping can't even keep my eye line for any longer than a second, I just think "I paid for the weed spray so spray the damn weeds" and then I shut the door, that's it.

A few days of bumming a few years ago when the kids were younger but starting school lead me to pick up Bruno. Bruno is a gorgeous red Irish setter with a charming personality and I truly love him, but like most love, contempt is right below the surface. I don't know if contempt is the right word, it sounds too harsh when I actually read it, disdain, loathing, disgust, I don't know, I'll get back to it. I started walking around the neighborhood with Bruno to burn off some of his puppy energy but after a while he'd fake sleep when I got up earlier and earlier to walk further and further, especially when it was cold out, he's not a stupid dog and if he wasn't a pain in my ass so often it would be funny, but he's a pain in my ass.

So, forty; the week was supposed to be James and I alone in a remote cabin with just shadows to hide our nether regions when we were feasting on one another like teens trying not to get caught. I was packed with what I needed and even though our plans were to be sans clothing, a girl needs options. James found it funny to still point out that I was taking two large suitcases, which in my defense I would still need lotions, towels, changes of clothes for whatever might come up, he was just trying to be playful I'm sure but he still came across as an ass. I was leery about spending the whole week with James, he was a good guy but as the kids got older and responsibilities mounted, we clicked less and less and we both felt it. I was intrigued to spend a week to get to know the man I was married to for sixteen years ago at that point; we had a lot of catching up to do.

A few weeks before I was supposed to take my trip with James, the company I work for did some restructuring. There was rumor that there might be some layoffs in the works when the top brass shuffled around some workers so of course I was concerned but James was confident that we wouldn't be shaken if I were to find myself unemployed for a short time. I worked in the afternoons four days a week, it was a bit tough going from full time stay at home while my kids were babies and into elementary school but James and I agreed that once the kids were in school full time, I'd return to work and replenish our retirement. I was nervous to return to the work life and especially hesitant about missing out on so much with the kids in the afternoons but it was good to make adult friends.

The first two weeks of the summer was stressful as the company rolled the shipping department that worked midnights into the first and second shifts and thinned the herd a little. I had four years organizing and routing orders for a manufacturer so I wasn't as worried because I wasn't top tier making top tier money nor was I a low level that they wouldn't feel bad for letting go, but I was worried about losing some of the girls I worked with. As bodies shuffled and moved around shifts there were some new faces, some of the groggier looking guys who'd spent years taking the physical abuses associated with night shift began to fill in some of the gaps in the shifts, and there was Ben.

I worked predominantly with four other office girls, we coordinated shipping orders as well as procured manifests for products and then made sure that each factory sent us the right orders and so on, boring blah blah. Hannah was a thirty year old married gal, she had three young kids and a doting husband she still loved immensely, it was cute that he'd pack notes in her lunches sometimes but some of us also wondered how much of that was a façade. Gretchen was closer to my age and reminded me a lot of my best friend Erin. Gretchen had long jet black hair and was more reserved compared to Lisa.

Lisa was the more bubbly and bubble gum popping girl but we all loved her. Reagan was the baby of our little office, she was twenty one and like Lisa, was still mostly single, I say mostly because she enjoyed the club life and was often coming to work without a bra on or minimal makeup after having applied it on her drive in. Lisa often wore her hair up and is an adorable girl, she was a good girl and even though she was twenty-six, she was still single and hoping to find the right guy. Reagan was bottle blonde but had the most amazing green eyes you could imagine, but she was ditzy and much more crazy than any of us could picture ourselves being but we loved her. Reagan was a shot of Tequila for breakfast kind of girl while I was a green tea while reading the paper kind of boring.

So, back to Ben. Ben worked the third shift for a little while before transferring down to my shift about three weeks before my birthday. Lisa noticed the strong armed man with light stubble as he walked into the warehouse section of our building, she nudged Gretchen to come to the window and stare down over the floor with her trying to find out who the new body was. "Dibs" Lisa shouted out to Reagan to ensure Reagan wasn't sliding his pants down and her skirt up in the parking lot on their break. Hannah slowly wandered to the window to see what the commotion was all about and was quickly calling for my conformity when she caught a glimpse of the guy in question. Everyone was standing at the window that overlooked the warehouse floor like it was a zoo display.

Ben was about six-two and an athletic one-ninety. Ben had broad shoulders and a smile that just made your underbits quiver. Lisa wasn't out to offend Reagan when she called dibs and she wasn't implying that Reagan was a slut or anything, but Reagan will admit she likes getting "dicked" and isn't ashamed of her free sexuality but she wanted a good chance at a nice guy. Gretchen and Hannah both chuckled that Lisa was starting to call dibs on a man that was beefy enough to feed all of us. Hannah was adorably in love with her husband and anytime anyone tried to goad her into admitting a guy was hot she would shrug her shoulders and just admit that some women like a guy like that, the coy was annoying more than not, almost a snub that she was eternally happy and better than everyone else for it, but whatever.

Ben was in his mid-twenties, his youth added to this appeal as did his bulging chest under his t-shirt. Gretchen so happened to sit by the window for the rest of the afternoon intentionally distracted by the work floor down below so she could report to Lisa his movement and whereabouts, it was like middle school all over again with the crushes and googling but it was cute. Half way through my afternoon I was tasked with heading down to the work floor and inspecting an incoming order to ensure that our newer distributer had sent all the right order. Lisa was wide eyed and smiling as she pushed and coerced me to move my butt to get out and introduce myself to Ben. Lisa was so overjoyed that her slap to my butt had much more zest to it than any before as she wanted me to hustle out the door and down the stairs.

Ben isn't his real name, I'll refer to him as "Ben" (as in Ben Dover) but that's for later. So the girls gave me the short straw to go and make first contact. Later on Lisa told me in secret that she didn't want Hannah going because she was so beautiful and she sure as hell didn't want Reagan going because she would have probably put her thong (if she was even wearing undies) in his shirt pocket before even saying "hi." The girls were giggly and funny, Gretchen even "oooh'd" as I pulled the door open to walk down the metal factory steps towards the back loading dock to begin my inspection. Watching my hands glide down the smooth railing I couldn't help but wonder if the expensive lotions were really worth the money, I wasn't even forty yet but my hands looked like they were sixty.

I wandered through pallets of boxes, down the rows of items being cataloged by the sparse afternoon crew and towards bay 3. The pallet I needed was shrink wrapped and still on the pallet jack, there was no sign of Ben. I looked for the shipping order to compare what was shipped, to what was ordered, and then also to what was actually on the pallet Ben had just offloaded. The shipping order wasn't on any of the sides and I was about to climb up on top to see of some jerk had put it on top when I heard; "May I help you?" from behind me. I had one foot up on the pallet jack and was about to hoist myself up when Ben rounded the corner. I felt my skin flush, there was an awakening inside of me in a warmth and it took half of a moment to catch my breath.

Ben caught me off guard, my foot nearly slipped off the pallet jack which would have probably sent me into the boxes or the handle, either way I would have made an embarrassing fool out of myself. Six foot two isn't all that tall unless you're five-six and standing right next to it. Ben let the corners of his mouth rise up with his greeting and warming smile. Ben had slight dimples when he spoke; I'm not sure what he was talking about at first because my eyes wandered his face and chest while my ears worked to unscramble what I was hearing. I felt like a cliché, old married woman taking stake at the new hunk at work but there was something about him. Once I noticed my heart beating like crazy I realized that I had to close my eyes for a moment to focus back to listening to him. I shook my head to try and ward off a slight dizzy spell and to gather my bearings again.

Ben lifted his hand up to show me that he had the shipping order and that he already compared it to what was actually on the pallet. Ben startled me a little but his charm and his voice are what left me reeling for a minute. My eyes blurred for a moment so like a dork I looked down onto my clipboard until I had my head on straight. I tried to hide my smile but there was no hiding my blushing, I felt my face get all warm and I felt a tingle wash over my body too. I blinked a bit with my head tucked and once my vision came back I realized I was staring at a blank clipboard. I realized I was super embarrassed and looking like an idiot. I felt like I was back in grade school and couldn't shake the notion of looking like a dork in front of such a hot guy. I looked around my feet to find the order sheet and quickly fumbled to retrieve it from the floor.

My pulse beat in my ears so badly that there was no sure way to know what Ben was saying, each time I looked at him I just wanted to watch his mouth move and it didn't click that he was actually saying anything. His hair was dark blonde, light brown, somewhere in between perhaps? I tried to keep my eyes locked on Ben's hazel eyes but I felt my eyes sink down to gaze on his arms and the bluish veins that seemed to wriggle beneath the skin on his biceps. I felt like such an idiot that my blushing was no way concealed, Max Factor couldn't make a concealer strong enough to hide my embarrassment, maybe a latex paint company might though.

I reached out to the shipping order that Ben had held tightly in his strong hands and I tried my best to keep my lower lip from quivering. Ben slowly moved his hand forward to hand me his paperwork when I finally regained my hearing; "I'm sorry for giving you a start, I honestly didn't mean for such a thing to happen, I am glad you didn't get hurt." I was so relieved that he didn't seem to notice that I hadn't heard a word in his two minutes of talking but rather was being super polite that it was him startling me that was causing my blushing cheeks. I spun around on my heel and tried to keep my speed under control as I walked briskly back towards the restrooms. I was too afraid to go right back into the office with the look of "hot and bothered" all over my face.

I clipped the papers together on the clipboard and made a beeline right for the girl's bathroom. I pushed the red door open where I met my reflection, my short blond hair had dots of sweat at the hairline on my forehead, my cheeks were well past rosy, actually they were almost crimson from my shame and my hands were shaky. I tried to take a few deep breaths to calm down but on my exhale I felt my chest shake a little while I shook my hands to fan my face. I stepped a few steps in each direction as I tried to look at the dull walls, I tried to think about the sinks and the drab colors to calm myself down with, each step made me want to step sideways to get a little more feeling but staying riled up wouldn't have helped anything, I was enticed.

I ran my wrists under cold water to calm myself down. I didn't focus on how long I had been in the bathroom until I heard a knock at the door. I looked at myself in the mirror to see that my hairline was dry and my hands were bluish from the cold water, they felt like ice when I pressed them to my face. I grabbed a few handfuls of paper towel to dry with and I shut the water faucet off. "You alive in there?" I heard Hannah speak out. I shook my head a little and headed to unlock the door. Hannah is a bright and cheerful girl and seeing the look of worry on her face told me that I was gone for plenty long enough. "You feeling ok, you look a little flush hun." I assured Hannah that I was indeed going to be ok, explaining that I just had a weird hot spell and wanted to make sure I wasn't going to vomit.

The warehouse can indeed get really warm and leaving our air conditioned office to the heat of the floor can sometimes mess with you but my spell was entirely man made, literally. I patted my forehead dry on my way back to the office as I followed Hannah. The girls and I joked that the constant up and down the stairs should keep our butts in tip top shape but just glancing at Hannah's as she took each step, I could tell that mine was much less ideal in comparison. Being a girl sucks, guys get older and richer and their tastes in girls stays the same, they want girls in their early twenties with bodies that haven't given birth, all the while we snicker and snarl at one another because we are jealous that we're aging and they young girls all show off their hot bodies and such. Hannah had her perfectly rounded rear end, it was smooth and without panty lines in her pantsuit, the tightening fabric of her pants thinned and seemed to hug her already firm butt with each step, I could feel mine still jiggle on each up step even when I flexed it.

I walked back into the office and was met with ample wide eyes, especially from Lisa. "Is he really that hot?" Lisa asked as she saw my rosy cheeks and sweaty complexion. I was caught and embarrassed. All I could think to say was "you'd better get on him, he won't last for long" as I smiled and eased some of the discomfort under my collar. Gretchen laughed off my little quip and I smiled to coax along the giggling but there was that small spark inside of me that was as serious as I was playful.

James is a good husband; he's been supportive of my jogging, my crafts, Bruno and so on. James supported me after I birthed him a son and then a daughter and worked extra hard to support us while the kids were still babies. I am grateful for James and all that he's done and together we've raised a house and made a good living for each other, as couples are supposed to. Every married person has that small crush, that actor or actress that you secretly hope gets topless on screen or has a beach scene so that you can eye their contours while wet, it's innocent and normal. I have had a small bit of simple crushes in my time as any other but there was something about Ben that had me imagining him more so than any other crush before, I felt a little guilty about it.

The safety about actors or actresses is that they are unreal fantasies. James adores Diane Kruger because of her adorable personality in that treasure movie, granted her cute body didn't hurt

I'm sure. For me I'd go Tyrese from Annapolis, the strong silent type, not the obnoxious and loud fool from the furious movies or Edward Norton, man that guy can act. The unattainability of actors puts them out of reach for anyone thus making them safe to joke about with our spouses, but the moment you mention getting steamy over a guy at work, that sets in motion an insecurity that can fester and go awry if you aren't careful. James has plenty of good looking women in his office, I've met plenty of them at office brunches and gatherings but he's never been flirty with any of them and there has never been any reason to feel insecure about them. Men are flooded with eye candy all day long, you see that girl on the commercial in skimpy lingerie, garters hiked up and her rock hard nips jutting out against her nightie? she's selling car air fresheners, what a nearly naked twenty year old model has anything to do with it is a good guess but most people aren't smart enough to see around it all I suppose.

So I'll get into some of my sexual history a bit later because it may or may not play into everything but for the sake of being thorough I will. The rest of that first afternoon the girls took turns heckling Lisa about what they'll name their first born children, Liam for a boy? Charlotte for a girl maybe? It was all in good playful humor but I caught myself heckling a bit harder than the other girls and I couldn't figure out why. I made two or three more trips back out and around the floor for various tasks and each time I tried to keep myself from veering towards Ben, I knew that the girls back up in the office would be watching me but I also wanted to catch a glimpse of him each chance I got. I felt uneasy, I felt like I was under a microscope as I walked around and I knew that my paranoia was my own fault but I couldn't shake the extra vigilance.

Ben wore faded blue jeans, a short sleeve dark grey cotton t-shirt under an unbuttoned orange plaid shirt and his hair was cut short and combed forward. I watched around any corner I could see for the telltale orange shirt, I just wanted to take a peek at him each time I ventured across the floor. Bed had solid legs that filled his bootleg pants, his work boots were clean and probably steel toed and he wore his watch on his left hand, err wrist, why does that matter you ask? Because I noticed the watch when I didn't see a wedding ring. When I first spoke with Ben I couldn't help but to stare at his strong forearms, no they aren't the most sensual of body parts but he had a large vein on the underside that bulged out when he brought his hand to his mouth when he yawned. Bulging forearms mean strong hands, which also mean a tight grip to hold onto you when you are entangled with one another and his large firm hands groping at you, it's incredibly hot.

Finally after a second round of introductions with Ben I convinced him to come up to the office and meet more of the gals, I was a bit hesitant on introducing him and Lisa because there was a slight tinge of jealously in me that she was single and I was forty but that's neither here nor there. I was forty and married so I did my best to smile through my bit of jealousy and encouraged them to go for one another. I sped through the introduction to Hannah, Gretchen and especially Reagan but I was sure to speak up a bit when introducing Lisa all the while waving my hand in a displaying manner to further help entice him to her. The introduction was short lived as he politely excused himself to get back to the floor to work but I was confident I sold Lisa pretty well. We all turned to watch him walk away, his ass filled in his jeans and as the pockets worked up and down with his steps his tall erect posture caused some of his thick back muscles to ripple and work under his shirt.

Gretchen and I plotted together that if Lisa gets to *Bangville* with Ben that we'd get the scoop on his down stairs business and that would help to fill in some areas that were missing from our imaginations. The afternoon spent gossiping about Ben and Lisa was in good fun, Lisa was a bit on the shy side but seemed to pucker up pretty well when Ben finally stepped into the office to make acquaintances, he was a nice guy and every time he turned his back to one of us, we'd eyeball the hell out of him. Gretchen and I are both married women with long time husbands, Hannah was married sometime in the last few years so they were still enjoying their young love but we knew what reality was like after long enough. Gretchen and I listened to Reagan boast and brag about some of the guys she'd meet and we'd coax details from her about as much as we could to prolong our home sex-lives, or what was left of our dwindling passions.

The end of the first night I met Ben I was livelier, I felt like I was breathing deeper and during my entire drive home I wasn't dreading walking into my house and getting attacked by Bruno and a sink full of dishes. It was tough going back to work at first years back but I learned to enjoy silent rides home, no music, no yappy talk show host, just the quiet ride with the breeze in the window on my way home, this evening was no exception. With the window cracked I let the summer afternoon air blow my short hair around and fill my shirt. I let the soft air fill my lungs, I kept my right hand on the steering wheel and my left foot propped up on the seat so I could rest my left elbow on my knee and rest my hand on my forehead to relax as I drove. I like to let the wind whipped hair dance along my fingertips, the smooth texture was fun to play with as the wind also kissed all over my body giving me goose bumps here and there.

The benefit of an SUV is the height; if I were in a car and sitting in such an un-lady like manner then who knows what other drivers might get a peek at me but sitting up a little higher had its merits, even though I usually wear slacks, sitting in this way in a long skirt was sometimes fun, draping my fingertips down my thighs to just scratch or rub along my usually sore legs was nice too. I watched as other cars passed as I turned off the highway and began my slow winding around the city streets to get to my cul-de-sac, the stop signs were bothersome but they also gave me a reason to get home a bit later, which meant a bit more me time. I lazily used my propped left arm to steer while I used my right hand to rustle my hair back. Letting my right hand rub down the back of my neck I felt the small hairs standing up from the slight wind whipped chill, it tickled a little.

Brushing my fingers down the back of my neck I felt the tingle course through me, my chest felt flush and like that I found myself turned on. Socially a girl is supposed to keep her sexuality in check, hidden and under wraps like it's some dirty secret, morally she is supposed to only lust for her husband and faithfully she is only supposed to think about her husband especially after they are married. My head felt warm as I traced the muscles along the side of my neck and ran my fingertips along my collar bone and under the collar of my shirt. My fingertips traced and teased a little, the feeling of my own touch seemed real this time, not that it was ever fake but I found myself newly awakened to it, maybe I was just in a mood but the corners of my mouth were raising up as I toyed a bit at myself.

Now speaking of morality I was raised to be a good girl, sit with your ankles crossed when wearing a skirt or dress, hands folded in your lap and always dress modestly. My mother was never one to speak of sexuality and when my periods first began, she was as bland in topic as I could have ever imagined. When my friends and I each began menstruating we made the code name "Doug" so when anyone spoke of *Doug*, we each knew in secret what was going on. I remember feeling ashamed of something that happens *monthly*, which is silly to be ashamed of something so natural. Growing up I tiptoed around my parents when it came to any topic that wasn't biblically strict, heaven forbid we're given ten fingers and one of them happens to get me off. I abstained from having premarital sex for a long time and even though I experienced the touches of a man before I was wed, I couldn't imagine that if there were a god that masturbation would be a sin.

I was born in nineteen sixteen-nine, the most sexually regarded year imaginable (for the immature of course) and I missed the sexual revolution of the hippie years and even in the stringing along seventies of still misspent youth, I was too young. I lost my virginity to a clumsy boy who was nineteen when I was eighteen and living on my own, I was scared and it hurt and it took a while before I was willing to go down that road again. My sex life hasn't even been cosmo worthy, let alone a "dear Penthouse" type of sex-life, but it's what I knew. James and I were a bit more vigorous in our earlier days and because I was later than my friends I sometimes found myself still wanting to have had more in my earlier days, now it takes pills for James to hang in there long enough or we have to schedule to time, it's just a lot of work now.

So my chest was hot and I felt sweaty, I pulled my hand from the top of my shirt and reached up underneath to play with my left breast for a moment, the touching was exciting and doing it while driving felt naughty and it made my pulse begin to race. It was late at night and plenty dark out so I had the comfort of the eve, plus with my left leg up against the window I was semi secluded. I was sweaty and hot from being turned on and even the taboo of touching myself while driving around made me a little hotter. I just played with my chest under my bra for a few more turns until I reached my dark and unlit house. I rubbed my fingers together to pinch a little at the bulge of my nipple through the soft fabric of my bra, it was a little beady from wear but it was still fun to entice myself, especially out and around. Even though it was dark out I felt adventurous.

When I first started working James would leave the front porch light on so I could make it safely from my car to the house, now it hasn't been on for me in years. I pulled my car in and shifted it into park, before I turned the motor off I switched the switch off so the light wouldn't come on when I turned the engine off, I just wanted to sit in the dark and quiet. I felt ashamed that I was turned on, although there was no real reason for it, not like I was reading some smut novel that got me going or even had I brushed up against Ben and was able to press his strong body against mine. I got laid three weeks ago, or at least I laid there while James did his thing. I usually just feel like a warm hole for my husband, I feel that it is my duty as wife to keep him happy which will keep him from looking elsewhere but where is mine?

I wasn't sure what in life I was missing but I felt there was something. I rubbed my nipple in my fingers and felt more blood rush to it to make it hard and erect. I imagined Ben was pressing it between his lips while flicking it with his tongue. I felt a little guilty that my husband was in the house and up the stairs sleeping, yet I was sitting in a dark car in the driveway thinking about a guy I just met at work. I held my breath a few times in excitement as I kept a pinch on my left nipple with my right hand while cupping the rest of my breast. I pinched harder and harder until it began to hurt a little, taking a deep breath in made my skin tighten and a riveting surge jolt down my legs, the touching was enough to curve my cravings so I rolled my window back up and took some deep breathes before getting out.

I could have easily went upstairs and fondled James in his sleep, even having something to play with a little while playing with myself should have been enough but hoping that I could have resurrected some life into his sleeping body was useless. It took ample coaxing while he was awake so it was a pointless ordeal to hope for a hard-on, I would have even blown him in his sleep for the time with his hard member until I got off but I knew that that wasn't going to happen. I pulled a small bit of egg salad from the fridge and made a half sandwich to eat while leaning over the sink, I was too lazy to dirty a dish only to have to wash it in the morning so I ate just leaning over the sink. I leaned over on my elbows and swayed my hips side to side. I stared into the bleak living room; the darkness was a blank canvas for my imagination so I let my mind paint.

I imagined Ben was standing behind me, his strong hands holding me firmly at the waist and grinding at me from behind. As I swayed my hips side to side slightly I imagined feeling him in his pants pressing against me as I arched my back in to push myself out more behind me. I thought about running my hands up Ben's shirt and letting my fingers ripple up his abds and towards his chest. I felt myself get warm, I was craving intimacy but I was alone at midnight in my own home. "*I'm alone in my own home*" I realized and thought to myself. When James and I first married we were as you'd expect young lovers to be, we were ravenous with desires and even though we weren't teens (I was twenty-four and he was twenty-six) we still spent our time as if we were. I loved it when James would step up behind me and just take me, roughly yanking my pants down easing himself into me before sliding his hands up the back of my neck to grab a handful of my hair and pulling it so that I'd look back at him as he grunted and thrusted at me, I miss the times he was a rough brute and took control.

James and I moved around a bit as we got our careers underway before we were ready to have children so we had our time to be alone and just a married couple. James and I experimented with locations and positions of course. My mother always said that good girls follow the bible and wouldn't partake in anything unnatural, I'm not sure what all she meant by some of her statements but there's plenty of priests taking advantage of little kids and that's as wrong as anything else imaginable so I'm pretty sure I'm safe masturbating.

I held my breath and waited for Bruno to return back to sleep in whichever kids' room he was in, he's grown lazy in that he'll hardly come to greet me when I get home at night anymore, I heard his footsteps through the ceiling for a moment when I first got in the door but not anymore. One of the kids will pet him to sleep and he'll stay there until he want's breakfast and then a run in the yard when I get home from my jog. The house was silent, other that the occasional creak and squeak of a floor board; everything was dead quiet and dark. I reached my right arm behind me and unsnapped my bra so I could feel my shirt against my bare chest. The slight tension of my bra let up and my chest felt more movable beneath my shirt as my breasts hung freely and my still hard nipples rubbed along the fabric, it was cooling to lean down against the counter. I rested my right cheek against the counter and returned to imagining that Ben was straddled up behind me and resting his large hand on my back near my shoulder blades, pushing me against the counter to pin me where he wanted me.

I slid my right hand down my warm stomach, my smooth skin was moist with perspiration but my own touch was stimulating as I was already enticed myself a little in the car. I let my hand slide to the fleshy parts of my and almost immediately upon my touch I was ready to writhe suggestively. I tried to keep my hand movements slow enough to hush the wettish sloshing sounds coming from behind me, the dark silent evening gave me no distraction from my thoughts and I continued to picture that Ben was the one pushing against me, my legs started at shoulder width but shortly I was nearly half way down to the ground and my feet growing farther apart. With my left hand I held on dearly to the counter as if I was on the Titanic and it was sinking. My legs quivered to close but my wide stance kept that from happening as I moved my hand around and around.

My breathing was sporadic; I took a bunch of short breaths as climax found me and with large exhales fought to keep my whimpers silent in the empty house. If James had caught me it would have been the best timing he might have ever had, I wanted him deep in me and I was extremely ready for him, but he didn't. My knees lurched up and down as I motioned, I rested my forehead on my arm and gritted my teeth while I let my hand continue to fill in for Ben's absence. I tried to raise up my right foot to keep from nearly ending up in the splits and I banged my knee on the cupboard door. "Woof" I heard Bruno, he totally heard me hit the cupboard and then jump to his four feet. With faster and faster thudding I could hear Bruno rushing to investigate the source of the sudden noise as he barreled down the stairs

I was committed to myself and right on the edge of where I needed to be when I heard Bruno's nails clopping on the tile floor. Bruno is a klutz, after four years since we put the tile in he still slips and slides into everything when he hurries. My motions slowed and I focused on what I was doing until Bruno swiped into me, jarring me behind the knees and nearly knocking me over. I held firm to the counter for a moment waiting for my breathing to return to me. I was extremely turned on, which was a rarity due to my earlier mentioned monotony and routines of life. I couldn't stop myself from smiling from the exhilaration.

I chewed at my bottom lip and immediately began contemplating how wrong it was that I just did what I did. I washed my hands off and returned to swaying my hips side to side to dry up a little. Bruno nuzzled my left leg for a moment and after a few pats I told him to go to bed, he just headed back up stairs. I missed my younger days of strutting around in the nude with James, the sight of me used to set him in a huff and he'd have to come and take me no matter what else was going on. Now I see my hands and see that my skin is getting thinner and I'm older. When dating I used to get a little Jealous if James would get aroused at some nude scene in a movie but once we were married I was grateful and used to totally take advantage of it, now I could put on an all-girl porn and I don't know if it would keep him from falling asleep, growing old sucks.

I have walked out of our bathroom in nothing but a t-shirt and James doesn't even roll his head over to take a peek at any of my exposed parts anymore, it's like having his two children has tainted my vagina for him. To keep from getting too graphic I do keep a tidy place for James, I keep trimmed and proper for hygiene and sometimes out of sheer boredom I completely taken it all down to the skin, I'm not sure how well I like the bald look but the feel is incredible. When we first married James and I would shave fun patterns and shapes into each other's nether regions, I shaved mine into a small butterfly once and it was such a turn on for him that he had to mumble his words to me for two days because his tongue was so worn out afterwards, those are the days I miss.

I am sure everyone goes through the stages; hating turning a year older each and every birthday, hating those stages that can't be reversed such as menstruating and developing and now hating the notion of drying up and becoming barren and infertile. I've dreaded turning forty since I could count that high. I viewed thirty as old when I was in my teens and it was a hard birthday to swallow but now forty was a nightmare. At fifty people see you as distinguished, at sixty you are adorable and even at seventy you are seen as noble, but forty you are thought up as drying up, becoming infertile, getting ready for hot flashes . Plus you can no longer say you have that twenty-something body, you can't even really pass off as mid-thirties, it just all changes,

Back to my empty dark house, I was alone, even though I had a husband upstairs, I was alone.

CH. 2

The morning after I met Ben I woke up still feeling alone. I went to bed without as much as a goodnight kiss from my own husband. I was feeling different than usual, I decided to forgo panties under my yoga pants, yeah yeah you are at risk for yeast infections and so on if you gather moisture down there and it's unhealthy but I was feeling like a small change, maybe a three mile run rather than my two and perhaps doing so commando style might boost my self-confidence. James hardly stirred as I got up and stripped. Out of pestilence I stood completely naked, cupping my boobs and wriggling my hips while staring at James as he laid there still as a rock. I spread my arms out and my feet apart and stood, spread eagle wishing that James would wake up and crawl across the bed to taste me as the first thing we did in the morning. James' apnea didn't even kick in to pause his snoring to even tease me that he might have woken up for a second, it was just more disappointment.

I stretched a little more before I finally gave up on the idea of an early morning romp, to be thrown down on the bed would have been a game changer so early that morning but James remained asleep. I gave in and put on my running clothes and just went. Once again Bruno didn't even bother to see me out the door, the bugger knew what I was up to and he didn't want anything to do with it so I was solo for my run and it was very early. Sometimes the rising sun on my jogs seems to be calming, the exercise makes me feel good about myself and that I am working towards improving myself.

I sought counseling for the support and things like that, I needed to be able to speak my mind as well as sort out many of my troubles for a while. I didn't think I'd end up where I am now, writing down everything that has happened over the last few months or so but her is my own story, for me to revisit and to take me back to each meeting, each hook up, each kiss and each heart pounding moment that I took the risk of getting caught by who knows and ruining everything I've done in the past eighteen years. Did I mention I dreaded turning forty, old lady forty at that. I abhorred the notion of forty, it seized me with anxiety and gave me the shakes, I just absolutely got sick at the notion and yet the date kept ticking closer and closer.

So on my jog I got not one but two honks from cars coming up behind me, childish I know but after thirty it becomes a flattering compliment. I've been athletic my whole life and it's always been important to stay lean and in shape but after I had my daughter, I always felt that my butt sagged a whole lot more and once I was no longer in my mid-thirties, it seems to be more work to keep in shape. I know I'm not the only woman on earth that isn't thrilled about her body, frankly I haven't met any women that are all that happy with themselves at all, we all have our issues and I'm no different but there are times I'm ok with my body, content, perhaps even satisfied but not often enough. I liked when James was constantly lusting after me, we'd be at it day and night and it was wonderful to see his full reaction to me all the time. I often wouldn't even have to do anything to rouse him, he'd just be rearing to go and we'd be at each other.

I wondered if I was reaching that "peak" that many women talk about. Fried Green Tomatoes referenced it and many other movies talked about a women hitting her prime much later than when a man can satisfy their lusts, or after she's lost much of her sexuality that she can't get her needs met? It's almost cruel that a woman of my age hit's their prime; James is at the point that he almost needs pills to function and that's if he doesn't fall asleep. Nothing beats the feel of a real person, the intimacy can't be replaced by some batteries and a motor and it's unfair that I feel trapped by my own urges and a husband that can't always throw me one on command anymore. James used to be a strapping guy, thick shoulders and rippling chest but that was fifteen to twenty years ago, now we're just an old married couple.

Gretchen sometimes thumbs through some of the tasteless books where the girl always gets the guy; it's all about reading porn rather than watching it for most women. James and I have had our turns picking out flicks to watch to get us riled up on our special nights, the girls are usually some hot little thing to get the guys watching all revved up but the guys *in* the videos don't even raise my pulse so it was usually one sided fun. Guys want to watch some girl get plowed like a cornfield, I want to watch some guy gently and sensually dote on a girl, sure it's fun to watch a girl get tossed around like an acrobat but after he's done he should knock out the dishes and the laundry so she doesn't have to service the house and the man, there's a fantasy movie that would sell.

Gretchen and I joke about Reagan and her youth but deep down I know we're both jealous of her firm little body and the long promise of time ahead of her. Each time my foot hit the pavement I tried to clear my head and watch down the road but each time my mind wanders through all sorts of thoughts and memories. I've spent the last several years grinding for everybody else, I know that is how motherhood is but it's exhausting. James typically busts his ass at work and when he gets home he lets the babysitter Kaylie off the hook and then he plays dad all afternoon. I get it that James has his hard work but he only plays dad for a few hours from after school to bed time the four days a week I work, I get the rest and the cleanup in the mornings after the kids go to school, perhaps I'm just being selfish and in need of me time.

The two car honks boosted my mood and with a faster pace I made my three mile loop through some of the woods near the house and back around the streets. My feet carried me at a fast enough pace that even the neighbor Joy and her yellow teeth didn't have time to stop and give me the breeze about Bruno barking before I made it through the door. I took long leaps up the drive way and over the flowers as Joy tried to scurry like a little rat across her lawn to catch me, I didn't break my stride as I took one last long leap up onto the porch and swiftly through my front door. The flowers even seemed perkier in the morning as I brushed past them and leapt up to the porch. I was forty but on the inside that morning I felt twenty all over again. As soon as I clicked the lock on the door my daily routine came back in an explosion of noise; Bruno barking, James trying to get out the door and alarms starting to go off to wake the kids.

I leaned against the door to pry my sweaty running shoes off, from the door I can see the pile of dishes from the previous night all stacked up by the sink, toys and clothes sprawled across the living room, all like the day before and will be again the next day. I barely had my balance while untying my shoe as James whizzed passed me, a kiss on my cheek and a slam of the door and he's gone. Bruno is running around with a sock in his mouth, I have no idea who it belongs to; the only assurance is it probably belongs to my house. I feel like I'm hopped up on allergy medication, that glazed over feeling that you feel like you're forever falling except I have the clear vision of being mentally present to my own life.

Once the morning rush of getting the kids up and dressed is done and they are on their way to the bus I get a few moments of calm. I start the dish water to get all of the dishes washed and Bruno dealt with. The morning hour or two is a tiring mess but then I do get some quiet hours to myself and that is nice. Once I get the dishwasher loaded, the dog fed and the living room cleaned up, it's my turn for me. I have to lock Bruno out of my room because he'll either steal my expensive underwear, or paw at the bathroom door because he wants to play in the shower water, I love him but he's a weirdo. One of Bruno's favorite things is waiting until I get into a bubble bath and then jumping so that his front two legs are in the water so he can bite at the bubbles, except he scratches the hell out your legs and if he eats too many bubbles his stomach goes bad and he throws up on the bathroom floor, which ruins a nice bubble bath really quickly.

Standing in my birthday suit two weeks before it turns forty was not unusual, except the forty thing obviously. Mandatory self-breast exam reveals no lumps but still smaller boobs then when I was half my age, and much less perky than then also. My hips are wider than my shoulders and my butt droops without elastic support, I look cute in my jogging pants and feel sexy in booty short, maybe it's true what they say; "clothes make the woman". Even my underbits looks different than they did when I was younger, not that things will ever be as tight as a teen but two kids have changed things, not that I'm hanging in the wind either, ok this is getting gross. The skin on my elbows is rough and looks like a rhino's nose, it also matches my knees. My love handles are a little squishy and faded stretch marks still hug around my waist and tummy, even from the side I can't stop staring at my little pooch and can tell you that is from my uterus being tilted twice in pregnancy, things on my body that will never be like they were.

With a turn to keep inspecting over my bare body I took a deep breath to take the hard look, my butt. The lower curves of my rear droop, they used to look like semi-circle smiles but now the edges sink downward. Using my finger tips to bounce my butt I watch the jiggle ripple a little, with a lift and squeeze the skin divots a little and shows some of the cellulite beneath the skin, it is not attractive like it used to be when my butt defied gravity and even in the nude I was firm and loved my form. Pulling my belly up a little I stare down at my pubis, I dread when my small pouch just seems to fall forward into that pannus, the wad of fat that women get that slowly tries to take over their nether region, oh yuck. Saggy boobs, saggy ass, different but still slightly saggy underflaps, loosening skin, constant tired look with puffy eyes and veins starting to stick out farther from the more pale areas of my body, yep, screw being forty!

Anyways, in the shower I propped my leg up as I usually do to shave and clean up down stairs, each leg gets the same razor treatment is has for years and so does my girl parts. Rubbing sudsy bubbles and lathering is always soothing but it wasn't as enticing as it could have been if I had someone to help. I know date night was due with James and perhaps he'd be up for something more than in the bed with him on top. I was feeling ambitious and the thought of the two of us revisiting our youth in a remote cabin in the woods was starting to grow on me. I was a little tired from my run but something about having only been awake a couple of hours after a night of sleep left me in turmoil, I was physically but not mentally tired so trying to lie down for a bit would have just been frustrating and pointless.

I found myself lying down on my comfy bed with my tablet scrolling through an adult site to find something to help me pass the time. I let my mind wander back to when I was first married, the honesty is that I was engaged before I met James, I spent a few years with a man named Nick that turned out wasn't the right relationship for me so it ended. So I lost my virginity when I was a late teen, much later than most but in my own way. Nick and I shared our time and after the first year of me not really wanting to engage in *relations* I slowly opened up to him. My experiences aren't grand nor are they even flashy, for a long time I would just lay there and pretend that everything was alright.

James helped me to become more comfortable with myself, the problem is that I still feel there is a bit of a mental hang up, I've had problems really letting myself be free and it's been an inner source of pain for me that I've kept deep down for all of my sexual years. So James and I have had plenty of our share of fun and I'm not complaining, we even waited a long time before having kids in order to have more of it, except I still don't feel like I've had enough. My mind drifted back to Ben while I was browsing through adult videos for my self-pleasure, I felt less guilty the second time around but the guilt free euphoria was short lived because it was in my bed; the one I share with my husband.

The second night at work was more controlled and the elation in my veins was a new and fun feeling. Each time I saw Ben I thought about him standing behind me in the kitchen, I know it was just a fantasy but it was a strong one. The girls continued to chatter and of course Lisa grew more certain that she should date Ben but I wasn't as sure that I didn't have a chance. I don't know why I was hoping for a chance at but I at least wanted to have him flirt with me to give me one last assuring compliment that might tell me that maybe I'm not past my prime or that my looks have begun to fade, I don't know what I was really looking for I just know there was something missing and I hoped that he had it. I felt a little dirty but there was something that controlled me, it called me and when Ben was around all of my memories of my husband James seemed to just get skipped over in my mind. I don't know if I really wanted Ben or if I just wanted to be the one frumpy office chick that the hot warehouse worker guy chose to flirt with over the others. I didn't want to feel like I was going out to pasture to grow old; I wanted to be convinced by a young stranger that I was still sexy.

My lifelong best friend's name is Erin, she and I graduated high school together and after college she married an amazing man named Charles. Erin and Charles were friends with Nick and I and as a pair of couples we all enjoyed dinner parties and growing into our twenties together. Erin was more supportive than I could have ever asked for when Nick and I split and I held her hand through her mother's passing. Charles was as solid of a man as I could have ever hoped for such a friend and they mean the world to me. Erin and

Charles are a fun couple, a little more open in the way that when they first got together one of their favorite things to do was engage in risky sex on hotel balconies to some people hollering or cheering from down below.

Erin was funny in that she was generally a bit shy with her body but it turned her on to no end to have people rooting and cheering for Charles to pound her and it made things so much hotter. Erin once told me that they visited a hotel in Spain that was surrounded by sexy topless girls and bronzed up guys and she couldn't help herself but to straddle Charles at the edge of the pool and have him. The looks and claps were fun for a few minutes until some waiter kicked them out, which was rough because Charles had to go through the whole ordeal with his boner waving in the wind. Erin liked that her husband had such an appetite for her body that sprawling out and having him take her in areas where they were seen or might get caught only escalated her passion for him, and he liked to show off how gorgeous his wife was. Erin and Charles were funny, they would never consider swinging but being voyeuristic seemed to rile them both up.

James always encouraged me to call and hang out with Erin when I could because she was my dearest friend; she is more than an hour away from my house and we worked opposite shifts so texting was the easier way to keep in touch. I tried to make plans with Erin once a month for just us but after working four nights a week, a date night with my husband twice a month, school performances and plays plus the relentless running on the weekends, it wasn't uncommon for Erin and I to go long stretches without even talking. When Erin and I did manage to catch up it was usually over s fruity drink in a small bar where we can actually hear one another. Each time we met up the drink was short lived and the night even shorter, it was depressing that you spend so much of your life for everyone else that there is nothing left for you at the end of the day. Erin always understood and she had plenty of responsibilities also, she and Charles grew real tame real fast when they had their first child and she often complained that the most exciting sex they had had lately was a quickie in the shower between shaving legs.

Sometimes I feel like once you get passed thirty that you are always running up hill against time and no matter how hard you try, you end up back at the bottom even more tired than you started out. Erin is such a sweetie, she was in the waiting room for both of my deliveries and even though she had kids of her own, she packed them up and came to stay with me the first week James went back to work. James and Charles knew of each other but didn't really bond the way that Erin and I hoped they would when we all started hanging out nearly twenty years ago, I guess you can't hope that boys will make friends. James always had nice things to say about Erin and Charles and Charles said nice things of James, they just didn't have enough in common to get along for the most part but so be it, it didn't stop Erin and I from being lifelong best friends.

So the second night working with Ben was a little more fun, I was able to better control my emotions so I was able to lightly flirt. I did my best to play it cool when I chatted with Ben on the floor; Lisa was under the impression that I was doing my best to talk her up but I was actually just getting to know the guy. It was easy to talk to Ben, he was down to earth and warm to interact with. Ben spent some time in the Navy before putting himself through school for business management so he was well rounded and intelligent.

Ben was stuck on midnights when he first arrived to the company; he enjoyed kayaking with his friends as well as mountain biking through dirt trails so having the days off was a plus for him. Ben's athleticism only added to his sexiness. I admired that Ben was outdoorsy and in good shape, of course I had James at home but he was only a few short breaths from needing a c-pap machine to breathe for him so maybe the contrast between the two made Ben more appealing.

Ben was good looking and had a very arousing voice but what made him the most attractive was how confident and assured of himself he was. Ben wasn't cocky or arrogant but he had good posture and through his shirt you could see his strong back muscles work in turn. Ben was easy going; he was respectful in his manners and diligent as he worked. Lisa and Reagan were funny in that they chattered about how many bad things they would do to Ben yet either had the stones to really talk to him. Lisa was shy, I get that but she seemed rather convinced that she was meant for him except that she didn't even really bother to try to start a conversation in which she might initiate any form of dating, or just to show interest and hope that he'd ask her out. I was surprised that Reagan respected the "dibs" put forth by Lisa, normally if she sees a guy she wants to take for a spin she'll flash him and lead the way to her car to put her ankles up.

Ben and I counted pallets and sorted some of the boxes and were easily able to talk about anything. Ben took interest in my kids and that James and I used to play softball with one of his firms a while back, I didn't mind pitching but I liked first base, Ben slid in a sly comment about being a "third base kind of guy" with a big grin. I was trying my best to be a good wife so I made sure than I didn't subconsciously hide my wedding ring or forget to mention my husband. I did my best to keep from swaying back and forth or even leaning over to far so that Ben could get a good view down my shirt. I felt comfortable with Ben but there was still the subtle awkwardness that I wanted to jump his bones. I tried to keep my mind on anything but Bens body as we spoke, when I began to feel my cheeks warm up and begin to flush I would avert my attention as fast as I could. It was hard to avoid eying the crotch of his worn jeans. The thin denim was slightly worn and faded in color but each time he stepped the bulge just called for my attention and it made my mouth water.

Lisa followed suit towards the end of the night and began to chat Ben up pretty well, Reagan encouraged Lisa to ask more of the personal and not necessarily "appropriate for work" types of questions. Reagan would text Lisa to ask about his Johnson as she spoke to Ben, Lisa would check her phone and from across the floor you could watch her face turn deep beat red and then shoot a death glare up to the window, it had to be endlessly embarrassing but it was pretty funny. Ben stood with a sturdy stance, his leg muscles bulged and flexed beneath his denim jeans and his rugged look was drop dead sexy. Lisa was smitten but to be honest, so was I.

I rooted for Lisa to find the courage to ask Ben out, I was afraid she'd wait too long for him to ask her and miss her chance. I found that I really wanted Lisa to date Ben so I could hear stories of him hoisting her up on a counter to ease into her or ruggedly manhandling her until she seized in pleasure. Gretchen sided with me when we snuck in small chats on our breaks; she also wanted to hear about the rowdy outdoorsman and the equipment he would be working with. Gretchen and I were the oldest two ladies of my office, she was a bit more reserved than I was but she wasn't also looking at the business end of age forty like I was. I did hold my tongue with most of the wording when I spoke to Gretchen, I wasn't about to blurt out that I wanted to take Ben twice a day like a prescription but I did admit to admiring his sturdy build and the rough exterior that constantly caught my eye.

I didn't feel weirdly hormonal or like I was having mood swings to I couldn't place why I was finding myself stupid horny for a man I had hardly met but his personality was calming and erotic at the same time. Towards the end of shift I found myself guilty about lingering around to "casually" see who I might run into. You know those moments where you know you are leaning towards doing something you shouldn't but your will to do the right thing is easily over powered by the urge to do the wrong thing? I saw myself like that as I accidentally "forgot" my keys in the office once I got across the warehouse floor; I walked out with the girls but had to turn back. Lisa and Reagan were dragging behind Gretchen and Hannah who were on their way to their husbands, happily. I felt a sense of dread wash over me as I headed back, I accidentally left my keys on purpose, and I knew at the time that it was the first domino to fall.

I wandered half way across the warehouse floor before overplaying my forgetfulness about my keys but truth was; I knew before I even pulled the office door shut behind all of us that I was up to no good. I wandered with the group of girls towards the parking lot with the intent to let them leave me behind. I know that the dillydallying was the first step towards poor choices but I was easily persuaded to forget the right thing to do for a moment, it was only for just one moment. Some of the guys that hauled packages and put shipping orders together were packing up to leave for the night also and one by one, there were less and less people in the building. I knew exactly where I left my keys on my desk but not having seen Ben leave yet I shuffled my feet in the office while I stared out the window that over looked the shipping floor until I saw that Ben hadn't left either.

I felt guilty about speeding up and then slowing down my pace in order to time it so that I walked up on Ben as he was trying to leave also. I wasn't really intending for anything to happen but by mere chance he was up for chatting a little on our way out (without any prying ears) then I would have been appreciative. The cool air was blowing in from the parking lot, the building was always as hot as an oven because the sun bakes it all day, even with exhaust fans it's always hot. Ben was wearing a light running zip up that was dark blue and had some worn through rips on the wrists, I watched as he swung his arms while walking out before I caught up with him.

"Hey, wait up for me" I called to Ben to make sure that he didn't get to much of a lead on me on his way out into the parking lot. I should have just let him go, I should have put my keys in my pocket and shoved myself into my car and gnawed at my inner cheek the whole way home, but this isn't a memoir of right choices. So I scurried to catch up with Ben, accidentally on purpose of course. I asked him how he was adjusting to the afternoon hours rather than the midnights, a harmless question sure but definitely one that could have waited until working hours. I found myself running my hands up my neck to hold my hair up, something I've done to flirt by showing off my bare neck since I was a sexy teen, my subtle way of saying step up behind me and bite on my neck and control me. I caught Ben looking at me a bit longer as I played with my hair a little; I used the excuse that I was cooling off from the warm shop by lifting my hair up and holding it there, keeping my arms up also slimmed my figure, accidentally on purpose.

Out of the corner of my eye I looked around to make sure the girls had all left so there wouldn't be any judging eyes in the parking lot to harass me. Lisa was contemplating going out with Reagan but she was often hesitant because she was much more conservative than Reagan. Reagan like to flaunt what she had and it wasn't all that uncommon to find her hiking her shirt up for beads or free drinks, or even grinding up with other girls for hoots and hollers, Reagan is definitely a wild girl. The parking lot was empty and the two other guys still in the warehouse weren't headed our way so it ended up being Ben and me for a few minutes to chat while slowly on our way to our cars. I milled around a little and found myself staring down at the ground kicking at rocks to keep from making it to my car too quickly, I was enjoying talking with Ben and I didn't want it to end all that quickly.

Ben was smiling as he looked down at the ground while he walked too, he was so comforting to talk to and I didn't find myself holding much back. "You're definitely a cute guy, I think you should ask Lisa out... since I'm married and all" I snorted out with a desperate laugh. Ben smirked off my suggestion to try and hook up with Lisa, she really was a sweet girl and a cutie but he seemed hesitant. I knew I was mostly pushing her on him in an attempt to keep from making any more advances on him, plus if she were to boast and brag after hooking up with him then Gretchen and I could get some answers and more mental imagery to think about every time we looked at him. I did my best to keep my feet pointed towards my car and not stop and actually point them towards Ben as we chatted but I found that I was swaying my hips a bit more than usual in a playful mood. Normally after the long shifts I am ready to go home and take off my bra and kick my feet up for a bit but talking with Ben seemed to energize me, I didn't want to think about wrapping my legs around him or running my tongue from his all the way down the front of him, nope, not going to think about it, I won't, no way.

Ben was a smiley guy, his hazel eyes were shadowed by the parking lot lights but I could still see that they were looking at me as we spoke. I kept my hands jutted into my pockets but every few words when I focused on what I was saying I would catch myself bounding on my tiptoes a little, and pushing my chest up and out a little more. Ben talked about how wonderful of a night it was and how he might go walking around his neighborhood to take in more of the air, one of the things he missed when I worked midnights. I inched my way with all of my might to convince myself into the driver seat of my car and I was certain that once in my car I could much easier drive away. I tried to inch bit by bit to put a gap between us, Ben was a charming guy and had a very soothing voice, shame on me for enjoying the conversation but the husband I had at home was snoring in his sleep by this point, I was lonely.

Once I made it to my back bumper Ben caught notion that I was trying to inch out and he bid me a good night then climbed into his jeep. I am not one for jeeps, especially since nine to five sissies and old guys usually drive them but Ben was a rugged outdoorsy guy and it made him sexier. I wanted to beat my head against my steering wheel for having purposefully towed the line and toyed with more flirting. I felt that I was only going to disappoint myself no matter what I did; I had to know that I was desirable but I knew I would also feel poorly if I got rejected, or hurt if I tried to behave and continued to fall for him, it was a lose-lose situation for me. I was raised in the church and any form of adultery is a sin and I had already taken thoughts of Ben into my mind while taking care of business myself. I lowered my head and flicked my wrist forward to start my engine.

"Knock "Knock" there was a sudden and startling tapping on my window. Looking up in a huff Ben was standing with his face squished against my passenger window. I jumped and shrieked so loud that I hurt my own ears, whacked my wrist on the steering wheel and nearly wet myself. Ben was staring wide eyed into my car and held a creepy smile on his face as I tried to kill him with an evil look. I hate being scared, I absolutely hate it and now I was furious at Ben for being such a jerk. My heart nearly exploded in my chest as I tried to calm my breathing after my panic by tilting my head back.

"Click Click" I heard Ben lifting on the locked handle of my passenger door. I squinted my eyes at him and debated for a minute whether or not it was smart to unlock my door for him. The instant flashed through my head as to whether or not I was making a smart decision, I was already flirting with the idea of indiscretion and each time I pushed the limit a bit further, I got sucked in more and more. I could actually see myself as if I were watching a movie of myself sitting in my car hoping that Ben would pull his pants down for me, I can actually see the movie of it happening and it was turning me on. I imagined Ben having a mildly groomed region, his rugged manliness wouldn't let him manscape very much but with as good as his manners were, I imagined he still kept a clean house *down there*.

Ben made sure I was ok since I waited a minute to start my engine, he explained that his mother raised him to make sure ladies get home safely, it only added to his charm even though his inner thirteen year old scared the hell out of me. You can't go and scare a girl like that if she's had kids, we pee a little. I felt myself getting hot that Ben was sitting alone with me in a dark parking lot, there were street lights but still in the dark corner there was enough secrecy to make for a wildly exciting romp between myself and this man that is like sixteen years younger than me. I wrung my hands together to keep them from shaking, my nerves were coursing through with shakes and sweaty hands, even my thighs were starting to shake, anticipating being touched by his strong hands. My womanhood began to tremble hoping that I would just give in and take his fingers inside of me, his breath smelled sweet, his cologne was subtle but also had a musky undertone that made my nostrils flare out to take in larger and larger breaths of him and all the while, I couldn't take my eyes off of his lap.

I'm pretty sure that Ben knew where my eyes were locked but I also hoped that in the shadows of the night that perhaps it wasn't all that obvious that my eyes were fixated on his package. Ben wriggled to adjust as he sat and in the slight lighting the images of *him* caught some the light and I could feel my mouth begin to drop open slightly. Ben's body was mostly hidden under the shadow from the street light but his mound rose up high enough into the light to look like it was being displayed for me. My mouth watered, I wanted to taste him in my mouth, that wasn't an urge I often had let alone in the last fifteen years or so. Ben leaned in to put himself in my eyesight, I felt my heart jump as he totally busted me staring at his crotch, I felt embarrassed and tried to play it off that I was just tired and having a hard time focusing but his smile was playfully joined with a raised eyebrow to tell me he wasn't buying it.

With a big smile Ben was letting himself out of my car while bidding me a pleasant evening. I was rife with guilt; what if James smells the cologne in my car? What if one of the girls at work finds out and I become ostracized? What did I get myself into? I huffed and puffed trying to calm myself down as I pulled out of the driveway, I hardly looked to check for oncoming traffic, luckily it's light this late in the evening; I was flying towards the highway to get home and away from myself. I wanted to sob in self-disappointment but I was also feeling frantic that I kept inching closer and closer to the edge of, something, living, an affair, cheating, elation, I don't know for sure.

I tried to fan my face as I drove; the open window wasn't strong enough to cool off my racing pulse or overheating body. I couldn't get cooled down enough so I unbuttoned my blouse. I reached for the top button with my left hand but it wasn't there. I padded across my collar bone and came to realize that sometime in the afternoon I had unbuttoned my top button, not that I have all sorts of cleavage to flash but I couldn't figure out when I had bared more of my chest, and did Ben notice? My mind raced at infinite speeds, I couldn't catch my brain nor my breath so I kept unbuttoning and continued my drive home. Vivid images flashed through my mind, what if Ben was brazen and scooted his bottom up a bit and slid his jeans down, could I have withheld from lunging at him once I saw his thighs emerge from under his jeans or would I have been on him like Reagan would have been had she been unleashed to devour him?

Once I turned off the highway and still felt my adrenaline surging through me a little. I remembered it was fun to be breezy and have my shirt totally unbuttoned with just a bra on underneath while driving. I felt like I was revisiting some of my younger years were I would take a road trip with either Nick or James and we'd titillate each other, sometimes I'd ride in just a bra or bikini and flash my driver to turn them on. With James I'd play with my chest to wait until he was completely engorged and then unzip him while still driving, I don't know how we didn't kill ourselves in a car crash; that would have been one weird mess for paramedics to find. With Nick he was younger and it was never a problem to get him aroused and ready for fun, one time it was so passionate that we pulled over on a side road and slid down into the ditch while cars drove by, I understood Erin's lust for the wildness that came with being a little voyeuristic.

I loved Taking James into my mouth and being so head thrashing wild that he would sometimes spread his hand on the back of my head to slow me down so I didn't kill us. I missed my wilder days, the days when I can say "I'm young, why not" and do plenty of the stuff that society deems wild and irresponsible. I used to take James into my hand and go crazy while going down on him; I'd pretend I was Steen Tyler with James as my microphone. Maybe I'm just in need of a change, maybe I need to shake up my life in a way that replenishes my soul and gives me reason to appreciate what I do have. Is that a thing, where someone teeters on the edge of death to appreciate life? Maybe I should try bungee jumping or sky diving, is there something without the heights?

The mental push and pull on my way home was daunting, I almost felt crazy, except I wasn't bad crazy, maybe just confused crazy or even like crushing on Ben crazy, like in junior high when you doodle your crushes name all over a notebook with scribbly hearts. I am nearly forty years old, how in the world am I crushing this badly, besides, Ben is sixteen years younger than I am, I was driving a car by the time he was born. Men date younger girls all the time. Men's lust is insatiable, their little divining rod will stand up for all sorts of girls, and it's just the more intelligent ones that control themselves. I have an entire conversation out loud convincing myself I'm not crazy before I realize I am talking to myself like a crazy person.

It's has always been nice to get winks, whistles, men revving their engines or even just smiling, I supposed I began to notice I was getting attention when I hit puberty. When I was in my early teen years I was awkward just like all the other girls; shy about my body and was unsure about the changes that were happening. In my mid to late teens I garnered the sly smiles and air kisses by some of the boys in school. I found it exciting to be lusted after and adding a little more sway to my walk or jeans that were a bit more form fitting seemed to further along the attention.

My mother was a good church going lady, always with her white gloves for Sunday services and in her best dresses. I like to wear sundresses and catch up with some of the other parents whose kids attend the same Sunday school as mine but it's a show, I honestly feel that it's a show for everyone, no one wants to be shunned for being the first to speak out against the herd and call phony. I can feel my skin crawl watching all of the fake people in their pearls and suits climb into their shiny new cars to upstage one another, a fake presence of happiness to lie to themselves as they head out to Sunday brunch. I loathe the other wives that push their bleached teeth through their smiles as they boast and brag about this tropic vacation or that, knowing all the while they just lounged their fat asses around a pool bar, desperate for someone younger and hotter than their spouses to even glance their way.

I find myself cynical wandering through the grocery store, I just browse some of the aisles and see random women clutching their high-end purses or bags while their kids sit neglected in the shopping cart. The same women that let their child scream in public but doesn't bother to take her eyes off of her myface on her phone drives me to a blind rage, the child just wants some love but she can't be bothered to pry her phone from her head because she desperately needs validation. I guess I'm not all that different, I like having the occasional head turn to look at me when I jog, or get the occasional smile when I rub elbows at one of the kids' performances at school. Sometimes I'll see a father at the school that hasn't let himself go and his quick smile is pretty flattering.

Women in sweat pants, or pajama pants and leather coats, these bored housewives that can't even bother to get dressed to go outside sit around while their husbands to all the work make me furious. I try to run each and every morning because I like my body, I told myself I wouldn't become some slag housewife that can't keep their man happy. Sad truth is even though I've nearly kept the same figure James married, he hardly notices me. I can't say that I should be miserable, there are wives with husbands over in the desert and those girls need way more sympathy than I do. James helps to keep up the house, he mows and does the fixer up crap to reinforce that he's a "man" but they are small tasks, it's not like he's been to war or served in the military.

I can't tell you when I grew tired of the same old routine, I should be happy with my morning kiss from James, I suppose he could just as easily high-five me or wait until I come into view before he packs up and heads to the gym. Years back James used to go and play basketball then come home to shower with me, to conserve water of course, and we'd fit in the time for some of our fun before he'd leave for work. James joined the YMCA to meet up with some of the other professionals he works with and sometimes they meet up with new clients, it's easier than trying to golf in the winter so now he just showers there. James used to work out with weights when he was younger and his strong build was one of the sexier parts of him when we married, but eighteen years later things have just fluttered out.

I know I sound like a total cliché that I looked outside of my marriage to make up for what was missing *in* my marriage but when you don't know what's missing it's hard to know that something was missed at all. James and I learned to get over our anxiety about communicating, we learned to rely on one another and we both put forth the effort to build our lives together as a husband and wife are supposed to. I have spent most of my marriage fulfilled in my role, I was elated to become a mother even though I knew the work it would take I knew that the outcome would be worth it. I spent most of my marriage happy in it, but happy was the makeup that covered over some of the many blemishes.

The notion of turning forty is terrifying, I don't want to let go of the vision I have of myself of being in my sexy thirties, I don't want to start seeing more and more veins through the skin on the back of my hands, I don't want to see my children graduate high school and then go on to college. What will it be like when James and I have the house to ourselves again? I have many questions and insecurities plaguing me, Erin is confident about herself and her future, me not so much. Each turn I take back home is just one more time I follow the same steps around and around again, how long can someone ride a merry-go-round, the same view, the same plastic horses and the same music, that's how I'm feeling about every single day.

Every morning starts out as a quiet moment as I get dressed to go running, I try to avoid moving cars or rolling an ankle as I cross over cracked sidewalks. I hit my front door and wait for the explosion of chaos when Bruno starts barking his furry ass off while James is trying to flee like the house is on fire. I love my little angels but I sometimes think I would be a better mother if maybe James and I were separated and I only had them half the time, maybe that way I would better appreciate them, or them me. I have almost everything I wanted when I was a teenager, except a popping rock album like Blondie but I still don't feel like it's enough, maybe I should have let go of my teen age dreams with my teen age years, maybe I should just hunker down and grow old, give in and give up.

When someone gets murdered the first person the cops look at is the spouse, what does that really say about marriage now a days, I know I probably shouldn't look all that deeply into that but is still speaks volumes. I like the occasional night where I can just have a few drinks, the body numbing warmth of alcohol seems to hide my issues. I understand why alcoholics exist, the nirvana that comes after a few shots is distracting enough from the day to day problems that it would be a nice place to live, but then there are the motherhood expectations, the wifely duties and societal burdens of having to function and hold down a job. One of my biggest pet peeves is addicts, everyone praises and parades when someone recovers and cleans up, well I never did heroin where's my goddamn sticker?

I remember not feeling right after the birth of my baby girl, I understood my hormones were out of whack but I was ok after my son. After my daughter I was slightly older, I was thirty-four and maybe that played a role in it but it did take several weeks to click back into *Ally* mode. I have noticed in the past few weeks that I felt a bit off, skewed in some way and my looming fortieth birthday around the corner has really become a pressing issue on top of it. Maybe I'll shake out of this mood, maybe I'll just wake up after my birthday with acceptance or maybe just submission. Maybe a week of getting screwed straight by James would straighten me out; maybe I just need a really good dicking.

Once again as I pull into my driveway my front porch light is off, the house is as dark and quiet as the rest of the neighborhood and here I am, just sitting in my car with a underlying feeling of dread to go into my own house, with my own family inside and to lay down next to my husband. I feel like a fake set of teeth tucked behind a fake smile being worn by someone with a fake tan and wearing fake bleached blonde hair, just layer upon layer of fake just masking contempt. Out of the corner of my eye I can still see the glowing images of Ben sitting in my passenger seat, his groin illuminated by the light and enhanced by the darkness around the rest of his lap, it all called for me to reach over and rub my hands along his strong thighs, inching closer and closer to the button that held his pants up.

I don't have the desire to pull the handle to let myself out of my car, the darkness seems soothing, maybe if I just slept in the car that James would skip his basketball morning and take care of the morning bustle and my day off might remind me that it isn't all that bad, that I am alive and the world could once again be beautiful. With my fingers resting on the silver door handle I notice that the skin on my fingers does look older, no soft pleasurable fingertips anymore, just stretched thin skin that makes me look much older than I feel inside, like I'm wearing old lady makeup and the only time I think about it is when my I don't recognize the reflection in the mirror. Aging is a bitch, I spend too much of my life doting on everyone else, there is no fun for me, I settle for jogging as an escape from my life but there is no comedy club with friends, no laugh sessions in a hot tub with good company, there is just the lack of kamikaze chaos that comes with kids getting ready for school and an out of control dog that wants to get out of the house too.

Maybe I just need one last whirlwind adventure before age takes over me. Maybe I just need one last hoorah to enliven me and give me a taste for life again. Maybe I should veer my car into a telephone pole and have an affair with death for a flash of a moment to reset my mind and make me see bright lights again, to taste zesty vibrant flavors again or so hear the crisp sounds that get drowned out but the humdrum of every day. I could easily let the steering wheel of the car take me into the back end of a parked car or one of the vintage looking lamp posts this fake city puts up to reassure the citizens that we all live comfortably tucked into a safe neighborhood, except I can only think about rising insurance rates, how inconvenient it would be to spend a few days in a hospital listening to beeping machines or to have to sit and answer questions about how everything happened, it would ruin my near death experience. Would James come take care of me in the hospital or would he convince himself that the kids and house needed him more and that since I was a big girl that I should have the ability to take care of myself, thus leaving me alone and lonely again.

I can't stop wondering if maybe Ben's power isn't so much his manly sensuality but rather his youth, his masculinity and rugged charm and perhaps that reflects the things I once had and perhaps still long for in my life. My garage door is black with shadows, my car is full of darkness and all I have to do is recline my seat to be consumed by the darkness, but I already feel I am. Each button I refasten reminds me that I am part of the buttoned down society, no long young and free. Each exhale seems to further deflate me, depress me and leave me empty. Even lightly flirting with Ben in conversation seemed to make me aware of sounds I never hear, especially my heartbeat in my brain. I seem to feel my fingertips shake and perspire with adrenaline and I like the feeling of the small rush.

I vowed to Love James when I was twenty-four, I still love him but I can't remember the last time I actually lusted for him. Maybe I am just supposed to keep wearing cardigans and frocks, then eventually heavy sweaters and shawls and just wither with age. Maybe once the kids are off to college James will spend more time in the garage trying to prove his manliness with small projects or hide away more and more to watch his sports while I slink away to reading books quietly and ignored. Will James and I just grow old in the same household, two people having grown apart who just share an address? If that scuba gear sounding breathing machine arrives in my room I am moving out of my bed.

Forty is a hard age to accept, forty is when I always pictured old age starting. "Click" (the door pops open with a tug on the handle) I suppose maybe I will just keep lying down each night and waking up a day older each morning, next to James and let my dull life continue. Maybe I'll just keep getting to have the close encounters with Ben and let that small spark remain in my loins, that slight tingle that tickles at me and makes my adrenaline thump. I know as soon as I press this lever to open my front door again that I willingly accept each day of age, that I willingly climb into my bed with James and shuffle my tired feet through yet another day of my life. Maybe Lisa will find the courage to talk to Ben more and they'll hit it off, maybe Gretchen and I can convince her to send him some naughty texts pics and maybe if he sends her some in return she'll let us take a peek.

I might be overthinking everything, maybe I am just tired or stressed and in need of a week with James to refresh our personal relationship with ourselves and then also with each other. Maybe when I wake up I'll appreciate the man that does help to take care of my kids and me. Maybe in the night I'll have some life changing dream that makes me aware of all that James has done and continues to do and maybe I'll feel love for him again.

Each time I work with Ben I catch myself checking him out, there is just so much that calls me to watch him. His slight smile, his strong hands and arms, and his muscular build, it's not too big just firm in his legs, back, shoulders, and chest. Hazels eyes are usually a take them or leave them for me, bright blue or green eyes are usually an attractive feature for me but even his eyes seem to have a smoky sexy appeal to them. I continued to find reasons to be near Ben, I noticed that I was a bit worse than Lisa, and she called dibs on him. Gretchen and Hannah both heckled me that I seemed to be trying to edge out Lisa in the running to get Ben into bed, in my defense I did mention Lisa a few times to him but she wasn't making much effort so it wasn't like I was sabotaging her. Gretchen and Hannah knew that I did most of the inventory so with that my proximity to Ben was more convenient coincidence than intent but that doesn't mean that I wasn't subtly finding reasons to see him.

Nights after work I would feel the high of getting flirted with, the rush of the taboo and inching close to the line of naughty or inappropriate. I was never a girl to push the limits and see how much trouble I could get in, I behaved and did what I was supposed to, as an adult you just do what is expected and be a grown up about it. Flirting with Ben seemed harmless but it also seemed to fill me with the rush that you get on first dates, feelings I have missed, butterflies and all. I felt my womanhood fill with the tingles of lust wanting him each time we interacted. I felt myself react to his voice when he spoke, goose bumps on my skin and the naughtier parts of me responding as well. Each time I pulled into my driveway I brushed down the small hairs on the back of my neck that still stood up and convinced myself that I got a small hit to feed my addiction but it was time to put it away.

On my long weekend James was still carrying on about our upcoming stay in the mountain cabin, it sounded lovely but I wasn't sure I wanted lovely. There was something erotic about standing stark naked on the front porch to greet the morning and to get taken right there, raw and wild and it turned me on. I was never into flashing myself for random strangers and the thought of getting caught in the act of love making was borderline shameful so I was curious why the thought of it was starting to excite me. I adore the idea of a quiet week away, no kids, no dog, sure the husband will be there but what can I do?

I like that James was trying to keep my ugly birthday a low key one, a week off from breakfasts and running might just be what I need to find my center again. Maybe James and I will do yoga in the mornings as the crisp sun breaks through the morning sky and then walk trails through the mountains in the afternoons and fall in love again. The thought of James maybe dropping to his knees in the woods and kiss me down there filled me with heat, the warmth in my lap made me pause for a moment and brought a smile to my face. A week with my husband would be a pleasant change; maybe we'll eat light salads and spend the week just quietly reading or actually get in the few love making sessions he's planning on. The notion of James climbing on top of my didn't arouse me much, the days of him licking at me like a dog at a water bowl were the days I had been missing, the days where his tongue would dance along between my legs until all of the muscles in my legs would cramp in excitement, those are the days I want back.

The weekends are an elongated chunk of time that are just like the mornings except I can't send the kids off and soak in a bath. James will rise slowly in the mornings and we'll try to have tea together, except I'll also be tasked with getting breakfast supplies ready for the kids. Depending on the season both kids will have soccer, James and I will usually share or split the chore of dealing with jerseys and game schedules and so on. The weekends are meant to relax but in all honesty, I can't really relax around James anymore, we have our lives and no longer just lay together to cuddle like we used to. The mad dash to get through the days are exhausting, timing meals and wrangling Bruno out in parks and dealing with two youngsters always clambering "mom, mom, mom, ma" and so on while James nods to strange guys and pretends he doesn't hear any of it, it has worn down my nerves to the point that I don't know if they can be repaired.

Each time I crawl into bed with James I can't help but feel that I might not miss him if he weren't here, his heavy breathing with sudden stops wouldn't be missed, his rustling that wakes me up in the night wouldn't be missed and his sweaty laundry in the basket every morning wouldn't be missed either. Maybe some time away from phones and endless calls and the chattering girls at work will help, maybe removing myself from it all will help me to find my bearings and then maybe turning forty won't be such a dread. I found that my unraveling nerves were a whole other level of stress, if I put Bruno out and tried to take a bath it wouldn't be long before he barked to be let in, if I laid down for an hour it wouldn't get half way before he was barking to be let out, it was tempting to send him to a kennel for a day just to have a day to strip down and lay sprawled out naked on my bed with the windows open to let in the sun and the breeze and pretend that I was alone on some deserted sandy beach for an entire day, but then I'd feel guilt for shirking my responsibilities. I'm trapped, stuck, miserable and now that I have finally admitted how I feel I feel bad for feeling the way that I feel, and I hate myself for feeling now too.

The week before my birthday was an emotional one, each night I worked I did my best to appease the girls in the office and play along with the girly notions of what each assembly floor guy might be like in bed, but each time I tried to picture it, it was always Ben. I knew I had missed date night last weekend with James but I also knew James was planning a big week of lots of romance, I wonder if he got a prescription of pills for such an occasion. Date night was often us just watching movies on the couch together, there was hardly any reason to go out, nor any real will too either. Going out is a hassle; find a sitter, get all dressed up and argue over where we're going to eat or what we'll see, it became easier to just put the kids to bed and then catch a movie for just the two of us, which of course meant falling asleep on the couch. At least when James falls asleep on the couch half an hour in it doesn't cost us thirteen bucks for his movie ticket, I often let the movie play out and just pull out my latest book to read.

Our occasional romances were well coordinated events. James would request some fun, then from there the variables ensued; a quickie was me just bent over the bed for a few minutes and then he'd leave me alone to go and brush his teeth and finish getting ready for bed. More involved meant shaving my legs or whatever and then he'd start with the same routine of kissing on my neck while jamming his fingers into me like he was plunging a drain. I'd move to find some comfort in James' jarring motion but it was more like reducing the discomfort. James used to take the time to caress and to entice me but for a while now there just has never really been the time, he was just in a hurry to get me moist enough not to tear at the softer skin on him while he just seized on top of me. I thought about maybe initiating date night fun last weekend because I could fantasize that Ben was mounting up behind me just like I fantasized about in the kitchen the first night but James would be done minutes before I was even really ready to start and I'd end up grinding on myself in the shower before bed so why not just cut James out of the equation and head right into getting myself off.

I learned more about Ben and he asked more questions about me as we interacted, he knew I was trying to sell him on pursuing Lisa but his interests seemed mixed. Ben was a single guy and Lisa was a cute single girl but her shyness inhibited her a little and I was trying to get them together, I didn't really mind being the girl that went to him to try to make it happen because it was a valid excuse to chat him up and get to know him better. Ben and I share ample smiles when we weren't talking, secretive glances that we would pass and a slight smile that we would share between us in private, just between us. I did my best to keep the girls from seeing my little advances because I would have been labeled a harlot and I would have been turned on by my friends in the office, plus it would have been a disaster if James were to catch on.

Don't get me wrong, sure I think about what it would be like if I weren't married, if I had a weekend a month to myself or the courage to tell Ben that I had a little crush on him. What would it be like if I threw away my life for a small fling? My new cars: gone, my nice beautiful house: gone, my children would be wrecked and I would be at fault; the temptress that ruined their lives. Not that I give a crap about the neighbors, especially the nosy Joy and her judging but it would be hard to be labeled as the whore that humped some pool boy or something like that and destroyed a nice man that did his best to be loving, I just couldn't be that kind of girl. Everything about Ben was charming and lovely, every part of me told me to steer clear and when he wasn't around I was more than convinced I would be strong and avoid any situation where I might be tempted to trip up, but when he was around every part of me told me to cover him in oil and use him as a naked slip and slide.

The week before my birthday vacation week Gretchen and Hannah were extra nice to me, they were smiles and sparkling eyes knowing that I was in agony about my pending milestone, they brought cookies and cupcakes for me, which was really super sweet of them except deep down I saw them as piles of calories and then had to calculate how far each cupcake would be in terms of miles to run off the fats and sweets. There was really only one person I wanted to hear "happy birthday" from, in his deep graveling voice; Ben. Reagan continued to party and club because that was what she did, she would have some of the wildest hookups and even though Gretchen, Hannah and I would shake our heads at her vivacious appetite for men, we secretly admired her for going out and getting what she wanted.

One night Reagan met with two *friends* at a club; both were tall, cute, athletic and very into her. I had only thought lightly about some of the things Reagan has done, her stories were fun adventures to have vicariously but never in a million years would such things happen but she "enjoyed the company" of both boys. Gretchen and I were full of questions, like the physics of how it all happened as well as sights, sounds, feelings, and so many other crazy questions only such a crazy girl could answer for two old lonely housewives. Reagan said that it wasn't a one at a time sort of scenario and that once there was some organization instrumented that she was able to focus on her pleasure of everything, two men completely infatuated with her and ravishing her body.

When Reagan was done telling our group of dead silent office ladies there wasn't a closed mouth among us. Each of us were blushed about what we were hearing, it was like a Showtime special or something. As Reagan showed and demonstrated to us many of the twisting and incredible things she was involved in, each of us had to adjust how we were seated due to being immensely aroused, I felt myself begin to sweat so I tried to think about Bruno chewing up more of my socks rather than two gorgeous sweaty men man-handling me and pinning me between them then roughly arguing over who gets to kiss me and where while my whole naked body becomes covered in hands and mouths. Reagan liked the attention and she wasn't going to feel ashamed that she was an adult and chose to do what she did, I admired her that at such a young age she had the confidence to admit what she likes and still hold her head up about it, I'd still be embarrassed to death over some of the PG-13 things, Reagan as at least one "X" if not two.

My lower parts were sensitive to my hobble as I awkwardly stepped down the stairs to the factory floor to inventory a new pallet, I felt swollen and engorged, ready for a go round to "make the tea kettle whistle". I tried my best to Lamaze breathe to cool myself off and silently hoped that Ben wouldn't show up out of nowhere, if I heard his voice I might have just soaked through my panties. I was on edge, I even tried to step lightly hoping that maybe silencing my heels a bit might make me invisible until I got my heightened sensual emotions under control. Reading those distasteful smut books was always something I thought those trailer park old ladies did, the ones that lay out all day with their big hair, reading while smoking poolside. I never bought into the long hair foreigners and my apologies to Diane Lane, but I'd take Richard Gere over Olivier Martinez, sure he's a hot younger guy but still, I never would have considered a tryst behind my husband's back and Gere was distinguished, not a sloppy student type.

I ducked between rows of pallets like I was running from a gunman, I have it in my head that if I can crouch a little that I might not be seen and by the time I can get my jinkies together, then I can forget the vivid stories from Reagan that had my dials turned all the way up. The paper order is still on the side of the pallet, shrink wrap is wrapped around the pallets a dozen times to keep all of the boxes tight and uniform so counting it takes a few minutes and I can scurry back to the safety of my all female office. I got my head on straight and hoisted myself on to the pallet jack to count how many boxes were on the top layer so I can multiply it by the number of layers and match it with the order sheets.

I was on my way to thinking about all the boxes and doing well forgetting about the extremely steamy session Reagan had with a pair of musculy frat guys when "hey there darling." His voice rumbled through me, not like the atomic bombing thunder of storms but the light little rumbling you'll hear from thunder in the sky miles away. Immediately I felt it; my most delicate of areas heightened, Ben's deep voice sent a shiver down my spine and into my panties. My knees nearly gave out on me; I must have looked like a freshly birthed giraffe as I fumbled to turn around to look at him while fighting to keep my legs underneath me. I don't know if the temperature in the warehouse dipped or my temperature spiked when I saw him but I nearly orgasmed from being so turned on and then seeing him.

I felt my hands tremble and could hear my words mumble as I strained to keep my eyes coordinated to see. My vision blurred a little and it took everything I had to keep from getting light headed, it seemed that all my blood rushed to my intimate areas. I pictured Ben stepping up to me, wrapping his strong arm around my back to kiss me as he pulls me in close before turning me in a way that leans me against the pallet before he slides my clothes down and then begins to kiss down my spine until he is kneeling behind me and tasting me from behind as I step up onto my tippy toes and work back against him. I wanted Ben to bury his face deep into me while I reached back behind me and pulled his face deep into me. I couldn't stop this train of incredibly hot and steamy visions from running their course through my mind.

So I'm sure Ben had begun to see my small nuances, my idiosyncrasies that might give a way that I want him in the worst possible way and I'm struggling to fight it. I glanced to make quick eye contact with him as he stepped closer to me and then I immediately shot my eyes in another direction to keep from any further bumbling like an idiot in front of him. There is a black piece of ground in chewing gum on the cement floor, it has no definitive shape but the glob was something to look at, better than at Ben's crotch I suppose. As Ben asked how my day was and if I needed any help I tried to keep from standing funny, my lady parts seemed to be swelling with desire and it was making standing still a challenge, each move I made seemed to send a quiver through me and I was afraid that if I moved too much or too quickly, I'd orgasm and burst out a pleasurable moan, surely embarrassing me to death.

I whipped my head around to face back at the pallet to resume inspecting all of the boxes to look for flaws or shipping damage, sometimes the pallets will tip and crush the whole side of a pallet but this one looked fine. I felt Ben set his hand on the back of my right shoulder, me left eye fluttered for a moment of weakness and my tail bone began to tingle. My whole body shook at his touch and it was just on my shoulder. I know I'm in trouble and maybe I need my week of having teenage like sex with my *husband* James to rebuild my defenses and sense of honor to the man I wed. I bent a little to duck Ben's hand on my shoulder; "this is a work place buddy, that could be harassment" I tried to play off my awkward bodily motion when he touched me but it was more so I didn't explode in my pants than anything else. I was dying of embarrassment inside but if I showed it even a little then I would die.

Ben dropped his bottom lip out and frowned while raising his eyebrows. I tried to ignore the puppy dog look from the corner of my eye but me entire body was craving his each and every touch. I struggled to keep my breathing a secret, it was making my lungs burn to ignore my pounding heart so I convinced myself that the girls were up in the booth and watching closely in order to behave. I made my count and page inspection as fast as I could, Ben began to crank up the pallet jack which lifts it up from the ground to make it easier to pull and move around. As Ben cranked on the jack the levels of boxes moved, causing me to have to start over.

My frustration at trying to hurry and count while inspecting turned off my tingling crotch. With a slight bit of anger I was able to face Ben to ask him to hold his horses without feeling like I was blushing or going to tinkle myself. I'm ok, I can now talk with Ben without gushing on him like a little girl, I can return to working and no longer feeling ashamed for wanting to violate my vows by throwing myself at him. For some reason I just wanted to lay him down, crouch over him and watch his face as I masturbated while squatting over him, it was a weird fantasy to flood into my mind but once again I was red hot with lust and I wanted to slap myself to get a grip on my head. I lost my thoughts for just a moment and they went to a very kinky place but I remembered that getting angry was a help so I got mad again at having to restart counting the pallet of boxes.

Ben chuckled because he was intentionally toying with me while I was counting; I was so focused on ignoring him and counting in a hurry that I didn't see the big shit-eating grin on his face as he cranked up the pallet with a cartoonish pumping of his arms. Ben continued smiling as he slowly pulled the pallet around, I wasn't done counting and his playful antics met a borderline disgruntled Ally mood. I was feeling angry enough that I didn't laugh along as he continued to cackle. Ben was being his charming self and my anger wasn't entirely towards him, it was also towards myself for getting wrapped up in the charm of another man, I was a married woman and happy... to some degree. When I was alone I was disgusted that I was school-girl flirting, ten years ago I would have been crushed to find James flirting in just the same way and yet, here I am behaving like a scamp.

I convinced myself that Ben should be with Lisa and not flattering an old married gal; I flashed Ben a big fake as hell smile and suggested he grow up. I tried to sound angry as I was slightly irritated in general. "How dare you, I say, how dare you make such a suggestion" Ben broke out in a southern dialect. His charm was winning me over again and I felt my mood lighten up. I felt like an idiot, I was smitten with a coworker and I knew that it wouldn't be hard for my other office girls to totally bust me. I felt all the muscles in my face let up after my forced scowl, I couldn't be mad but I wanted to be, I wanted to be man at him rather than hate myself for cooing for him.

"Ben, you're sweet, a bit of an ass, but sweet, ask Lisa out and irritate her" I tried to say confidently to convince both him and myself. "You think I have a sweet ass" Ben responded with his choppy question. I was stunned, unable to respond and feeling like a fool. My right eye began to burn; I can feel the tear beginning to well up. I can feel anger creeping back up in my throat, sweet Ben is just being his charming self but in thirty seconds I jumped from turned on, to angry, to furious, to hurt and on the verge of crying, what the hell is wrong with me? Maybe I am a nut case. I was frustrated that I was struggling to convince myself that Ben was no good but he kept proving that he was. I was fighting my urges to rip his clothes off and taste every part of him with every part of me and I was losing.

I half ass counted the levels of boxes, Ben stood in silence as he could see my face turn beet red, I'm sure Ben noticed my eyes gloss over with the beginnings of tears, I tried to hold my brave face but I was hurt. I turned to wander down the rows of shelves and pallets but at the bottom of the stairs I didn't go up to the office, I headed to the restrooms to cry for a moment. I held back my anger, my hurt and my tears as long as I could but the last three steps before the restroom was the breaking point and I began to sob. I can't pinpoint what brought on the waterworks, I know I was holding on tightly to too many emotions, the test of my marriage was a huge one but I want to tell myself there was no real test, no challenge to myself or what I held dear, I am honorable and I wouldn't betray my husband.

I wept for a few big old crocodile tears and like that it was over. I sniffled away my runny nose and opened my mouth widely to stretch my face before lightly slapping some color into my cheeks with my hands. I stared at myself in the mirror, my eyes were slightly puffy and I am sure someone saw me look a bit upset so I searched my mind for any halfway logical excuse for my behavior, crying or being upset for no reason wasn't good enough. Was I upset because I was embarrassed that Ben knew that I liked him or was it that I was losing my self-control, or even that it was taking all of my energy to keep myself going day to day that I just needed to leak a few tears out and keep going? *GUM*.

I thought that if anyone asked why I looked so upset then I'll just say I was chewing gum and either bit my cheek, or maybe thought I cracked a tooth, yeah, almost cracked a tooth, a molar, in the back and it freaked me out. With another hearty sniffle I was smiling and ready to brave up. To my relief there wasn't anyone waiting for me when I exited the bathroom, the hallway was clear and I easily returned to the office to enter in my counts and tallies. I was super paranoid for the few steps from the restroom hall towards the steel steps up to the office, I was on guard with my excuse if someone popped around the corner, but nothing happened.

Hannah was filing her nails while yapping into her headset, some client in California was giving her an earful on why they are so prestigious so their small orders should trump some of our larger clients, just to get an order a day sooner and the usual self inflated egos that go with running businesses. Gretchen was running a pen through her long black hair rolling her mouse along her desk and Lisa was slowly typing on her keyboard, no one seemed to have any notion that I had an episode to myself and it was such a relief. I averted my eyes from Lisa because despite what just happened, I still wanted the man she had dibs on.

Reagan must have been away because she wasn't at her desk when I returned. I was surprised Reagan's story of being the filling in a hot guy sandwich was so involving, usually I can listen to her stories and not get so caught up in them, for some reason her story of the sweaty bodies, the moaning, the suckling and fondling, it all just sent my mind across the porno world and back. I was days away from leaving for my week of husband and wife time, maybe I was just desperately in need for James and didn't really realize it. I kept a low profile for the rest of the afternoon, I felt like my emotions were all over the map after having cried (I hate crying) so I just kept to myself a bit better.

Gretchen chatted a little about my upcoming week; she poked and nudged with winks and smiles about what all I had planned on my time with *just* the husband. I assured Gretchen that I planned for yoga twice a day with walks through the woods with James during the day, I wanted quiet and as nature filled as I could get, I wanted to decompress. I wanted the peace and I wanted to reset my mind to focus on being his wife. Gretchen admired that I was refocusing my efforts on my husband, she is also a firm believer that retaining a long loving and lasting marriage does indeed take work, I was less than honest with myself about my standings but I also figured if I faked it enough, then I could make it.

Hannah's husband was some big PA at a hospital so she was gone nearly a week a month to some warm climated place, she was polite and didn't boast or brag and often brought us small keychains or recipes of the food she tried. Hannah was a sweet girl and worked because she wanted some of her own independence. I respected Hannah for working even though her husband made more than enough to support her to stay home, she always said:" why stay home, my ass would expand and my hips widen, then he'd leave me for some hot young thing." Hannah was silly, she knew her husband would never leave her but because of that she felt it was her job as his wife to stay in trophy shape, like how I felt.

Towards the end of the night I pushed that Lisa really needs to make a move on Ben while I was gone. I told Lisa that I wanted gooey romantic stories of the two them when I get back, in a week I didn't think she'd bang him but I had hoped that maybe she'd buck up and get some juicy details of things that we all wanted to know about. I also deeply hoped that maybe if Ben was taken then something in me would turn off and I could breathe easier. Lisa shied away a little at the topic, had I spoken to her alone it might not have been so on point but in front of the other girls she was on the spot. I bid the girls all a good night one at a time as the evacuated, Reagan and Lisa left first and Hannah shortly afterwards. Gretchen was going to wait for me but I let her rush ahead so I can pull all the recycle bins for the night cleaners.

I wasn't purposefully stalling nor trying to time it this time to bump into Ben, in fact; *he* was waiting for me. I watched the girls walk in a line through the warehouse to the side door and out as I was stepping out from the office door and getting ready to lock it. Looking down the stairs I saw Ben. Ben was actually sitting on the steps and hunched over, his small movements looked like he was picking at his nails or something to pass the time. The girls had just walked down the stairs to he must have just sat down for a minute, my body froze but my heart erupted in chaotic beating in my hands. I felt each surge of blood expand my arteries in my body with each beat; the pulse was making me feel like I was swaying as I just stared down the stairwell at Ben.

"I know a Korean girl that can give you a wicked manicure, fix you right up" I broke the silence as I began to step down the stairs towards him. I let my fingers trail along the top of the handrail, I didn't hold on all that tightly because I was wearing flats instead of heels so I was at less risk of falling to my death on the metal stairs. The railing was smooth on top as I traced my fingertips along the top on my way down, the paint long worn off from repetitive use. Some of the overhead lights were off so I had more of Ben's outline in my view than his actual self, shame because I couldn't make out his flexing back muscles as he twitched and dug at his fingernail.

"Sorry about earlier" Ben spoke up. I stopped in my steps for a moment; I hadn't expected him to apologize. I thought I hid my being upset pretty well. "I..I..I, what do you mean?" I puttered out. I shirked off any sign that I had any notion what he was talking about as I tried to gather my wits. Ben stood up as I neared the bottom of the staircase and he turned to me. Normally Ben is wearing his hat on the factory floor but he had it removed and shoved into his pocket, the sparse lighting shone through his short crew cut hair. Ben was showing his charming manners that it was polite to stand when a lady nears and I was befuddled, I wanted to appreciate his grace but I was also mad that it was that same charm that had me smitten for him in the first place.

"Pssshhh" I snarked with a half closed eye and a Popeye look. I didn't want to let on to Ben that I liked him in any way, nor show that I was at all vulnerable and especially that I cried so I pushed all of my feelings down and brushed it off like it wasn't nothing. "You sure we're good" Ben replied after we spoke for a moment. I rehearsed my gum story a few more times in the office and had it practiced so when asked if I was sure that all we ok, I hit the play button. Ben nodded as I spoke and seemed to buy the story. I smiled up at Ben and he over to me as he led the way to the parking lot door for the two of us to leave for the night. The warehouse manager Dale was still wandering around and somewhere in the background his boot steps could be heard so I kept an ear out assuming that I had a babysitter to force my behavior.

If Dale hadn't been in the building somewhere I could have easily knelt down in front of Ben and pulled him out of his zipper, his caring about me being upset (over a stupid reason, if there was one) was endearing. Going down on a guy wasn't an urge I've had for years, your jaw gets tired, if there isn't enough saliva then you are just tugging skin, your arm gets tired of trying to keep a rhythm, if you lose your balance you end up punching your guy right in the sack, and it's much less romantic when he's farted so bad in his sleep next to you that you wake up dry heaving, the romance fades quickly after you say "I do". If women had wet dreams I'd name them after Ben, I would have pantsed Ben on that floor after an eight hour shift and gone at him like a pro, that was how badly I wanted him, my lust was just as carnal and animalistic as it was in my youth, but also having had several experiences and come across a long list of things I might like to try... I'd have a go at him so wild it would live in my mind forever.

I didn't feel shaky after talking to Ben, as I followed him out of the building I thought about just speeding up my pace and then "accidentally" bumping into him at the door and getting my grope on for a second. With each step behind Ben my thoughts kept getting dirtier but my heart didn't jump up into my throat, my pulse didn't race and my mouth didn't go dry, there was a new calm in me around him and it was soothing. I thought about purposefully stepping on Bens heels before it hit me; I was still flirting. Having childish thoughts and urges was still flirting except I was back in control of myself. "Sorry if I seemed upset earlier, you are a sweet guy and Lisa really does like you, I keep telling her she should scoop you up." I lagged behind in the parking lot after Ben held the door open for me; I was still trying to convince not only Ben, but myself that he should be with Lisa, not with me alone in this dark parking lot where it would be easy to let a small indiscretion happen. Small? Did I just tell myself that doing anything with someone that wasn't my husband be a *SMALL* thing? Oh shit I might be in trouble.

Ben just chuckled a bit when I spoke about Lisa, I couldn't figure out why it was comical so I prodded a bit. "Lisa seems like a nice girl, I'm attracted to her because she is a cutie but I might be a bit more than she can handle, I still have a bit of a wild side and might not be all that ready to settle down just yet, but you ladies in the office can keep flirting and checking me out all you want, it's sincerely flattering." I was taken aback, I didn't think I was all that obvious I was flirting, and I certainly didn't think anyone else was either. Ben explained that in the break room Hannah smiles and inches closer to smell his cologne, Reagan is often looking over at him from the office window and sways her body a bit when he makes eye contact like a lioness staring down at a gazelle she wants to desire and Gretchen always finds some lint or a hair to brush off his shirt with her hands whenever she sees him.

I was impressed that Ben had the awareness to pick up on some of those things, I was even more impressed that he hadn't taken Reagan like a wild animal, she's the naughtier sort of girl that bad boys like, and not to knock her but I bet she has more panties in the back of her car than in her apartment. I made it from the parking lot door without football tackling Ben and having my way with him, I would have just melted if he would have turned and held me though. I took long blinks to close my eyes enough to try to convince myself that my teasing with the line was just as bad as crossing it and if I wasn't careful then I might end up in trouble; like buck-naked rodeo right there in the parking lot kind of trouble. I always used to believe there was only "happily married" and "unhappily married", but lately I wonder if there's "happily married" or "married and happy enough" and it pings at me.

As we neared the end of the parking lot Ben turned to me and extended his hand. I wasn't sure what he was up to so I hesitated at reaching out to grab on. I reeled my head back and gave Ben a suspicious eye wondering if he had an angle or was being sincere. Ben twitched his hand and insisted that I could trust him. I reached forward and clasped my hand inside of his, his hand was warm and even though he had big manly hands, they were soft and comforting to hold. I felt my body relax and my tension leave my shoulders, the delight was tender and delicate, not like a alcohol buzz but something like eating that comfort food from your childhood. Ben stood tall in the parking lot lights, he blocked the direct light beams streaming from the glowing white orb up and above so I was standing in his shadow, I felt wrapped in darkness and the skin on my chest began to tighten a little, it felt like blood was rushing to my breasts, engorging my nipples waiting for his touch.

I knew better than to sit around in my car and wait, I knew that any minute Ben might pop up and if he slid into my passenger seat again, I don't know if that would be the last thing of mine he'd slide into. I scuffled my feet a bit across the parking lot, Ben had harder thudding steps in his boots than my small feet in my flats but I tried not to look over towards him. I was on my way to a week vacation of having rambunctious time with James and I was hoping that it would be enough to satisfy whatever there was in me that needed to me satisfied and then perhaps when I return I can just go back to being normal. I fought against myself to get into my car, I always thought it was cheesy and pathetic that you read some of those mushy stories in cosmo about situations being so overwhelming intense that you give in to your primitive urges and these young girls sleep with their boyfriends' best friends and all that drama, I am an adult and I can put myself into my car and step away from Ben, I refuse to be some "Dear Jackie" story.

I sat in my car relieved that I had my dignity. I have my composure and my character is intact but I don't feel all that thrilled about it. I am proud of myself for holding out but I also feel like I missed out on something, something that could be really really good in fact. Backing out of the parking lot was ominous, I felt the same old routine kicking back in and I felt my heart sink to my stomach. I tried to keep my window open on my drive home but there was no great smell to the air, no whipping breeze that caressed me under my shirt nor yearning to listen to the wind blow; I just drove. Each turn towards the highway and then off just made me reflect on Ben, his strong jaw, watching the muscles bulge in his cheeks as he clenched his jaw, his high sharp cheek bones that made his eyes stand out like they didn't have any reason to judge a thing you've ever done or even thought to do in your life, he was sincere and I felt like I could tell him every dirty little secret I was afraid to admit to James, or even myself, and he would listen intently and make it all alright.

I laid down with James after my normal routine of undressing from my work clothes and into soft cotton boxers and a t-shirt. I tried to notice if my body looked much different as I changed; as each day grew closer to my stupid birthday I grew more concerned that I'd wake up with droopy tits and a need for aloe injected creams that can overpower the smell of any room. Of course I applied my skin toning cream nightly and brushed my teeth topless while I waited for it to dry, even with mild brushing I hardly jiggled much, good for my stomach not so good for my chest. Each night was lonely, James snored in our bedroom while I walked around without any clothes on and there was no notice, there was no snicker or sneer, I was invisible. Early in our marriage James would always find some angle to peer at me, he would always crawl across the bed to give me a "special kiss for a special place" any time I was without pants or panties, now I could probably go and sit on his face and suffocate him and he still wouldn't budge.

I'm not sure I can think back to when James stayed up late enough to talk about my day with me when I got home. I try to catch up with James on the weekends, we nutshell our week to save time but by that point it becomes quick highlights of what we can remember, it's an exchange of quick intel to feel like we're keeping up with one another but the conversation quickly turns to the kids and their week. On Fridays we talk about what the kids did. On Saturdays we fight our way through sports practices and rounds of meetings or birthday parties. Sundays are prep for the coming week, I try to make one or two meals ahead of time but usually I'll make dinner during the day so all James has to do when he gets home is reheat and serve unless I prep it on the crock pot to dish out. I have a bit more time during the days so I feel obligated to prepare what I can for James and his afternoon with the kids.

Our sitter Kaylie stays with the kids until almost five Monday through Thursday, she is a cute blonde teen that has been with us for over a year, she helps get the kids off the bus and does her own homework while waiting and makes sure the kids get their snacks and so on but she only really has them for two hours till James gets home then it's all him till bed time. James does work hard all day so I know it's my job to clean the house and do laundry and dishes and cooking during the day so he can navigate the afternoons but I feel like he gets to enjoy the kids in the afternoons, on my off time it's after my late hours when I'm having a drink and giving myself a run in the kitchen. Taking time for myself once or twice a month makes me feel guilty because I already miss out enough time with my family so more often than not I pass on chances to have a drink with Erin or even take myself out to a movie.

To feel like I'm eating with my family when I am at work I take a serving with me to eat at my desk. If I make a Cajun lasagna, I can enjoy it with my family remotely. When James and I said "I do" we meant it, /meant it. I think if James and I renewed out vows right now I would decline, sure it can be a romantic gesture to renew but right now I don't know if I would go on being married if the opportunity came up to just stop. It's sad to stand topless in just a pair of cotton boxers next to a man and there isn't *any* sort of response. Is there a thing where you can just cease a marriage, no ugly fighting or tiny-peckered attorneys making a fortune on the misery of others, just two people that sign on a dotted line and undo a marriage just as easily as they did it?

I slide my hand down my stomach and under my elastic waist band, maybe if I play with myself five feet away from him he might wake up and ravish me. I notice a bit of my stubble but cruise my fingers right on past and to their intended target. I keep brushing my teeth with my right hand and let my left explore me for a minute to get me in the mood. The heavy breathing I hear is of an asleep man I married sixteen years ago, nothing special. I'm bored in my life, a few circles between my legs and I still don't feel anything. I was insanely turned on earlier but there isn't anything I can think of now to get my engine running so why bother trying to finish.

I tried to imagine Ben as I pinched my nipples and shook them up and down a bit with a firm hold, the painful pinch the other night did hurt a little but like a good hurt, a pleasurable pain that I kind of liked. I'm not some weirdo into the crazy spanking or being tied up and humiliated, that stuff turns my stomach but I did like it when I'd be on all fours bucking with Nick holding on tightly behind me and a wide handed hard slap to the ass can send a painful surge mixed with the pleasurable ones all along the body and once that split second of hurt pain goes away the pleasure seems much more intense, I miss that once in a while.

I've seen enough clips and movies to have my mind expanded, there are things I can remember seeing ten years ago that with James that raised his eyebrow for a moment but looks plenty wrong for me. I detested the notion of one of the positions that we saw, things aren't meant to go that route and I put a quick stop to that sort of thinking, except now I wonder if that pleasure mixed with pain would be all that bad. I thought about revisiting some idea with James but his stamina and interests were coming up short in all bedroom departments, plus there are some things I might be willing to try once, just not with him. If I were to try one thing with James I'd be worried that he might like it and want it all the time, despite my dislike for it, I would hate to start a habit, or worse, maybe he would think I was a slut or something for wanting to try something new, or he might even ask where I got the notion to try such things, although I would just say that Reagan had one man in front of her and one behind her when she was enjoying two guys at once and that she loved it. I can usually blame some of my own curiosity on Reagan; she does have some wildly fun times.

I couldn't find the ambition to finish myself off, it's pointless to try and force it and I'd just end up with a wrist cramp or a soreness that wasn't worth the poor orgasm. Washing my hands and rinsing my mouth out with blue mouthwash is the last step in yet another night of mind numbing routine before I pull a loose and worn t-shirt over my head and go to bed, essentially alone.

The weekend before we were supposed to leave was as hectic as always. James' parents agreed to stay the week but we asked them not to come until Sunday afternoon. Saturdays are crazy with the sports and so on so we decided to save them some of that crazy running around. James and I packed what we needed on Sunday and spoke with the kids about what we were intending to do, the time frame of which we'd be gone and how we expected them to behave. I was growing more and more fond of the idea of walks through the woods and hopefully waking up stark naked next to a man rooting around in my downstairs, only to awake to a climax. I wanted to wake up one morning to find James so hard that it only took him a moment after I climbed on top of him before he finished, I know these are immature hopes but these are the fantasies that I had for our week.

James was energetic as he packed and helped the kids to set out a list of things they can't wear to school (little princess likes her Barbie bathing suit all year round) and how they were expected to get their work done and to behave for the school week we'd be gone. The prep was done and the kids were warned so we packed his truck and finally made our way to our destination. I knew it wasn't going to be a short drive but we needed the road trip and we were beyond in need for some husband and wife time. I even looked forward to pulling the sheets back and going down on James until at least that part of him woke up for me to enjoy while the rest of him slept. I was feeling younger at the idea of a week alone in a cabin in the woods without any clothes. I ignored the small voice in the back of my head that reminded me of all the scary killer movies where people got butchered because they were in fact naked in a cabin, I just put those thoughts far away and focused on having a sun kissed body.

James and I spent a few hours trying to catch up on our time at work and things going on, I tried not to think about Ben, or the girls, or even if Lisa finally got him or not, I left it all behind me. It was strange trying to reconnect with James, almost as if we were just strangers that once knew each other. James and I agreed to find a nice restaurant for dinner to treat ourselves and to continue on with the rekindle. I liked the romantic gesture, that's the kind of man James is, candle light and pasta blah blah, things that still represent that we're upstanding adults but sad proof no longer horny young kids in our twenties anymore.

I thought about taking my top off or just taking my bra off in the truck and pulling my shirt up to let James grope and paw at me, hoping to get a rise out of him. I wanted him to want the things I wanted but without having to be told. I wanted him to last more than six whole minutes when we did make love and it not lead to me being so bored or disgusted with him or myself that I can't even finish myself off if I have to. I planned to eat quickly so we could finish our drive and still perhaps have some time for a sunset from the front porch of the cabin overlooking a mountain valley; I was very excited about that. I felt guilty that I should have just told James about feeling neglected but I knew that he would just tell me that we were passed that teenage romance stage and in a mature relationship, but I wanted to be finger banged in the front seat of his truck by him because he wants to, not because I want him too.

There was a part of me that was already dog tired of the silent driving, we lightly talked about any news at work either of us might have bothered to remember and of course I didn't speak about Ben, even it was about lightly trying to hook him up with Lisa. James and I spent more time just watching cars go by than actually interacting, back in the day his desires for me were so much that he hardly kept his hands off me and if I was even a little hesitant he'd whip himself out and start without me, which then of course I'd have to help finish him off so he could keep both hands on the wheel for safety. I even wanted James to just lay a hand on the seat or reach over to just play with me, I have felt so neglected that even just being lightly fondled would have meant a lot to me.

The meal was nice, the waiter was nice, it was all… just nice. I don't know what I had expected with the dinner, we were two people eating, there wasn't much conversation of note, James spoke more to the waitress than to me; I was just there. I tried to figure out what I really had expected as we left the restaurant but was mostly coming up blank. Did I expect an actual date; one where we stare into each other's eyes and get gussy about the future? I hoped maybe we'd at least discuss tentative plans for getting to the cabin or how we were going to spend our week but we just eyed the menus and then just ate dinner together. I crunched at my salad and just watched other couples, nothing different than hundreds of other meals but it was hard, it was hard to sit in utter silence with a stranger you happen to be married to. I was sad that I was the only one feeling the strain; James didn't seem to be bothered as he just browsed the menu over the top brim of his glasses, hardly even looking in my direction.

James and I rode the rest of the way to the cabin, the small GPS said left or right and when to turn but that was the most talking that happened. I left behind my home and the routines of it only to find that they had come with us on our trip. The cabin was quant and tucked away at the end of a narrow dirt driveway up a long steep dirt road. James and I both unfolded ourselves from the drive and spent a moment stretching our bodies among the pines once we arrived. The birds and critters chirping and chattering in the distance was a relieving sound compared to the cars and barking dogs and noisy kids of the subdivision. James and I both nearly fell out of the truck when we finally arrived, I left all my nonsense in the truck, I stepped out onto the pine covered parking spot and tried to imagine that I was a million miles from home.

I tried to put behind me that I was endlessly stressed and on edge earlier in the week, it wasn't a topic James would have liked to hear about and who knows what kind of hell would have come up if I admitted to masturbating to thinking about Ben, although if he could get the wood in his staff he's probably spanked it while thinking about Kaylie (our hot little seventeen year old tart of a babysitter we hire to be home for the kids until James gets home from work). I'd probably want to kill James if he did cheat but then again it would be nice to know he has more use for his pecker than taking a leak. James wants his once a month five minute humping but that seems to be just to say we were still intimate at our point in life and not for actually being *intimate*.

I wished that James had desires, lusts, even if he watched Kaylie in her bathing suit and I walked in on him rubbing one out or caught him watching porn, I at least want to know he's still a man. Stretching in the open woods was relaxing, I was a bit angry that I have felt ignored for so very long but he did make the effort a few months back to put in the requests for the time off at work and arrange things to make a majority of this little vacation happen so I'll focus on being grateful. I was excited to see if James got a prescription for some blue bombers (pills to put some lead in his pencil) and perhaps he'd last for more than a few minutes so I can get off with him. My climaxing has always been an issue, from the beginning I am a hard woman to get off, in fact it never really happened during sex, usually just with manual or oral help so that's why I just lay there to let James have his fun.

Long before I even met James I had sex, it's not the dirty secret that everyone advertises that it is. I didn't mind losing my virginity after a while, it was painful at first and awkward and I was nervous and all the things that everyone deals with when they don't really know what to expect. When I got together with Nick he made it much more fun, strip games on car trips and a little more adventurous in our ways, nothing crazy but there were times I'd go down on him while driving and that was pretty wild for me. James is a little more conservative but in our younger years we did have good fun, but as the years have passed so has most of the ambition to keep having the same kinds of fun.

Sex with Nick was exciting, I can't say I orgasmed all that often when we were going at it, something about actual sex never really hit the right buttons and I've just accepted it since then. Nick introduced me to oral and the first few times the notion of him putting his tongue down there was just gross. I was totally weirded out that Nick wanted to spend time just looking at my crotch, not that mine is all blown out or flappy but it's a vagina. Maybe I was just weirded out because it was new or maybe that he just liked the way it looked and felt and tasted, either way it was new for me.

I never really got off during sex so I guess that is why I never really cared if James took forever to finish, it was usually his mouth or his fingers that made the most progress but it still felt good anyways. Once I learned what getting off really was instead of just feeling pretty decent I had Nick face down on me a lot, I know it's not the most tasteful subject but wow, that boy was like a hound dog and an ice cream come and I loved it. I tried to carry over some of the techniques from Nick to James; it's not about thinking about Nick when fooling around with James it was about getting across the finish line once I started the race.

The cabin had faded and weathered wood siding, the view from the car alone was spectacular and being surrounded by the woods meant privacy to get a little racy. James hauled the luggage out from the back seat of the truck and began to hobble towards the cabin. The air was settling and the sky was beginning to dim. I decided to initiate the fun and reached up under my shirt to unhook my bra before taking my top completely off. I was feeling exposed as I begin to pull my arm into my shirt but the risk of being spotted excited me more than it scared me. I let my heart begin to beat a little faster, I was glad that I found a way to get my heart racing that didn't involve being face to face with Ben while forcing myself to refrain from reaching out and latching onto him through his jeans.

Yes I've seen Deliverance, and no I would not be thrilled to be mauled or raped by hairy toothless yokel, especially those whacko inbred duck killers that are always talking stuff on TV but I wanted to throw caution to the wind. I had been on good behavior all week and it was time to embrace vacation. I slid my left arm into my shirt and with a swoop of my right arm I had my shirt and bra in my right hand and there I was. Immediately I wanted to shield myself, all of my instincts told me to cross my arms to cover myself and run indoors but I fought it. Standing tall and topless among the woods was a young and wild action I did in my later teen years, myself and some girlfriends decided that skinny dipping in a lake late in the evening would be a crazy and fun adventure, which it was until realized how badly mosquito bites on your naughty bits were.

Blood rushed to my nips as a slight breeze tickle along my bare skin, the large goose bumps in my areolas stuck out and became extremely sensitive. I caught myself looking around with a little bit of panic waiting for someone to pop up out of the woods but I did my best to keep my shoulders rolled back and feel free. I usually slept in a t-shirt, no bra. Every gal knows how restricting it is to live with your boobies all holstered up all the time but gravity is also a nasty bitch and if you have much of a chest to talk about then you want to keep them up and where they belong as much (and as long) as possible. Going without a bra seems like a small victory and occasionally I'll give it a go, usually if I'm wearing a sweatshirt but for the most part, I'm imprisoned in a brassiere.

I rubbed my free left hand around on my stomach, blood rushed to the surface of my skin, I had tanned a few times in the bare but lying on a tanning bed is not standing in God's country and showing my gifts to the birds and the bees like right now. After my brazen eight seconds of courage left me I felt the shame of standing topless in the wind, I was nearly on the top of a mountain and anyone with a pair of binoculars had a straight skin tugging view of me. I was half excited and half nervous about going brazen but my inner young girl wanted to prove to myself that I was brave enough. I felt a little childish for committing such an act but I was also convincing myself that this week was going to be for revisiting my younger days with my husband and that I was still bold, sexy, and strong.

"Holy hell" James echoed out from the front porch of the cabin. The sudden voice made me shutter a bit and brace to cover myself before I realized it was him that was ruining my moment. I whipped my head to see him standing with his arms folded across his chest and a medium grin with open eyes under his raised eyebrows. James looked pleasantly surprised at my bold declaration to nature that I was still pretty comfortable with myself. My skin had that tightening feeling from being slightly chilled and exposed but I tried to enjoy the feeling of each skin cell stand up in the form of a goose bump on my skin interacting with the air around me.

I spread my arms and took a few large deep breaths in to expand my chest as I began to step towards James and the porch, I was ready to see the accommodations James had arranged for us for our quiet week. Blood continued to rush to my already hardened nipples as I walked; my freshly released breasts still had a nimble bounce to them with each step, making my nipples even more sensitive and engorged but I like the free air flowing up my chest and against my bare skin. James leaned against the side rail of the porch and just watched me walk towards him, his grin convinced me he was pleased and I hoped that leaving our busy routines behind meant that we could revisit our younger years for a few days and I could work on completely forgetting about forty coming at me like a freight train.

James didn't reach his hands out to embrace me as I stepped up on to the porch, I was a little let down to glance at James' crotch and not see him ready for me, in fact he didn't even have a partial. I let my arms drop to my sides as I stepped up to push against James, I wanted to be kissed, I want him to be so overwhelmed with passion for me that he can't keep his hands off of me. I want James to be filled with lust for me, I want him to live up to his plan of waking up early with me and stripping me down on the front porch in the morning and watching the sun come up as we climaxed together. I want him to take my right here and now on this porch, just slide my pants down enough to get in me. I want to be wanted so bad that he can't even wait until my pants are off to be inside of me and I want his thrusting to be so energetic it borderlines on brutal and leaves me holding onto the rustic porch railing for my life.

James wrapped one arm around me and pulled me in to him, he didn't even graze my chest with finger tips or even start to kiss down my neck; he didn't even bother to grind against me at all to start some sort of foreplay. I feel my mood turn sullen and dreary, James is warm on my skin and some of the dwindling sun rays warm spots on my back but what was the real point. I dreamt about having the courage to strip down and even up tan lines on a beach or even just inside of an open screen door back at home but the thought of a neighbor catching an eye full of my goodies would embarrass me to death.

I texted with Erin a few times during the week, I didn't want to distract her from her work and sometimes I needed reassurance that maybe the lows I was feeling with James might have been normal, she also experienced them with Charles but they had every afternoon together so it wasn't as severe as James and I. Erin assured me that once the honeymoon period is over things slow down and mature, everyone experiences that. Then when you add kids to the mix things usually are all about them and their needs and the needs of the parents usually slides into the ditch, it was all disheartening. Erin knew all too well about lows in the sex life, she had been through it and tried to encourage me to speak up about it, but with my work schedule and his being out of alignment, what was the point, there was nothing that could be done.

I can't look back and pin point a time where I can definitively say that James and I began losing steam trying to stay a passionate couple, I guess it all just started to flutter as kids happened and lives continued to put pressure on our ability to stay young and in love. I rested my face against James' chest, which was a simple gesture but one that also hadn't happened in a long while. It was nice to feel James' hand on my bare back, our intimacy was so strained that even his measly touches were longed for. James let his fingertips trace up and down along my back. I longed for his touches but it wasn't just his touches that I thought about.

I wrapped my arms around James, I tried to put my longing feelings behind me and just focus on the fact that even topless, my husband wasn't willing to run the bases on me. I tried to convince myself that I was still desirable, youthful and sexually attractive but I wasn't feeling so. I couldn't even get my own husband aroused, I had gotten myself off a few times in the last few weeks but it didn't curb my cravings, I still wanted to be touched by someone else, touched by a man, especially *my* man. I wondered if maybe in fact James had diddled himself or even Kaylie our babysitter maybe he was getting some action on the side and that was why his sex drive was completely gone for me.

I know when James and I were in our twenties we went to his cousins wedding and that night was our first good night of hotel sex and we went at it more than half a dozen times, we were aiming for a full dozen but by six am and alternating doing it on the bed and the shower we were absolutely exhausted. I know having the memories of such an intense sex drive makes out lousy once a month look pathetic but I can't help but to think that maybe it isn't his sex drive that has broken down but maybe his sex drive for me? I often feel like our piddly once a month little sex session was more of a chore, I'd either lay there and think about chores or he'd grab on really tightly around my waist and hold on as I bent over the side of the bed before we got into bed for the night, it was measly and I really did only feel like I was doing my duty for him to use to please himself with, no different than if he just used his hand.

James' lack of sexual energy or willingness to even toy with me a little put the idea in my head that maybe he already spent his juices this week. I would have been more than receptive if he would have been willing to try, anything, if only he would have just attempted. Giving a blowjob doesn't excite me, it was fun in the beginning when things were new and we could use our tongues to rock each other's worlds but over the last ten years it's become a pointless exercise, he'd get off if I just tugged him more than twice so where was the fun?

I liked having the power to go down and then stop or whip my hair around like an eighties rock singer and thrash to get James near the edge and sometimes I would just hold it until he would plead, it was fun to have that power but now I knew each and every breath hold and what it meant, there was no excitement in any of it, nor has there been in a sadly long time. Once I gave birth to our son, James no longer seemed to drool at the thought of rooting around in my crotch like a pig in the mud, it used to me exciting when he'd kiss down my neck, between my breasts and keep going down past my belly button and into my honey pot.

I've always done my best to keep James satisfied; I always took my job as a wife seriously and put forth every effort I could to be a wife that he would be happy with. Watching adult films with James was fun for a little while but in all honesty seeing some of the girls on those films made me feel a little self-conscious but it was worth it after he brought his increased stamina and energy into our bed. Erin and I chatted a few times about possibly going to a strip club to get our husbands all riled up, the thought taking that adventurous step was terrifying but if it meant James would have brought his thick and ready self to me then it would be worth letting some hot young girl grind all over him, plus perhaps I might learn some hip swaying sexy moves or some sort of wild hair flipping.

Erin was way more confident than I was; she had actually followed up on taking her husband to a hooter-hut, of course I admired Erin for being so brave and I had tons of questions. Erin admitted seeing the scantily clad bodies strolling around in high heels was nerve racking at first but once she stopped over thinking it and focused on Charles having a good time, she began to enjoy the music and get all blushy flattered when more girls offered her dances than him. Erin went full in when she checked out a bunch of other girls, she realized that none of these girls had what she did, a man that happily went home with her.

Charles was committed to Erin and because of it, Erin was willing to let go of her insecurities and go with him to a booby bar. Erin put aside her reservations of the club; she worried about cleanliness and all the usual issues when facing groups of naked people but once in she sat and enjoyed the music and the lights. It took a few dances before Erin got into the atmosphere and even found some of the sultry dancing to be appealing enough to want to learn it. At the end of the night Erin was willing to let Charles get a private dance since there was no touching, together they had admired and spoke about some of the more private-part landscaping artwork they saw and once she was at ease, she found her comfort with her surroundings so she was willing to let Charles go into the private dance room.

Erin took a deep breath and waited for Charles to pick a girl he found the most attractive, she was hesitant on letting a girl rub her ass all over his hardening crotch but she also looked forward to getting him home and having one of the more wilder nights in their marriage. A petite tanned girl wearing neon pink lingerie strolled around a few tables and made eye contact with Erin. Charles sat up a little and watched the girl take sexy sleek steps towards them and begin to smile. Erin felt her heart begin to thump in her throat as she compared herself to the younger girl, this girl hardly looked eighteen, not thirty-nine like Erin was, her tits were fake and firm, her ass wouldn't have dropped or sagged if she took her thin lacy panties off and from a look through the sheer material, she was an avid waxer.

"Sincerity" stepped up and took a stance a bit wide for a girl in only skimpy lingerie; her legs were muscular and long. Sincerity stood tall in her crazy tall looking high-heels and she swayed her hips side to side. "Either of you like a dance?' she spoke up with confidence that Erin could only fake. Erin nervously pointed to Charles and forced out a smile. Sincerity moved her eyes and started to make eye contact with Charles and before her tone leg muscles flexed to step closer to reach for his hand, Charles pointed back to Erin. Erin's heart stopped. She had no idea what she was going to do and she felt her cheeks and ears flush with blood. Sincerity reached forward to clasp Erin's hand, her long dark brown hair fell down around her shoulders and all Erin could do was stare at her slender collar bones and tendons connecting to her neck.

Erin couldn't put the words together to politely decline before Sincerity had a tight hold on her. "Can he come" Erin requested Charles to join so she wasn't alone in some big chair in some shady back room, she was afraid to be alone. Sincerity motioned for Charles to follow them and Erin went back to being partially comfortable. Sincerity danced and took some extra time to show Erin some moves for when she gets Charles back to their bedroom, slightly pulling her panties to the side to offer up a naughty peek at her nether bits before covering back over to twirl around and continue dancing.

Erin watched Charles but he was also watching her, she thought he would be fixated on Sincerity's bits and trying to look up to see her cervix when she turned her back to them and bent over to touch her toes, but he watched Erin. Charles piped up and told Erin it was hotter to watch *her* watch the girl than to actually watch the girl himself, it turned him on watching her get turned on because he still loved her that much. Erin shelled out a few more twenties and sat back, growing more comfortable watching the girl with tiny areolas flick her hair and do her dance, all the while Charles was nearly seizing from being so turned on watching his wife watch another girl strip and expose herself.

Erin said that it didn't even take her lips reaching the base of Charles when she began to go down on him, the ease of work was incredible, she couldn't remember the last time Charles exploded so much in her mouth and it wasn't even twenty minutes later and he was rip roaring and ready to go again. Charles wasn't done after his first shot with Erin and the second time around he lasted almost three times as long as his average before when his intensity for her was wild and unhinged. Erin was nearly hooked on taking Charles to a strip club once or twice a year to take things to a safer lever and to strengthen their bond. Erin grew fond of looking at naked girls, not as a competition with her aging body or for the attention of her husband but as proof that her marriage couldn't be tested by some young hot bodied girl. Erin took the risk of going to see naked women with Charles and rather than spark an insecurity that could have raged out of control like a wild fire, it actually comforted her by reassuring that what she had with Charles was real and amazing.

I thought about taking James to a strip club to get his libido revving but I just couldn't get passed the rage that gave me a slight pain in my chest at the imaginary picture in my head of some girl bent over at the waist backing up to James's face and then he just sticking his tongue out and diving face first into her backside, it just made me mad. I tried to get over the notion of James being aroused by other girls, in my younger years I was less concerned because we were at each other plenty and I still had my hot body, sometime in the last few years when my body began to age and I found many of my interests dull I picked up insecurity about myself. I hated the notion that turning forty meant I was no longer sexy, I wanted the mature secure marriage but I still wanted the hot and heavy passion also. The last ten years since my son was born I could feel a decline in our passion, I felt a sincere drop in my own hunger for comfort but now in the last few months my sex drive has returned, but my partner hasn't.

I worried that maybe I shunned or turned away James too much over the last ten years, maybe not being in the mood too much just turned him off or maybe even he just learned to go without all that often. I say that we've averaged once a month but if I really thought about it it might have been every other month, or maybe a little longer since. Thinking about how often I get down and dirty with my husband now requires some hearty thinking, I am pretty sure we had sex at least once this year, I think. Am I to blame, have I gone so long without validating my husband that maybe he just no longer has any urges? Here I am standing topless pressed up against my husband and he won't even kiss me, he's just rubbing my back and staring out into the great outdoors.

I convinced myself that during my vacation in the cabin that I would spend days with James and we'd go without clothes, reconnecting. James rubbed my back to try and warm me up but it wasn't his hand rubbing that I wanted. Since James didn't even follow the contours down my back to even cop a feel on my backside I just pulled my arms in to cross my chest to start warming myself up, it was pointless. I dropped my head and let go of James, he dropped his hand and turned for us to walk inside. I couldn't decide if I was going to stay adamant about remaining unclothed or just try again after dinner, I was feeling pretty let down about everything now.

I pulled my shirt back on while James started a small fire in the cast iron stove to give us some background heat for overnight. We had a few dim lamps and one couch in the main room, it was romantic so I hoped once the sun was fully set that maybe James would feel energized enough start our fun. I tossed my bra on the back of the couch and shoved my cold toes under James' right butt cheek to warm them up. James scrolled through a news app on his phone and hardly paid any attention. With a huff and a puff I finally decided to speak up, I wasn't all that mad but disappointed enough to finally stick up for myself.

"What's going on, you promised life changing and vigorous activities but I pop my knockers out and can't even get felt up. I know we've hardly connected and a majority of the last few times we've spent quality time together you grunt and groan for a minute and it's over for you, where's mine?" I might have had more attitude in my voice than I should have. James jumped on the defense that I didn't appreciate what all he did to keep up with the kids in the afternoons but he didn't even acknowledge all that I did either. Our conversation turned south pretty quickly. Two people that don't show one another appreciation can get pretty ugly pretty quickly and we were no exception. Even after sixteen years of marriage you can't instantly feel appreciated.

I only grew more angry as the argument grew louder. I kept most of my anger inside because I was trying to salvage some of the romantic appeal to a remote cabin in the woods but it wasn't working. I wanted to brush off the emotions brought out by James as he talked about his long work days and getting up early to get ready for work and then helping to wrangle two kids when he gets home until their bed time but I felt my temperature rising quickly. I was appalled that James wanted so much credit for his afternoons with the kids; I did it the other three nights a week and still did a majority of the cleaning and so on during the days. It hurt that I hardly get so much as a text at work that dinner went well or how the kids liked what I prepared. I was a ghost in my own life; the expectations of me to keep up the wifely chores had me broiling in anger.

I stepped out of the truck ready to get stripped and humped, violently, and now rage was the only feeling in me. James grew red in the face and yet he hardly even bothered to look at me while we argued, his damn phone was a higher priority to him than I was. I was fed up, all week I wanted him to pin me against the couch, the wall, the shower, the sink, random trees on our hikes, basically I wanted him to go back to being twenty-six and a full time walking raging hard-on, but he was just a tired old man with no will to think past himself. Like most arguments things got heated; James and I agreed when we'd start arguing that we'd stop for a few minutes and think really hard about the root reason why we were really fighting, often times outside factors were talked about and our fights lightened up, this time there was no pause and we barked back and forth for a bit.

I got fed up with being talked to loudly, I already had enough to chew on and I was throwing plenty of it back at James. My chances of feeling loved and being made love to in a romantic cabin had zeroed out and it was obvious so I stopped holding back. I didn't bother to say anything about Ben or feeling so neglected that my vows from our wedding had begun to fade and were almost non-existent, but the emotions of it all made my eyes well up. I kicked my feet out from under James and rolled to my side, I needed some air. James' voice quivered as he spoke angrily, I'd say he was shouting but he didn't raise his volume enough to constitute it as actually shouting, it was just full of anger and frustration.

I jammed my feet into my shoes and shoved my way out through the rickety screen door. It's a crappy thing to do to storm out during an argument and I was guilty of doing it but had I stayed in the room any longer I would have blurted out how badly I wanted Ben inside of me to thrust away until all of my problems disappeared. I was hurt, I was angry and I was frightened about so many things, especially possibly growing old with a man I hardly knew any more. The engine of the truck still clicked as it cooled off as I walked by, I didn't know exactly where I was headed but I needed to storm through some dirt paths and push at branches in the way to calm down for a bit. I took in deep breaths to vent out my steam into the open tranquility of the wilderness, the strong scent of pine didn't sooth me fast enough and actually the thought of being stuck out in the cabin for a few more days with James being such an ass only further infuriated me.

After leaf kicking and storming down a pathway for a few minutes I let myself start to cry. Emotions flooded through me and all I wanted to do was lean against a tree and just let it all out. I bent at the waist and leaned back until my butt hit a large oak, the woods smelled of pine and with my hands on my knees I stared down at the browned leaves and pine needles carpeting the forest floor. I heaved my chest in and out to slow down the tears that were welling up in my eyes and then falling to the ground and making small pitter splat sounds below me. I let out a dozen large tears before I began to sniffle, I was tired of being emotional so I stood back up and started to scan my surroundings. I shook my hands to get out a little more anger, the breeze blowing through my fingers tips helped me to calm down after a few moments.

I was alone, purposefully this time, but I was alone. The woods still held enough light to see the trail and squirrels could be hears chattering all around me. Looking through more of the trees I can see pine trees and other large trees in nearly every direction, but not a single person in sight. With or without James I wanted to have a lively week and right now he was ruining it. I had been in charge of my own orgasms for many many years so this time wasn't going to be any different, I didn't need him. I let my right hand explore up my shirt to start pinching while my left hand unfastened my jeans to reach down between my legs. The earthy smell of the woods was different than in the city, no exhaust, no cars driving by and no dogs barking across the street. Part of me was afraid to fully clench my eyes shut to focus on thinking about Ben sliding my pants down and begin kissing at my knees before working his way up my thighs but I quickly glanced around me to double check I was alone and I let myself go.

The small twig snapping sounds in the distance started being a distraction but I tried to imagine I was pleasing myself to let Ben watch from a far, the thought of putting on a show for him made me even hotter, and wetter. As I thrusted my pelvis back and forth on my left hand I felt air wisp across the top of my ass, my pants slid down a little and grinding my backside against the tree while thinking about Ben holding me up with his masculine hands while kissing me roughly made me swell and perspire. My breathing grew faster as did the rhythm of my body, the thought of Ben reaching beneath me and the touch of his hands on my intimate areas only made the privacy of the outdoor even more erogenous.

Once my breath was gone and my muscles all strained my legs felt wobbly. I pulled my hand out of my pants and eased myself down to sit right on the ground. I was so wet I felt like I sat in a puddle but the euphoria that overwhelmed me seemed to wash away all of my other emotions and bring me peace. Something about my hand holding my breast and rolling my nipple between my forefinger and thumb brought me pleasure but with the intensity of my orgasm I had pinched my left nipple so hard that even the feeling of my shirt rubbing on it kept sending surges of sensitivity up my chest, causing my shoulders to twitch a little. A cool rolled over me and covered me with shivers, the coolness on the back of my neck tickled. I tried a pixie hair cut a few years ago, I wasn't completely sold on the absolutely short length of it at first so I let it get a bit longer but I still wear is very short for ease, it is also cooler in the warehouse because it gets real hot. So the shorter hair comes in handy to hold up to cool off or now to flirt with Ben a little.

I almost ran my left hand through my hair but most of my fingers stuck together and it reminded me that it might not have been a great idea. I was still alone deep in the woods, critters still rustling around me but I still had complete solitude. I thought about wandering around some more but it was probably safer to get back to the cabin before it grew much darker, even if it meant I had to face James. I decided on my way back to the cabin that there was nothing to feel guilty about, men watch porn to get a little extra fuel in their engine, they get to watch some girl crawl all over someone else and it turns many guys on and there's nothing wrong with it, I refuse to feel guilty about just thinking about a ruggedly attractive guy with a heart melting smile and beautiful eyes. I didn't actually touch Ben nor had I let him gaze upon the parts of me that belonged to James through matrimony but I sure thought about it.

I didn't want to keep denying myself the fun of life, James came up short in the stamina department, he tried to hold in there but to be honest he wasn't ever really in it for the long haul since we started having children and I was tired of just being a way for him to get off. I wanted this week to avoid talking about my pending birthday, I wanted this week to get humped thoroughly and I wanted lots of attention for myself, it looks like I'm going to be the one to do it all, again. My left nipple was still sensitive from rubbing against my shirt on my walk back, I walked slower than when I left because I wasn't in much of a hurry to get back and deal with James or the silence that was waiting for me so I just kept thinking about my nipple freely rubbing against my shirt, I thought about if I worked one night without a bra if maybe Ben would admire the view down my shirt in secret or how it might be exciting to catch him glancing down my blouse, on accident of course...

The view was spectacular, I did enjoy the outdoors and the effort James put into our get away. I tried to put the ugliness behind me and focus on the ideal parts of my upcoming week and maybe in the morning I can be woken up like he promised, on the porch being stuffed like a turkey. When I was twenty it was fun to go at it all the time, Nick was a lean guy with ample skills that made it plenty of fun to get down and dirty with. I enjoyed Nick after my initial reservations were behind me and I slowly learned how to enjoy myself in the bedroom.

My mom hardly brought up getting laid; it was a taboo subject because good girls don't bring up bedroom activities and blah blah blah. I was uneasy for a long time even touching myself for a breast exam, I felt there was something to be ashamed about with my body until Nick brought out the fun of walking around in the apartment we shared in nothing but a smile. I slowly came out of my shell but there still that underlying hesitation about speaking up about what I wanted. I didn't think much about being wild in the bedroom, a few positions or risky places such as the kitchen or living room was on the more adventurous end of the spectrum for James and I and even when we watched adult movies together, many of the things on the screen made us both uncomfortable.

Looking back over the last half of my life I found it more shameful that I was ever ashamed of my body than there should have been and shame in myself at all. It is a shame that girls are expected to be so covered up, not that everyone should be running around with floppy boobies waggling all over the place but standing in the nude shouldn't make anyone want to scurry away and hide. I loved the feeling of the open air on my body when I was riding around with Nick, I was scared to get caught but the exhilarating fun was there. I enjoyed taking my top off when we first arrived but that shudder that struck when James spoke out scared me for a moment. I have much more confidence in my body now than when I was a teen, I feel bad that I have been ashamed of myself for anything and if I could have one wish, it would be that women would never feel ashamed to be their strong selves.

I took a few deep breaths before yanking on the screen door to step back in to the cabin to deal with James, my blood pressure settled down after getting off but it was climbing again as I stepped up onto the rickety wooden porch. Some of the wood cross pieces were split from the harsher weather, the screen was an old metal screen that was grayed with dirt and the handle was old and rusty that required a bit of muscle to. My hand reached out to grab the handle while I took a deep breath in and readied for whatever was going to happen, this was it. Stepping in the door my eyes met with James', he had his light jacket on and there was no luggage on the floor anymore. James looked sick, his face was beet red and it looked like he had been crying since I left. "What, are you surprised that I stepped out, you made all these promises for this week, for *my* birthday week, and then I went back to being invisible again, it hurts that I miss being loved and you get mad when I bring up the fact that I popped my tits out and you didn't hop on them like a suckling baby."

I started back into my fight with James, I wanted to throw the first punch to get things rolling so I felt like I had an even ground to stand on and then wait for him to retaliate. James and I did our best not to fight all that dirty, the old saying was to keep fights clean and the sex dirty except that our sex didn't exist let alone get dirty. James struggled to take a deep breath in his face was bright red and his eyes were puffy and I began to fill with worry. My stomach was already knotted from the first fight and even getting myself off didn't completely quell my nerves but the level of excitement with my climax certainly helped to relive a lot of my tension. James took a deep breath in and began to speak: "Charlie died."

The first night of my vacation started with a fight shortly after arriving and it caused me to storm out and end up fingering myself deep in the woods to an erotic fantasy starring Ben again. When I returned from my solo session of taking care of myself James was waiting to tell me the horrible news that Erin's husband Charlie died in a car accident. James had the truck packed and as soon as I got back to the cabin he delivered the news that completely knocked the wind out of me. I had known Erin since like high school and shortly into college when Charles met Erin one night, Erin introduced him the next night and he became like a brother. Erin and Charlie lived for each other, their lives and everything they did in their day to day was *for* each other. I took a lot of pointers and tips on how to conduct my marriage from them and now he was just gone.

Charlie was on his way to pick up their kids when a housewife in a big SUV plowed through a stop sign because she was on her cell phone and right into the Charlie's car. Erin called my cell, which I left behind to go for my walk in the woods, which James answered. Erin said that the SUV struck Charlie in the driver's door and he lived almost twenty minutes afterwards, he passed away on the way to the hospital. It has been a week since Charlie passed, I can't tell you how many times or if I even showered until two days ago when the funeral happened. James said he scooped me up off the floor of the cabin and let me cry in the passenger seat of his truck as he drove mostly through the night until we got to Erin's, everything has been a blur to me.

The days around the funeral blurred together into a melting pot of crying with Erin. James made the run back home for what we needed, he was supportive and waited on both of us hand and foot for days as Erin tried to make arrangements and comfort her children while struggling to accept the fact that the love of her life was now gone forever. The shock of losing Charles was honestly too much to take in, he was a tall handsome man with a bright smile and above all things in his life; he adored Erin and their children together. When Erin and Charlie met he was half living out of his car trying to get through his last few classes to graduate with his degree, his priority was paying for classes before his own rent, he was betting on himself big time.

It seemed fast when Erin and Charlie met and were almost instantly living together but they smiled and canoodled through their first few months together and that was their beginning. Erin and Charlie spent their time apart with business trips and family obligations but each moment they spent together was rife with hot passion and I've been jealous of her and her marriage for twenty years. Erin and Charles had an amazing life together, I don't know how many times she'd remind me that it isn't about having the best relationship but rather making the best of what you've got when it comes to making any relationship perfect.

The first day I spent hugging Erin in her bed, all she could do was shake and cry at the magnitude of everything. James took the task of helping to comfort their three kids as well help to make sure that anything Erin needed was taken care of, be it mowing the lawn or fixing meals. The long days went by quickly and during the weekend before I was supposed to be back to work some of the haze slowly began to lift. Erin was still a giant mess but her parents and her in-laws signed up for alternating weeks of staying with her to help fill in the gaps to help in her healing times. There was so much chaos that flooded into Erin's life, losing her life-mate and the love of her life left her borderline catatonic. If it wasn't for Erin's children and their needs for her to be strong then there was no telling how long she would have remained slumped in the gloom of despair that shrouded her.

There was so much going on at Erin's that after two days of lying with her in her bed trying to just cry with her and dab her tears that I hadn't had time to think much about the week that James and I were supposed to have. The depressed week clouded over the lust filled revisit to our youth that James and I were in need of but that's how life goes. James returned home a few times towards the back half of the week when I could better take up helping out Erin on my own. Life often throws plenty at everyone, my hardest fought point was that I hardly felt like a priority to my own husband and that was the biggest underlying key to many of my unhappy days, and now I was trying to help my absolute best friend marry her husband of twenty years.

The week I was supposed to return to work was a rough one, I was supposed to pull my big girl undies up and get back to my life but I just couldn't do it. I called in the first two days because I couldn't function well enough to get out of bed. I just cried and remained rolled up in my covers, that was all I could do. I didn't want to eat or drink and trying to sleep just flooded me with memories of all the times I had with Erin and Charlie and the sadness was hard to contend with. James helped me to shower so I wouldn't end up really funky and gross, he was gentle and delicate as he'd sponge me with a wash cloth and hold me gently to comfort me in the process. It was nice to have James caring for me. I felt helpless and the thoughts of Erin losing Charlie completely took the wind out of my chest.

I spent a day convincing myself that I needed to get out; I needed to stop sulking and return to my life. It was a hard struggle to convince myself into the shower and then instead of returning to my pink plaid boxers I sleep in, I pulled on my running pants and chanted in a mantra to just take another step. I had almost two weeks of eating take-out food and lying around in bed, I needed to get some sun on my skin and some fresh air in my lungs. I couldn't muster up the energy to put any bounce in my step so sluggishly I stepped down the porch and just thudded onto the pavement. Each step I took seemed like I was trudging through mud, my legs were heavy and even the bright sun seemed to try to convince me to return to my bed for the rest of my life.

I continued chanting "one more step" and I took steps one at a time. My heavy legs lightened up once I left my driveway and even though my chest remained tight, I continued walking out of the cul de sac. I should have done a better job taking a third person look at my life, I should have done better at acknowledging everything that James had done for my during our entire marriage, but instead I thought about Ben. I thought about Ben and his firm chest muscles under his t-shirt, his muscular thighs in his jeans and his rugged hands, roving my body. With each step the clap of my feet on the pavement seemed lighter and a slight bit of bounce slowly returned to my feet.

The air toyed with my hair as my feet tapped along the pavement. Dogs barked in the background but it didn't seem as loud, cars passed but I didn't even bother to look over at the drivers, I just jogged. My body let up and so did some of the tension on my chest and it was a relief. The gray heaviness that clouded my mind cleared a little as I walked and jogged, I tried to organize my mind and make more and betters sense of everything since my argument with James at the cabin. I can't tell exactly where the argument went nuclear but it was tempting to pull the pin and let the rubble all come crashing down before I decided to storm out. Erin was dealt a life altering blow and some of the shock reverberated into my life and it washed over whatever problems James and I were beginning to uncover.

James went to work of course so I had the day to lounge about in bed and wallow in my self-pity some more. I lost a friend in Charles but Erin was truly the one who lost something special. I didn't know how to handle everything that had happened. I was grateful that I was still married but also sad that I was still married I still thought about maybe stopping my marriage and starting new again. Thinking back to the crazy idea I had about maybe bungee jumping or doing something that might bring me to the edge of life to give me something to re-evaluate my life, losing Charlie wasn't it. I was sad I wasn't happy, I was sad that I was sad but I wanted to be happy. I couldn't figure out why I was struggling with so many emotions and none of them made any sense to me.

I could have taken another day off of work to hide away from the real world. I could have tucked into my covers and not emerged until the following week to return to work but I was out of bed and sweaty enough that I needed to shower. Returning back home brought a funk back, my heart sank as I stepped back into my home, even Bruno was more docile when he nuzzled my leg, he wasn't wagging like a crazy critter or pouncing around trying to get me to play with him. As I reached my front stoop I could hear Joy pulling into her driveway and I was quick to jump inside to avoid the old hag. I was sticky sweaty so a shower was my next step and since I was going to get showered up, I might as well try to keep with my momentum and drag myself through a work day.

My beige bathroom seemed more gray, darker tints didn't go away with the bright flickering lights but a thorough cleansing of myself was badly needed. I removed my tank top and feared looking at my body in the mirror; I was forty now and it was any day now that I'd discover an old body under my clothes. I pulled my sports bra off and to some minor relief my chest looked and felt the same as it did two weeks ago. I stuck my thumbs in the waist of my yoga pants and slid them down my body. Working my legs back forth to ease my pants down my body informed me that two weeks of not shaving my legs left them prickled like barbed-wire.

Shaving away the lathered foam on my legs also seemed to help shed away more of my funky mood. I started to look forward to going to work, even if it was just to converse with the girls. I wondered if Lisa found the courage to entice Ben, maybe she got ripping drunk and sent him some saucy crotch pics, her all spread eagle and showing him all of her glory, only to rile his loins so he'd track her down and man-handle her one night after work, lucky girl. I knew Gretchen would understand the looming depression, she knew my dread of turning forty two weeks ago and probably chalked my absence to avoiding life. I texted Erin every day to check in but I know that the texts I got back were more of the "fake it till you make it" sort. Hannah was often too self-involved to do much more than lend a friendly ear but beyond buying cupcakes for the occasional potluck, she was more focused on her life.

Reagan really was a sweet girl, she's be the young and wild one of our little group for some time now and is usually entertaining, although sometimes I can't help but roll my eyes at her antics. Reagan has a partner in crime named Sha-sha, and yes it is pronounced Sha sha. One night earlier in the year Reagan and Shash (yes her nickname) were at some club when a girl stepped to Rea(gan). Rea is a charming little blonde and never had any problems attracting the attention of any guy that looked her way, her slender dancer body moved and grooved and Shash was almost the same. Sha-sha was partly Latino and used her heritage to justify some of her fly off the handle types of ranting's but generally they behaved together. Some girl once stepped to Reagan in a club because her man was eyeballing Reagan, which prompted Sha-sha to go outside and stand up on the hood of her before squatting down to pee on it, yeah ok she's trouble.

I wondered what clownishness Reagan had achieved while I was gone, I secretly hoped for some good stories to help me laugh, maybe losing a bra to a carnival ride because it somehow managed to get away from her while entertaining a friend or maybe even taking a man to the zoo and convincing him to pin her up against the glass at the primate exhibit to show the monkeys how people do it. I hoped to hear something hilarious or dirty, either one might help me to shed this layer of gloom and try to return to my life. It had been almost two long trying weeks and although the notion of returning to my plush duvet and hiding away sounded overwhelmingly ideal, albeit unrealistic.

I hardly ate, James tried to make food for me and brought me snacks and breakfast bars in the mornings as well as dinner in the afternoon, but I had no appetite. It was nice to flake on my responsibilities a little longer than I should have. To be honest I felt burned out on the rigors of every single day, jog, wash, cook and clean and then work. I won't lie and say I didn't enjoy being relieved of my household duties but I was also so amassed with the dark dread of losing Charles that I hardly noticed. My two weeks of mourning seemed all a haze but finally getting a spark of life back in seemed to make a small improvement.

My feet felt heavy, even standing in the splashing droplets of water from the shower they seemed to throb. It was my heavy feet that would wear me out dragging them through my work shift and cause me to slip back into the groove of my worn down path of life. I began to dread the routine of getting dressed, grabbing a quick bite of a meal and then getting into my car and driving to work. The same old same old was already coming back to me and it began to sink in my gut. Rubbing the bar of soap together to suds up even seem mundane, repetitive and boring. I imagined the bar of soap was Ben in my hands and suddenly I was moving it up and down a little with a tinge of a smile break out of the corners of my mouth.

Easing a bar of soap up my legs felt dull, the soapy film bubbled up and then the small bubbles took over one another and then they would create larger and larger bubbles on my legs. I raised my left leg up onto the corner of the shower to begin dragging my orange handled razor up my shin to clear away the small forest that began to sprout in the weeks since I showered well enough, I was clearly in dire need. I hardly felt the razor nip and nick at some of the more persistent hairs that refused to go down after the first pass of the blade. Growing up my mom always warned that with razors you go up and down, never side to side. Everyone has nicked themselves shaving, woman have some major square footage to keep sexy and smooth so a nick or two was inevitable.

I neared my mid-calf on the inside of my left leg and something inside of me convinced my hand to move side to side. I kept my hand straight and made sure not to swoop but as I pulled the blade toward the back of my leg, bright red blood began to bead up. I watched the blood pool up in large beads before some of the small streams of water running down my leg took on the red tint of the blood. I don't know what prompted me to cut the shit out of my leg but I didn't feel it. The bloodied water splattered onto the ground at my feet, small red dots freckled my legs but I was entranced to just watch. Soap in my open gash on my leg didn't burn, it didn't ache nor have any feelings whatsoever, but neither did any of the rest of me.

I washed the rest of me and even easing my fingers down between my legs even the more sensitive part of me was without any feeling. I tried to think about some of the more fun times James and I had, I hoped that recalling some of the intimate times I shared with my husband might bring some feelings to my tenderbits, I wanted to feel some life and I wanted to crave the man I said *I do* to, but I couldn't. I felt ashamed the first time I got myself off in the kitchen, writhing against my own hand while day dreaming about Ben holding my hips and grinding against me. The solo performance for the chattering squirrels dropping their nuts in the woods was so freeing and livening that there was no feeling guilty or ashamed anymore, especially since the enjoyment was cut off early when I got the bad news about Charles.

Sometimes when I wash my body I think back to some of the different stages I have grown through. Being forty now you kind of just have accepted your body, some women don't fret what their bodies look like and heave themselves into a bikini or bathing suit that flatters each roll, each dimple and each glob of cellulite that seems crammed below the skin. I have too much self-respect to shove myself into yoga pants or a skimpy suit that jiggles with each step I take to just strut around in public, but I feel I'm also in pretty decent shape for my age. I never thought much of when I was a little girl; you wash what you're told to and try to find more time to play with your dolls before you go to bed. As a teen you spend more time exploring more of your budding body. You notice your skin getting softer in areas that are shifting in shape or size, you try not to be obvious when you glance at some of your friends in the locker room to judge your progress compared to theirs.

My friends and I all agreed that when we got our periods that we'd be revolutionaries and use the code name "Doug" to refer to our time of the month. When I reached my twenties Nick was really comforting about my body and his attention brought me confidence. Nick desired me in any way but he was charming and even though he'd never once turn down some activity or look away if I was changing, he was tasteful about it, not just some horndog. I loved my early twenties, Nick and I talked about getting engaged and were ravenous like monkeys as often as we could be, but it wasn't enough to carry us through and things faltered. When Nick and I fought it became nuclear, we brought out the worst in each other and during the worst of it, holes appeared in walls and half our stuff would end up broken. The days of gut wrenching anxiety and distrust with Nick sank us. You can't build a life with someone that leaves you twisted-gut sick because you can't predict when the next blow out is going to occur.

One positive with Nick was once he was done I learned quickly all of the things I never wanted in someone I intended to marry. I did learn some of the things I liked about myself during my time with Nick also. I learned that I could be as sexy as I wanted as long as had the confidence to support it and that was all dependent on me and my attitude. I also learned that even though I never really got off during sex, that there was no reason I couldn't orgasm whether I had to do it myself or not. I am a hard orgasm, it takes more than a few minutes of someone sweating on top of me to get my jollies off but I learned that I could take my own pleasure into my own hands if I had to. Sexual independence is an amazing thing. I have never actually orgasmed during sex, I don't know if there are mental hang ups or what but I often get to the cusp but have never gotten over that edge from just manual sex, it's pretty sad actually but I can compensate when I need to.

James made it his mission to get me to the "BIG O" when we first started dating. I felt a little guilty that James would nearly give himself a heart attack staying on course trying to get me off but we never got to that point together. Nick had introduced me to oral sex; let me say that at first the thought of a slimy tongue down there made me quiver more with icky feelings rather than joyful bliss, at first. Nick was adamant at making sure that I enjoyed him, he would take his time and go through the alphabet with his tongue against me until one day, we were lying on the sun drenched floor of our tiny apartment and my toes began to curl.

Nick had my legs propped up on his shoulders and a small pillow under my tush while he worked. After a few minutes of Nick bobbing his head between my legs I felt a small rush down there, there was a tickle that stretched from my crotch down to my toes. My toes curled and made fists trying to grab hold of the carpet and my mouth wrenched open so wide it nearly touched my chest. My hands rustled through Nick's hair and my back arched so hard that I thought the muscles spasms would snap my spine. I wriggled and twitched until finally my legs snapped shut and nearly broke Nick's neck by alligator clamping down on his head.

Revisiting Nick going down on me or the mere fantasy of Ben holding around my sides didn't get my blood pumping; I just stared at the red water mixing with bubbly suds just circling the drain before disappearing. The water began to run cold before I realized how long I had been staring blankly at the drain. Toweling off just further proved that I was numb to feeling. I watched myself towel off in the mirror, the towel draped to my curves and contours but watching the mirror could have just been a movie, I couldn't feel the towel brush across the top of my feet or the small loops of the plush terry cloth on my skin. Staring into my own eyes in the mirror brought me nothing, I couldn't even really tell you what side of the mirror I was on, maybe I was the copy in the mirror staring back and the real person with the life and the feelings and the happiness?

      I felt like one of those realistic paintings of a bowl of fruit, so lifelike yet no life at all. Looking closely at my own face it was hard to see much life in my eyes, my pores haven't changed in years and the feel of the skin on my face retained plenty of the stretchy elasticity to the point that I didn't have many wrinkles but I supposed that is mostly because of the expensive creams and lotions that I spend half a fortune on. Wrinkles or not I didn't really feel like I existed, I was just a blank person now, a forty year old blank person.

      When I was worn out and physically taken through the wringer of childbirth I still didn't lack motivation this badly, I found no point to shaving or bathing, nor even leaving my bed for days. Maybe I was a copy of a copy, maybe this sad routine was just playing out in my head and I was really still lying in bed. Maybe I'm still really just lying on the floor of the cabin and the entirety of the last two weeks was all just a played out scenario in my head as I still try to wrap my head around what James just told me about Charles. Maybe Charles didn't really die and this is all a dream that is supposed to slap me in the face and make me take better notice of James and how well he really has treated me, or maybe I'm supposed to find present awareness that maybe I haven't been in love with my husband in a very long time and my wanting Ben was just my inner voice speaking up.

I rub some concealer into my cheeks to give my grayish skin some color and some medium shade lipstick to give my lips a fuller appearance, if I couldn't fool myself then maybe I could fool the girls in the office. I used to enjoy going out, getting dressed up so James could twirl me around the dance floor and show the entire room that I alone was his. James also enjoyed that the best way to puff up your lips is to go down on your husband; he smiles the entire night and your lips are swollen up and pouty. For my own benefit I decided to wear matching sleek undies and a bra, no there was no intent to show anyone it was purely for me, a facade to lie to my own self that even though I was now forty, that maybe I could find a way to try to feel good naked. The dark was probably going to be my only trick to achieving sexiness any more but I was desperate to find some way to feel good about myself.

I sent James a text that I was barely mobile but planning on making a courageous attempt at a work day, of course I didn't get a response, I never really do when he's working but what-evs. I slipped into a nice pair of slacks and a loose fitting light sweater, it was white with navy blue stripes, one of my favorites. I put my work flats on and dragged my feet towards my car, each step was full of dread as I stepped further and further from my bed. The sun was stupid bright in my eyes so I kept my head hung low as I crossed my walkway and then my driveway. "Helloooo there" I heard the beckoning call above the usual day to day noises. My heart just sank when I recognized the tone. "Hello Joy" came out of my mouth while "Oh hell, what now Satan" rung through my mind.

Joy was standing near our white fence with a blue flower patterned blouse on with her fingertips tapping on her crossed arm. I'm sure in some way Joy meant well and all and it is always a big plus when your neighbors take good care of their property because anyone who owns a home agrees that property should be an investment that should be taken care of a nurtured but she was a hag. I ground my teeth together and waited for Joy to spread her lips and begin to rag on Bruno as she so often did. "Few weeks off with the family huh? You and Jimmy taking plenty of time off, you two spending all the time together or just getting caught up on errands and stuff?" I nodded to pass the idle chit chat as I fumbled to unlock my door. I tried to hurry into my car as if Joy was about to pull a gun, she was never any more than passive aggressive or nosy but she still raised my anxiety at the mere thought of running into her. I smiled off Joy's squawking and slammed my car door behind me for silence so I was safe.

I had no will to listen to the radio on my drives into work in a long time, the thought of listening to some pompous deejay blab on about sports or boobies while some half stoned all brain dead bunch of nincompoops chuckled like idiots in the background. The flashes of light beams flickered through the tree branches and then refracted through my windshield, the strobe effect seemed to nauseate me for some reason and I was on the verge of just pulling over and curling up in my back seat to take a nap. I arrived to work after a few more agonizing streets, it was hard to keep my eyes from crossing and my head from bobbing with the road noise from my tires, I just felt ill. The big beige building didn't look any different, I suspect the piles of pallets and boxes inside hadn't changed at all either, just rows and rows of stacked piles all being reshuffled and then moved around.

I made it to work on time for my shift but there was still no will to actually go in, I dreaded all of it. My chest was heavy but there was nothing I could do about any of it, if I sat here much longer than any number of my coworkers would come rapping on my window and begin peppering me with questions and so on. To save myself the hassle of being interrogated I yanked the handle of my door and heaved myself out and onto my feet. My shoes made small uneven scuffling noises beneath my feet, it's not that the scuffling squeaking sounds bother me when my sneakers are wet, it's that they sometimes squeak unevenly and then I fixate on an uneven gate or worry about one leg being longer than the other or if I'm walking funny, not as much of a worry when I'm wearing flats or heals but I do get hung up small things like that about myself still.

As I stepped lightly through the shop, the cement floor often echoes each step anyone takes (when it's silent) but on any usual day when there is staff and there is commotion going on I was able to float through like a ghost. I tried to keep my head down as I glided through between the stacks of pallets to avoid being spotted, any number of the guys or girls that worked the floor could have gotten me and started to chew my ear off, I didn't want anything to do with it I just wanted quiet. I made it to the bottom of the stairs that lead up to the office that sat high above the warehouse floor without having been spotted by my coworkers, I felt lucky. I wanted to curtsy just for smiles and just get through my afternoon with minimal interaction; I doubted I'd get through silently though.

I grabbed the worn smooth railing of the stairs, I was tensed up to pull myself up one step and then I heard my name. The hairs on my neck stood straight up and with my short hair it was hard to hide. My legs began to shake and it quivered where they met. I felt my blood rush and my nipples harden beneath my bra and light sweatshirt, sure enough there was Ben. Ben was making his way out from the small hallway that housed the restrooms, I was busy watching over my right shoulder and didn't notice him making his way from my left, I was caught and there was no where I could go.

Ben spoke my name again, my knees wanted to give out and with my heart beating violently in my throat I couldn't speak. I swore I'd smile through anything that came up today, I planned to bear down and pretend that I was immune to the pain that filled my heart but Ben broke right through all of it just by calling my name. Ben was only a few feet from me when I started to frantically swallow, I couldn't get the lump of emotions balled up in my chest to settle back down and I felt like I was beginning to choke. The corners of my mouth went up as I tried to speak up to greet him, I knew of all of my sins but no one else did and I tried to just smile like none of them existed.

Ben was wearing his worn out "D" hat and a blue and black plaid shirt that had fine lines running through it, he was a sharp guy with a comforting and sincere look on his face. I hardly spoke to Ben much but there was comfort to him. If Ben had been ten years older or I ten years younger I would have known in my heart and my loins that we were fated to be together, but I've been married longer than the age gap between us so I had to pretend my feelings didn't exist and it made my heart sink. Ben's long smooth arms flexed as he swung them gently with his steps, the rest of the warehouse seemed to disappear as I just gawked as he stepped closer and closer. I couldn't take my eyes off of Ben's biceps as they bulged against the short shirt sleeves with each step.

After a few failed attempts I finally managed to get a deep breath in me, my chest was tight and with my adrenaline beginning to pump I could hear my heart beat in my ears. "How are you" Ben started our conversation. I couldn't find the right words but I could force a smile as I tried to unscramble my brain words. Ben reached his left hand out and placed it on my shoulder, his fingers touched my shoulder blade and his thumb wrapped around and rested on my slender collarbone. I could feel his warmth through my shirt and it made me tingle under my clothing. My skin twitched and tingled as I fumbled for words but kept coming up empty. My emotions finally boiled over and while I kept eye contact with sweet Ben, they began to well up.

Before Ben could even raise his other arm I was quick to bury my head in his chest and unleash all of the feelings that rumbled inside of me. My shoulders started bobbing and tears burst forth from my eyes and all I wanted to do was hold on to Ben and keep his warm strong chest against my face. "I missed you" I said before I even realized I was talking, I wanted to melt into Ben, I wanted a week of lying with him in a bed in some small town hotel that lined a beach so we wouldn't even have to get dressed to go get ice, just stroll down the empty halls in our birthday suits and not have a care in the world.

Ben engulfed me with a hug, his arms were large and warm on my body, his heat even began to make me hot. Ben rubbed my back to comfort me but in doing so I found myself pushing my pelvis into him. I was body to body with Ben and feeling like our clothes were a curse. I forgot for a long moment that we were even at work, there was no noise except his beating heart against my head nestling against his chest and my arms tucked in between our bodies. I let my fingers slowly and intimately explore the rippling muscles around to Bens back for a moment, the small taste of touching him just made everything worse and I craved him, I wanted him and to hell with Lisa, I had to have him.

Ben broke our contact for a moment and that was when I snapped back to my surroundings and it hit me with a bit of a shock. I completely lost track of where we were, it didn't click until I pulled my head back from Ben to kiss him that the corrugated metal walls registered in my vision what was going on, I was filled with surprise that I had completely fazed out. My hands trembled, what a stupid mistake. I am such an idiot and now my eyes are dumping tears by the bucket load because I was about to die of embarrassment.

Ben tried to speak but I pushed away and scurried up the stairs to the office, there was no undoing my stupid mistake so all I could do was to hide. I burst through the office door like I was John McClain hiding from Hans in *Die Hard*. Gretchen looked up and smiled at me with her phone pressed to her head, her toothy grin let me know that I was missed while Reagan threw a hand up to wave. I was trying to wipe my eyes clean of my tears and settle my nerves because if Lisa would have turned to look at me she could have read the guilt all over my face. I took some deep but labored breaths and found smiling wasn't so much of a challenge as I returned to my desk for the first time in weeks.

I fumbled through all my login passwords and slid into the remote headset for my phone so I could oversee many of the workings to coordinate most of the logistics in the warehouse. Some more deep relaxing breaths helped me to feel back in my place as I set back into my old work mood and mentality before the girls started up with some of the usual gibbering. Hannah was out on some new adventure with her husband so there was one less body asking me to relive the last two weeks, the first was supposed to be a marriage renewing vacation but it was sadly interrupted with Charlie's tragedy.

I fielded some calls to customers before I caught on that Gretchen, Lisa, and Reagan were all holding off their phones until I was finally done with my calls. As soon as I hit disconnect on my last call each of the girls turned to me at almost the same time. I caught three sets of eyes on me and there was nowhere for me to hide. My face flushed and my hug with Ben flashed through my mind, I was paralyzed with fear that they might have seen my embrace. My ears were hot and all I could do was stall by burying my face in my hands for a moment and rubbing my eyes so hard I saw spots.

I popped my head up and sat with an expressionless face until my eyesight returned from seeing reddened spots. The three gals were all swiveled towards me waiting to talk. I lifted my eyebrows and wondered if maybe I missed hearing someone speak, they looked like they were waiting for a response but I didn't hear a question. My eyes darted between the girls, I felt my mouth drop open but once again, nothing came out. Each girl had a serious look on their face, oh shit they saw the hug with Ben. Shit shit shit I am screwed. I got careless and I completely screwed myself, aww shit.

"How are you sweetie" Lisa piped up first. There was a knot in my stomach and I felt extremely ill. Lisa is such a sweet girl and an absolute darling, honestly I adore her, plus she called dibs on Ben so I knew I betrayed her. I felt my mouth begin to salivate, my guts began to wretch and I felt sick. "What's wrong darling" Gretchen followed up after a long moment of not speaking. I began to calculate the cost of evil, the amount of everything I risked to feel alive with Ben for a half second hug, I had done it to myself and it was all flooding through my mind and making me start to sweat.

"What the hell" I blurted out as I felt a wet finger in my ear. I jumped to my feet and was ready to elbow someone to death until I caught the sight of Reagan and her bright blonde hair and giant grin. "Just trying to cheer you up lady, don't throw any cats at me." I had no idea what in this crazy ass world she was trying to prove but Reagan got me to my feet and out of my mind with her little prank. My ear hole was as wet as, well, never mind, but this was gross. I tried to wriggle my finger in my ear to soak up some of the girls' spit and was thrust into talking already.

"I am so sorry" I began my plead. Gretchen and Lisa both reached out to hug me. As the girls clamped hands around me I realized it was for condolence not aggression. They had no idea I hugged Ben or slipped and told him that I had missed him, my brush with death gave way to a relief that I was back in a safe area and it took a large chunk of pressure off my chest. I explained how my vacation week started out, the quiet truck ride to the cabin, our quiet dinner and our ugly fight that commenced almost as soon as we arrived. I even admitted to my brazen bit as a nudist in the driveway trying to get James on board to a week of teenage like debauchery. Gretchen and Reagan were proud of me for instigating my antics, Lisa parted her eyebrows with an "awwww" at how sweet it was at our age. "I'm only forty you brat, it's not like James is hoisting me onto the arms of his wheelchair in the senior center" I playfully rebutted to Lisa's comment.

I came back to myself during my shift, I got to sit with Gretchen and judge Reagan about having somehow lost a bra and thong in the back of a squad car without having been detained or arrested, or having had sex with the cop, the night was a crazy blur from her end but somehow some guy she let pick her up got them into the backseat of a cop car for long enough for her to lose some of her unmentionables, Gretchen and I could only shake our heads and fail at piecing everything together from the crazy story. Gretchen was glad to see me because she and I are the older, more mature married ones in the office and on her own she felt like she had been babysitting the other three. Hannah's once again off on some world wind adventure with her husband and we'd all get to hear all about it when she returns so it wasn't a full office for my return.

I glanced out over the floor looking for Ben each time I neared the window. It was a bit of a tease for my own emotions but I sort of felt like maybe I was building up my immunity by seeing him. Lisa said that she took my advice and found the guts to ask Ben out for a beer shortly after I left for my break with James, my heart sank. Hearing that Lisa actually found the courage to talk to Ben nearly knocked the wind out of me. I couldn't figure out why I cared so much because I was out with my husband of sixteen years and had no rights to Ben but I was jealous. I felt the corners of my lips roll down as Lisa spoke, they went out for a few beers twice already but hadn't let anything go passed that. Lisa blabbed on and on about her two dates with Ben and how great of a guy he seemed to be. Originally I wanted Lisa to go out with Ben so she could report back all about him and his bedroom activities; I wanted to know his favorite position, his downstairs techniques and all the other dirty details but then wanting to hear about it turned to wanting to be the center of it all, and then Lisa stole my chance.

I tried to mask my jealousy with excitement for Lisa, she was normally a shy girl but James taking me out to a quiet cabin for a week of romance prodded Lisa to dig deep down and finally get a conversation started with Ben. I was proud of Lisa but also found my adrenaline causing my hands to ball into a fist as she spoke. The rest of my work shift was phone calls and evasive conversations with the gals, none of them caught on that I was chewing back a little bit of guilt. I tried to avoid having to go back out to the warehouse floor but as the hours passed the odds of keeping up my luck were against me. I tried really really hard to focus on my phone calls in order to distract myself to keep my head from spinning out of control.

I had to go and do an inventory match with some of our computer records with less than an hour left to go in my shift. I was stricken with blushing again because from what I could tell it was Ben and one other worker out on the floor, and I'd need the help of one of them to move a few pallets around. I hoped to cross paths with Frank first, he was a heavier set guy a little older than me with short black hair that really thinned in the middle. Frank was a quiet guy on average but a nice guy to converse with. I tried to watch out over the floor as I took each step down the stairs until I reached the cement floor, I was nervous and my hands trembled. I couldn't figure out how to face Ben, he was being courted by Lisa and I dumped a huge amount of crazy on him earlier in the afternoon, I was so embarrassed.

Of course because karma hates me for the bad things I've done Ben was right around the first corner I turned. "I have to apologize" I tried to stutter out before he said anything. "SHHH, it's ok, I missed you while you were gone also" Ben reassured me with his kind eyes and gorgeous smile. I tried to talk in a whisper as we searched for our pallet, my legs were shaky and it was hard to focus on the item numbers on the pallets. I was such an idiot and I just could've died. Ben told me that there something about me that he was intrigued by, he even admitted to having *thought* about me once or twice (he was biting his lower lip and smiling) which gave me a fun little shiver. I was surprised at what I was hearing, the shock kept me quiet but I wanted to come clean about everything., especially my time in the woods thinking about him.

"I'm forty, and married" I tried to curb our conversation before things got out of hand and continued down a path that might prompt me to continue to make reckless choices. "Neither bother me, I just want to have you if you'll have me, not forever but at least once" Ben spoke out as I was searching for my ability to speak. I turned to face Ben as he told me he found our pallet, the boxes were stacked high enough that there was no way the girls in the office could see us and I stepped right up to him. Ben's hazel eyes met mine and I knew.

With my beating heart and a warm feeling surging all through me I knew that there was no good way to go anywhere, if I stepped back I would regret missing this opportunity for the rest of my unhappy marriage. If I kissed him I don't know if I could stop, if I continued to duck around and enjoy the titillation of being secretive but there was no telling how long could it go on before I've had enough. What would happen if we fell in love? Could we just kiss a few times and stop or would we get caught in some cheesy motel and then I lose James and the kids? I have always tried to balance risk versus reward in my decisions but everything is on the line and I'm the one risking it all.

James and I hadn't really connected for a long time but I feel that a small part of it might have to do with my stressing out about turning forty and all the drama that comes with being emotional about Charles. I wanted to taste Ben, I wanted to take him into me and I wanted to have him in every way like I've never had anyone before. I tried to stammer through some of my thoughts as I reached up to put my hands on Ben's large forearms. My hands shook like leaves blowing in the wind and all I could do was stare at them blankly. Ben leaned in and kissed me again. I could have melted within the strong kiss because it was so passionate. Ben braced his right hand against my cheek to caress my chin with his thumb as our tongues took turn passing each other's lips. I came to life. I felt an electric spark rush through my privates that could have lit Las Vegas for a month.

The buzz that toyed within my naught parts nearly dropped me to the ground. I felt shaky and weak but I didn't want to let go, everything seemed right for the first time in my life. I was terrified of so many things before and after that instance, but in it, I was at peace. I don't even know if there is a list long enough for all the things I worried about but yet, none of it mattered.

Ch. 6

After I kissed Ben on the warehouse floor I had to excuse myself to the rest room, I was so excited that I could feel myself walking funny, I needed desperately to clean up and calm down. I hid my blushing cheeks with cold hand pats as best as I could from Lisa and Gretchen, Reagan was too young and naive to be certain of anything but I still tried to keep discretion on my side. I sat at my desk and tried to figure out if I felt dirty, ashamed, pathetic or in love. As a teen you can understand some feelings but it's hard to decipher much of a difference between lust and love, or even a strong passion and desire from just being lonely. I've had run-ins with lust, you see a hot guy with his toned abs and thick shoulders and you let your mind wander down his stomach for a moment to what he'd be like in bed. Everyone has those movie celebrities that you'd search the internet for nude pictures of them to satisfy a small craving but never are any of them worth the risk of what would come after: guilt, shame, loss of family and so on.

I could never have considered a day where I'd betray my vows. Most of the time isn't a chance where I could pull the plug on my marriage and permanently scar my children but in the last two weeks it's only most of the time, not all the time. If I ever caught James cheating then there would be a different story but I couldn't ever leave my family or screw everything up on purpose. I loved James, he has been a good husband, but I can't admit that he's been great over the last few years. I feel like perhaps my need for attention or real romance might be the reason I ever considered a fling with Ben and maybe if I had been happier at home then there would have never been such an opportunity, except it's a lie. Ben was a beautiful man, thin athletic build with a strong chest and even stronger jawline. Ben had immaculate posture and I could always see the rippling muscles of his back under his shirt as he walked, and I could watch him walk all day long.

After my strong passion filled kiss ducked behind a stack of pallets like two high-school kids hiding under some bleachers trying not to get caught, I was hooked. I couldn't think straight, the taste of Ben on my lips was merely a glimpse of what I wanted, the kiss told me many things, and all without saying a word. Ben wasn't bothered that I had a husband at home, his self-proclaimed "bit of a naughty side" had my imagination running wild after we parted, I couldn't wait any longer. My legs quivered and my underbits hungered to feel Ben and his touches, all of them. My cravings for Ben were insatiable and a mere tryst couldn't be enough to keep my urges at bay. I was lost even though I knew exactly where I was.

My mind whirled as I toweled myself off in the restroom, I tried to hold my breath to keep from getting caught panting as I wadded up my third handful of toilet paper to dry off my panties. I wasn't entirely sure at what point I let myself end up hand drying panties in secret in a restroom at my work, but here I am, squatting down and wadding up handfuls of toilet paper around my fingers trying to sop up some of my mess. I played solemn around the girls and even though I had to sit in my own damp undies, I played off my awkward sitting as just restless.

The longer the shift passed the more I felt the heat beneath me, a hunger for Ben that was unlike anything I had experienced in my mediocre sexual history had me antsy. I tried to pretend I watched myself from an outside point of view, it was easier to see myself motioning through my shift rather than be myself and sit conflicted about what I was on the verge of getting myself into. My mind raced, I don't know how many phone calls I answered before I realized I was out of breath from speaking so quickly. It was a matter of time before one of the girls caught on that I was acting so funny and I couldn't help myself.

I missed the butterflies that disappeared after experience with James and now they were coming back to me with Ben, and I was loving them. Each first time you get to experience somebody, you get all the jitters and shakes when you unbutton their pants and slowly ease them out of their jeans while they ease their hand down the front of yours and start to touch you intimately. My mind raced with all the usual urges I had had before, except it wasn't enough. I knew that I was going to grow old with James, I was going to get gray and wrinkly and eventually watch my kids grow old and then James or I will wait around and hope that we pass away first to avoid having to live without the other person. I convinced myself that if I was going to have one little fling that it was going to be such that my vagina would quiver with the intensity of passion for the rest of my life, until now I didn't think it could ever actually exist.

I wanted to feel that I was still craved, that I was desirable and that I hadn't sunk into the category of old and no longer wanted. I needed this young sturdy man to ravish me, to take me like a brute caveman because he's so engorged and overcome with a hard-on that he loses control and has to have me. I wanted the snorting and rooting animalistic sex that would leave me walking funny for a week. I wanted to have such an erotic time that no matter what stories Reagan brings in to the office, deep down I can smile to myself and think: "amateur." I sometimes found myself browsing through some adult clips online during my quiet days, I hadn't sat around much a few years ago but recently I really got into some of the more taboo things now, taboo to the point that I had no idea why it aroused me so much.

After my work shift I dragged my feet again, the gals left chuckling and Gretchen hung back to check on me. I was caught once the girls were all gone but she turned at the last minute at the door, she wanted to talk to me but I was dragging my feet to hope to "accidentally" run into Ben (on purpose of course). Gretchen grabbed my hand and spoke with courageous words to assure me that god had a plan and that maybe Charlie was in my life to help me appreciate James and all that he had done for me. All while Gretchen spoke I couldn't stop thinking about going down on Bed in the middle of the office while Lisa watched on, jealous that I had him first. The thoughts of his bulging in my mouth made me salivate and I tried not to smirk. I thanked Gretchen for all of her kindness and gave her a gracious hug before readying to head to my car and go home. I stepped slower and slower toward my car, secretly praying that I would hear Ben's boots hit the pavement behind me as Gretchen moved ahead, she made it to the outside door a few yards before I did as I faked fumbling with my phone pretending to text somebody.

I started my car and leaned back in my seat for a few minutes, my heart raced and my lungs burned with the hard thumping in my ears. The adrenaline rush that came with the tiptoeing around and having such a large dirty secret to myself was exhilarating. I hated the drama that came with working with women, Gretchen and I laid down ground rules against cattiness and being petty when we first started, we lorded over the younger girls and they abode pretty well but we were also vigilant to make sure things stayed comfortable in the work environment. I enjoyed many of Reagan's dirty stories, the girl was much more bold and brazen than I could have ever imagined myself being but it was fun to live vicariously through her. I thought about many of the things I missed out on, there is a long list of things you just don't do when you're married, there is a long list of things you don't do when you reach your forties and just because you haven't done the things on that list, doesn't' mean that you don't have an interest in them, it just means you go without.

Some women who get divorced in their thirties go out and live, they'll find some younger guys and take the "cougar" brand for a while until some of the forbidden things on their lists are crossed off and the last breaths of life are taken in before settling back down to grow old with someone. The women that don't get a divorce don't get to have a wild year or two, they are also often uptight old bitties, like joy. I didn't want a divorce, the messy fighting and separating and hiring douche-bag lawyers that drive Volvo's, the same ones that linger around in the nude in locker rooms and scam on little kids, I didn't like the notion of any of it.

There was something about Ben that made me think about my list, there wasn't much that I didn't do with Nick, mostly because my list was very short but also because we didn't get started until later in our relationship before we started fooling around. James was older when we met so he was a bit more tame but Nick was the wild one I had many of my adventures with. There was plenty I was unsure of trying in my twenties, in my thirties there was just an overall lack of interest, but now at forty, there was a spark in my loins for so much more. Lately James just seemed like a roommate I shared a bed with, like if I had ever spent a semester abroad then it would have been like that, but maybe on a cot in some grungy foreign county just to say I did it in my life. James and I camped in our twenties but there comes a point where even sleeping on an air mattress you still needed a day to recover and I've out grown it.

My will for life seemed to be clouded, like the smoke film that covers the inside of a candle after you blow it out, sure the first layer is thin and hardly anything but the more it burns down, the darker the layer of soot, much like my life. I was a candle, a mere flicker of life left in me but hidden away behind a thick layer of film and I was burning away. The hippies had their sexual revolution, topless in the parks and free love and all of that. The unclasping of bras that signified sexual oppression of women and the freedom from the men that sought out to keep us under their thumb was a freeing change in history, and I missed it. I was born at the ass end of that revolution, perhaps my parents enjoyed those group experiences in the parks while people sat around in a drum circle and cheered them on. I wanted to feel free with my body, I wanted to experiment with myself and others and not feel overly judged by it, I wanted so much different than what I had

"Knock knock" the sudden tap tap on my window nearly caused me to soil myself with the surge of panic that ripped through me. The parking lot was dark and nearly empty except Ben was standing by my passenger window with a huge "know it all" shit eating grin, he knew I was waiting for him. My downstairs immediately came to life, my hands shook as I tried to fumble for the unlock button to let him in (in more ways than one). Ben hurried into my passenger seat and continued to smirk, "hi" he started. I leaned back against my window to keep from hurling myself at him; I had to keep up the courage to speak before I could let myself do anything.

"I can't leave my husband, I love him but I need one last fix, a rush and an experience that leaves me satisfied for the rest of my life" I began. "I understand, there's something about you that has me excited, I don't want emotions involved, like I told you, I have a bit of a naughty side and I don't know if you can handle me" Ben tried to dissuade me. "I just want to try you a little, see if I can figure out what it is about you that I need to find in my husband again" I attempted to convince both of us but I think I just had to say the words to feel like I tried. Ben smiled through my ramblings and assured me that he was not looking to get tied down nor ruin a marriage, but he was curious and ambitious. Ben nibbled on his lower lip when I talked, he was so cute doing so that I wanted to just grab onto his crotch and work it like Steven Tyler works a microphone.

"Once or twice if our schedules align, if we sit and do the math maybe can get each other out of our systems, we are smart adults and this is just a small little crush" I tried to continue on and convince the two of us but I felt like I was talking more to stall than to persuade myself of behaving. Ben nodded in agreement to all that I was saying but his adorable little smirk just made me want to rip his clothes off and ravish him like a wild animal. I had to ask, my curiosity was causing delirium, I had to know what his naughty streak entailed, I just had to know and I didn't care the cost, I wanted every naughty dirty thing to do with him and now. I dug down deep and tried to think of some of the dirty things that I had seen in porn, I tried to think of things I once thought were vile but have grown to accept that people do, I let the taboo turn into possibilities and I found that my mind exploded with twisting writhing positions all tangled up with Ben. "Have you ever tried the.. "You know" kind of stuff?" I started to mumble out to ask. The topic disgusted me before, the thought of the pain and the mess of it all, *gross* but the thought of Ben being there to give me pleasurable pain and to ease me into something so scary overwhelmed me with the desire to have him.

"I love it" Ben responded to my question, his smile growing even larger. I often shuttered when I heard people talk about the back sort of action and the thought of it grossed me out but hearing that Ben enjoyed it, it turned me on. "Come up with three things you really are curious about, we'll make it all worthwhile" Ben assured me in his gruff voice. I wondered if one tryst between us would be enough to satisfy my every craving for him, or his for me. I told Ben that in no way could any of this ever get out, that he needs to keep chatting up Lisa and that there was no way in any hell that I'd risk my marriage to my husband over our small minor fling, but I wanted him and to have him. I knew I was lying to both of us, my desire for Ben was insatiable, he was a fire that I would run into and happily burn to death. I knew deep down I would risk my marriage, I would trade all of my unhappy times with James for an earth shaking orgasm with

Ben tucked up behind me and to have his strong arms wrapped around me.

Ben was willing, normally it's easy to tell if a guy is just bullshitting to get laid, most of them are guilty of it but Ben and I were reaching an accord, two sided agreements and starting to make requests of one another. We would talk one on one but never at work and not on the phone. Ben would flash four fingers on one hand sideways if he was up for a romp, then we would discuss whether after work for a teenager banging or wait and meet up the next day before work. The dirty discussion in my car was endlessly enticing, to talk to Ben about intending to sleep with him was starting a flood in my lap and I tried to fight off shifting to avoid looking like I had to pee. To have the comfort and the guts to tell Ben that I wanted him to kiss up from one knee and then get lost between my legs was oddly calming to think about it was wild but to actually tell him, I was so insanely turned on that I could have exploded right there. I was almost scared that I could talk to Ben so easily; all of my insecurities and fears just fell from my lips without hesitation.

Ben *listened* to me, he didn't just hear my words but he understood my deepest fears and listened, like actually listened. I can't remember the last time my own husband even left the front porch light on for me after working second shift for years, and here Ben was listening. Ben was often expected to be the alpha male, the big strong guy but he wanted to know what it was like to have a girl take complete charge, and he wanted me to take in a large chest full of air and be honest with myself about what I would want, it was amazing. I found it strange that Ben would request that I be honest with myself, I felt that I was the most honest with myself of all the people in my life, but maybe he was on to something.

Ben leaned back and put his left hand on the back of my chair, his boyish smile and charm grew slightly confident as he leaned back, he almost knew what was happening but maybe he was just really really hopeful. I fought it as long as I could but I wanted to kiss him again, I wanted to seal our deal with a moistening kiss in hope that the light touching of tongues would be stronger than a handshake. I leaned in but Ben held firm, he smiled and let his tongue flick at his top front teeth, looking at his tongue move side to side made me want it inside of me. I wanted all of him inside of me and in every possible way. Looking at Ben leaning back in my passenger seat was intense, his was over six foot, not some short troll looking guy but an athletic cut young man with a slender torso I wanted to run my tongue up and down.

"So now what" Ben asked. Ben shared that he was in fact interested in Lisa but it was me that he urged for. Like me he didn't want any hiccups at work, no giveaway winks or flirty smiles. Ben didn't want any sign that we were any more than coworkers as we had been and that in absolutely no way, was anyone to find out anything for any reason, he felt as strongly as I did about the entirety of our potential but that absolute silence about it all was necessary. I was beside myself thinking that Ben still wanted Lisa, sure she was a cute girl and had a nice body but I felt my heart sink that he wanted both of us, I felt a little jealous that I wouldn't be his one and only desire but I forced myself to accept that I had James at home, which meant I had no real excuse to get jealous or upset if he had other flings beside me, except I didn't want to be a fling, I wanted to be his.

Had I never crossed paths with Ben then there was no telling how many things could have been different, except we did in fact intertwine our paths for a short while and each time we connected it was an amazing bliss that I would gamble my life for. Ben and I straightened out details about how we would further handle interactions but under no circumstances would we risk our careers by doing anything stupid at work. In the back of my mind I had an inkling that I wanted Ben to bend me over against the glass of my office, I wanted him to thrust deeply into me from behind while I stared out over the work floor. I wanted to be raw, exposed, and there was a small bit of spite in me that wanted Lisa to look up from the work floor to see me, bare tits swinging to the rhythm of Ben slamming into me and everything. I wanted to see the look on her face that I had him first, not to be mean but I wanted to know that I was hotter than the twenty-six year old but I knew that was just a fantasy.

Ben put his hand on my leg above my knee, the mere tease of his fingers made me antsy. My butt began to dance a little in my seat, I wanted to slide forward until his hands met me in the middle of my legs and I could finally feel his touch where I needed it. My legs moved uneasily together, his hand remained still despite my needing it to slid up my thigh and touch me. My nipples pushed out against my bra, they were hard erect under my clothes and in the shaded darkness in my car I could still see the difference in contrast on my chest. Ben had the slightest of smiles on his soft beautiful lips; the light stubble of his light colored facial hair glistened in the bright white glow of the parking lot light overhead and my pulse raced.

My eyes moved up and down Ben's body, his full chest muscles and bulging shoulders were welcoming, nuzzling my face against his chest earlier in the shift was soothing and settling and was also enticing and arousing; I wanted more of it, just without any clothes in the way. I never had any interest in trying drugs, from the way some of the kids in high school described some of them I could never have tried any drugs for fear that I might like them too much, Ben was about to become my drug. Turning forty was nearly impossible and it stalked me like a predator. My thirty-ninth birthday was full of family and loved one but as soon as it was over I began counting down until I turned the big four-oh. The bulge in Bens pants kept calling to my eyes, I was sure as caught as Ben watched me stare at him but I wasn't embarrassed, I was free.

I couldn't take it, the long minute of letting Ben sit with his hand on my lap was all I could take, I placed my left hand on top of his and slowly eased his hand up my leg. Ben's smile grew larger, as did his pants. More than my mouth watered, I was turned on that

Ben had such self-restraint that he didn't rip my clothes off but there was a little glint of wonder as to how he was able to hold back, maybe he didn't want me as much as he said he did, or as much as wanted him. Maybe my suspicions were right and I lost my desirable appeal. "Let yourself go" Ben began to tell me. Ben wanted me but he wanted me to want to let go and want him also, he wanted me to take the lead and to let myself take him.

Ben's strong and sturdy hands didn't move much as I rubbed against his fingers, his eyes deadlocked on me as I began to thrust my pelvis against his touch. "Am I not hot enough for you" I asked because I had to know, his lack of physical responding was distracting. "Watching you take what you want has me turned on, what I want just a bit more is to take you the right way, to romance you and strip you down and gaze upon your nude body and then taste all of you before I take you" Ben explained in his deep voice that he had always been the one taking, and now he wanted to be taken. Listening to Ben speak only made me hotter, I couldn't keep my eyes open as I thought about his strong and hard hands grabbing at my body while sliding my clothes off of me. Ben wanted me to do what I wanted and to use him as the tool to do it, he wanted to know what I would want, what it would be like to enjoy me at my utmost unhindered and free. I was a little hesitant on blurting out everything that came to mind, I was always raised to be conservative so casting aside all of my person restrictions would be nearly impossible but the comfort that I felt with Ben made everything ok.

It took a while before I was comfortable enough with Nick to let him gawk at me in normal lighting, intimacy was supposed to be hidden away in a dark bedroom so finding the courage to let him stare at me and all of my flaws made me self-conscious for a long while. Nick would often leave the bedroom curtains open at night so the street light would cast long shadows along my body at night, seeing Nick kiss of my dark body and watching as out two outlines met in our most intimate of areas was enticing and sometimes I think back to those times. Even when Nick and I showered together I was averting and embarrassed to let him just stand and watch me wash up, Nick was in good shape and his body was most enjoyable but when it came to some of my more private areas I was shy. Nick was patient and in time I learned that there was no shame in my body, I grew confident in letting Nick fondle me or remove my top in the car while driving or fool around in a parking lot here and there in secret, nothing as brazen or bold as Erin and Charlie but I tried.

James and I shared a fair amount of toying times in the daylight, we'd get courageous and see who lasted longest on drives of masturbating together on road trips or playing with one another as secretly as possible at some parks sometimes but it still took little while to grow comfortable enough with him to get to that point. I wanted Ben to watch me get myself off, like I fantasized about in the woods two weeks prior. I wanted to sit back in a chair without any clothes on and watch Ben lay on his back and get himself off while staring at me. I even wanted Ben to sit at the edge of the bed just inches from my crotch and just watch me get myself off just to excite him to the point that the moment my mouth wrapped around him he would explode. I wanted more things with Ben than I have ever wanted with James and Nick combined, there should have been guilt reeling me back but my mind went full speed into fantasies I never thought I could have had and the more taboo the hotter it seemed.

I imagined standing behind Ben, right hand wrapped around him to tug on him while my left hand reached up underneath him to cup and grope at him from between his legs. My fantasies started out hot and erotic but still pretty tame but as I writhed against Ben's hand my eyes closed and my mind continued to wander further into depravity. Something about slathering Ben and I in massage oil and then sliding all over him with my legs spread seemed both oddly enticing and sexually appealing at the same time. Sure I could rub my crotch down onto him but I wanted to slide my crotch up and down his oiled back muscles and all the way down his muscular legs before turning him over and sliding along the front of him. I wanted to straddle up behind Ben and direct all of his actions, his movements and motions of what he did to me or to himself, I liked the idea of being in control, not just a participant.

I wanted to rub my nipples along Ben, I wanted to cup my breast and trace all of his facial features using my hard nipple instead of a fingertip, especially along his luscious lips. Rubbing my hands along Ben would be hot but being slathered in oil and rubbing my body along his flexed muscles turned me on and I couldn't understand why. My breaths grew shorter and harder to hold, Bens fingers curled lightly and his hand gripped on to the inside of my right thigh so I could grind on his extended index finger and thumb and like that, I was exploding in sensations and trying to hold my breath enough to keep quiet in my car. I kept my right hand on Bens hand to keep it pressed against my privates, my head was rolled back and my back arched while my legs kicked and hit against my steering wheel. My left hand pinched and groped on my chest as my legs spread and jostled in my seat. Using a guy's hand to aggressively molest you in your own car in the parking lot of your workplace was not the most delicate nor lady like thing to do, but because it was far from appropriate it was intense and exciting.

Ben hardly moved but each time I peeked to watch him watch me he was in a trance. I jerked and spasmed on his hand, I could feel myself soaking through my clothes but I couldn't stop twitching on his fingertips. My entire body twitched, there was no rhythm to the motions of my pelvis, just convulsions following each of the intense electric jolts that shot through my body from head to toe. Ben had a large smile on his face when he finally pulled his hand from between my legs. Ben admired his fingers in the small light beam coming through the windshield, his two fingers glistened. I looked at how wet Ben's fingers were as he brought them to his mouth and touched his tongue out to taste me on them.

Watching Ben watch me sent my mind whirling, I didn't care to bother how silly I may have looked as my legs kicked and my body writhed, I thought about how hard he must have been throbbing in his jeans and what he felt like. "What do you think, honestly" I had to know what he was on his mind, I needed a little reassurance that it was all ok. "I love strawberries" Ben replied as he licked his teeth under his lips. I wanted to straddle Ben's mouth, I wanted to feel that light stubble tickling at me down below and I didn't want to wait. "Take yourself out" I asked, or rather instructed Ben. I just had to touch him, I wanted more than his fingers rubbing against me but I also wanted to wrap my hands around him, now. My body still jolted with intensity and trying to sit up a little in my seat caused me to have to roll side to side, any touching just sent me back over the edge and it caused me to whip my head backwards a bit.

Ben reclined his seat a little and kept his eyes locked on me while he unbuttoned his jeans. Ben's pelvis was mostly in the dark behind the car door, the window barely shone much light through but I could make out details in the subtle contrasts in the dark. Ben pulled his shirt up a little to show me some of his tight abs and I couldn't stop myself from placing my right hand on him. My left hand continued to rub and toy with my right tit under my shirt in anticipation. Ben's hip bones popped out from under the waist of his jeans as his slid his jeans down below his ass, his boxer briefs still hid what I needed to have. I strained to see the contours of him under his underwear, it was leaning towards me in the crease of his hip but I could still make it out.

My mouth watered and my hands trembled as I slowly eased my hand down his stomach. I played with the light trail of hair below his belly button as I worked my index finger under his elastic band to lead the way for the rest of my hand. The happy trail of light hair stopped under the elastic, it was bare and smooth and the surprise made me gasp. Finding smooth skin near his privates was new, it was exciting and the mystery of what I still hadn't discovered was making my heart race so fast that I began to sweat. I let my fingers inch slowly down to where I wanted to be, I wanted to grab hold like I was hand catching fish but I also liked that the excitement in my mind was making me dizzy.

I tried to hold my breath to contain some of my excitement but my choppy breathing was all that I could control. My fingertips found him. I raised up some of the fabric from his boxers to guide my hand over him more and when I finally got to grip him, he was so enormous that my fingers didn't even wrap around him. I let out an awkward half moan exhale when I grabbed him; I froze for a moment to try to full comprehend what I held in my hand. The smooth skin was overlying bulging hardened veins, the ripples and contours seemed to go on and on as my fingers continued to trace him. My chest let out all of my air and all I could see in my eyes were spots with a dark background. I felt light headed and the surge of orgasm ravaged through me again.

My toes curled in my shoes, my mouth fell open and my left hand clenched down on my breast so hard I was sure it was going to bruise but that piercing pain entangled with intense pleasure seemed to take me higher and higher. Ben shuffled a little in his seat, I popped my eyes open to make sure that I wasn't holding on too tightly or hurting him. "It's all yours" Ben instructed as he wriggled down his boxers to below his butt to join his jeans. It was pretty dark but the sight of Ben was breathtaking. Ben was shaved bare and he was enormous. My hand looked so small wrapped around Ben as he laid back and gave me complete control. I moved my hand left and then right to further inspect him, I began to doubt if I could fit my mouth on him but I was sure going to try.

I couldn't stop inspecting Ben as I leaned over the seat, it was almost mythical but I could feel his pulse in my hands so it had to be real. I let go of my chest to cup him with my left hand as I began to lean down towards him. Ben's muscles flexed as I eased him into my mouth, his size was immense but I had to have him. Ben seemed to glide in my mouth, I struggled a little to work my way down him but no matter how far I got, I had to have more of him. Ben didn't thrust his hips but small muscles twitched in him and the faster I worked my hands the faster I felt his throbbing in my mouth. One of Ben's free hands roamed the back of my head, his fingers running through my short hair turned me on, I wanted him to grab a handful of my hair and take over to get him off but he just played with my hair instead. I liked that he moved me in rhythm to better please him as he had to me, the other free hand ran down my right side and inched around to my breast, his large hands easily grabbed at me, his hands were gentle and his touch further set me wild me with passion. I focused on using plenty of spit to keep him wet as I my hand and mouth worked together, I wanted him to just release so I could taste him.

Ben thrust his hips a little and I could feel his body shake in my hands and mouth. I found the moment I wanted, where the warm rush filled my mouth as I got to really taste Ben before swallowing him down. Ben pushed down on the back of my head gently, pushing more of him into my mouth as he quivered sporadically for a moment of elation. I continued to swallow Ben down, I felt full as I continued to slurp and gulp him while he strained, I wanted all of him in me and even though I had him, it wasn't enough. Ben was amazing, his body might as well have been carved in marble he was so smooth and perfectly contoured and here I am, nearly swallowing him whole in the front seat of my car in the parking lot where we work. The naughty and dirty of what I was doing was almost as big of a rush as that "first time" exhilaration that comes from someone new.

My blood raced, my ears were hot with passion and even after finishing, Ben was still upright and ready to charge the mound, (or mons perhaps) again. Ben reclined his seat a bit more so that he was lying flat but he sat up to take a safe look around. "Come here" Ben suggested as he pulled me over the middle and towards him. It was difficult to keep my head down and step towards him but I left my shoes on the driver's side floor and began to make my way. I wanted him in every way, I wanted to just not go home to James tonight but follow Ben to his place and let him ravish me over and over. I wanted Ben to lay me spread out on a bed and stand at the foot and tell me each and every move to make, what to do and when to stop until I was quivering and ready to orgasm and then I want him to enter me and send me to that land of orgasm from sex, a place I had never really ben.

Ben's pants and boxers were still under his butt, his shirt up under his arm pits and the rest of him covered in my saliva. James would need a power bar, some pills and a nap before he was ready for a second inning but Ben was still up to bat. Ben eased me onto him, my back lying on his front. Ben let his hands roam up my shirt, shoving my bra above my chest and letting my tits out into the light of the parking lot and so we could be skin to skin. I let my hands hang down to my sides to clench into the skin of him as he kissed the back of my neck. The open air on my stomach and chest were a relief in the warm car. I wasn't ready to be done with Ben yet so I decided to slide my hand down the front of my pants and open the button and zipper.

With Ben hard and pressed against me I wanted to get off again, I was too engulfed in the moment to focus on getting him into me so I thought I'd finger myself while his hands explored the rest of my body, my excitement was still near its' peak and it wouldn't take much touching to get me back on cue. Ben's strong legs were pressed against the back of me as I worked my hand down the front of my pants and under my panties. I slid my fingers into place to rub and slide back and forth. Ben used his large hands to cup and fondle my chest while continuing to kiss at my neck, goosebumps riddled my entire body. "Let me taste your fingers" Ben whispered into me ear, his voice took my breath away, his instructions nearly sent me over the edge.

I reached my hand back so Ben could taste me on them; he sucked on my fingers and licked all of me off of them before I reached back down to continue. Ben slid his hands down my sides and inserted his fingers under my waist band to slide my pants and panties down below my tush so we were skin to skin on our midsections now also. My pants were too tight around my knees to open my legs up much and my fingers were working feverishly as I took in all of the feeling of Ben below me. I had no worries, no cares and no looming burdens hanging around my neck as I returned to the climax of my womanhood with Ben right behind me, still rubbing himself against me.

I tensed up again on Ben, his hand joined mine and as I jerked and twitched I had to just let all of my muscles turn to jelly with my release. I suddenly didn't have any bones or ability to move as I continued to exhale endlessly. My words slurred and I felt immediately sloppy drunk as I tried to just melt all over Ben. My chest muscles twitched, my left neck muscles seemed to pull my head towards my left and if I hadn't lost all of my bodily fluids between my legs I might have begun to drool. I didn't even have the power to breathe right and if I hadn't been lying on top of Ben as his meaty chest heaved up and down, I might have just suffocated but his inhaling seemed to force me to as I just became completely numb.

I had lost all ability to think, my body was just a warm sort of numb as I lay there on top of Ben. My body fluttered and twitched in random places and none of it made any sense to me but I didn't have a care in the world. I don't know if I've ever had such a feeling, there were no words that any writer in history could have strung together to come close to even remotely being able to describe the feelings surging through my veins. I was hot with passion while my skin slowly cooled in the dark air in the night. Each breath I released out of my body seemed to take with it any negative thoughts I had ever had in my life. My fingers tingled and my toes remained curled in my socks. I could only feel Ben's warmth below me and nothing else as waves of heat ran up my body and caused my eyelids to flutter. I felt like a shaken pop can that finally was finally opened and able to release years of pent up pressure and stress and immediately I felt that my life was sure to change forever.

Ben pushed me up with both hands, my body didn't know how to work still but he told me that it was probably getting really late and suggested I get back to my family and my husband to stay in line with our agreement not to screw things up in our personal lives. I didn't even know what Ben had going on in his personal life but I didn't have to care; he wasn't my husband or even my boyfriend, he was a toy with a pulse and I felt unchained from any sort of burden of attachment. I could drive home and have no concern for his feelings.

There was a part of me that did in fact care for him, I wasn't sure I could sleep with him and trust him with my heart and body without having some feelings but I was also forty, married, had kids, and knew that I wanted him so badly at least once that I was willing to take the heart break and risk it all for those intense minutes with him. I tried to think about trying to drive home while hanging my backside out the window to dry in off but I couldn't come up with a logical way of doing so. I had to drive home sitting in a puddle but I couldn't even think straight enough to worry about it. I tried to find a way to angle my vents to blow down near my lap as I kept my pants down for better aeration, I was a mess and driving home late at night without pants on was just proof that I was being stupid.

I took long ways home to let myself cool off better, I had all of my windows open hoping to air out my whole sweaty body. I thought through every moment of my time with Ben, I worried that I would be caught with his cologne on my back or on my neck so I began to drum up excuses, I came up with excuses for excuses and began to make sure I could cover every angle James might come at me from to make sure my story was as solid as it could ever get. I kept it simple; I got plenty of sympathy hugs for having to deal with things with Erin and Charlie so I planned to play it off as many hugs creating such an aroma on me if there were any questions. I felt guilty having to plot and plan to lie, it was unclean and grotesque and I felt began to feel badly as I neared my home. The high that came from touching Ben and then the elation of Ben finally touching me was unlike any wild erotic fantasy that I could have dreamed of but now the low of guilt after ward was manic and shitty feeling, I dreaded that I was such a loser for having betrayed my husband, my vows, and my sense of self.

I pulled back into my dark driveway to a dark house yet again. The dark rooms reflected my personal life, no lights on inside and nothing stirring. Bruno was waiting for me in the living room this time, he was often asleep in one of the kid's rooms upstairs when I got home so it was strange that he was waiting for me with his tail wagging, luckily not barking his furry butt off. Bruno was curious and his tongue went crazy on my hands, I guess trying to figure out some of the new and strange smells I carried into my home with me. The house was dark and as usual, James was sound asleep while I changed out of my clothes. My groin was still dripping wet from Ben as I stood naked in my bathroom mirror, I reeked of sweat so I decided to quick rinse before climbing under the sheets with my husband in our marital bed.

The shower cleansed me of sweat, saliva, and other things but it didn't wash away my shame. Away from Ben I had self-control but once he came around my urges to have him completely took over my brain and turned me into another cheating idiot. Cheating spouses either get caught or have to live with the guilt and I finally did something worth feeling poorly about, I threw away what my husband ever meant to me, I made a joke out of my vows and above all, I just risked the mental wellbeing of my children on some stupid wild crush and a chance at a small fling, there wasn't enough soap and hot water in the shower to wash away my feelings and I had to now figure out if I had enough of Ben to curb my cravings forever or it I would soon miss the high from being with him and trip up again.

I felt out of sorts the whole weekend after I gave in with Ben. I had a hard time focusing on many of my tasks first thing in the morning so I took Bruno with me for a jog just to force myself to focus on something. Bruno was often reluctant to jog with me; he was a lazy bum and would sometimes lag behind after the first mile because he knew he could but I just tugged him along. The jog didn't really clear my head, the fresh air was enlivening but the same worn path and same looking houses just seemed to pass me by without much notice. Bruno stopped at every fire hydrant and telephone pole and it quickly grew annoying as hell. I jerked and tugged Bruno to follow me as I trudged my way back home to ready the kids for school and so on. Taking Bruno with me for my jog didn't change up enough, everything was back to the same old routine passed the same old houses and I was back to the same old me.

I tried to breath heavily as I readied to open the door, I wasn't sure what to expect when I opened the door because I had Bruno on a leash so he wouldn't be ready to pounce on me from inside the door. I opened the door to reveal James, he wasn't rushing out the door with a small peck on the cheek like before, the look on his face was different, he was waiting for me. I had a split second to fake being startled when I walked in to mask my freezing panic that stopped my heart in my chest. Bruno barked as he tore the leash from my hand to head inside and rile up the kids before they were off to school. My hearing stuttered and sounded like there were pauses for a moment as my heart began to skip beats.

Bruno charged in and passed James, he hardly flinched as he stood tall and kept his arms crossed. A lump larger than Ben appeared in my throat. In sixteen years of marriage I hadn't ever done anything that made me think I was in any trouble. My mother always told me that if you don't do anything wrong then you can't get in trouble and you'll never have to worry about that deer in the headlights feeling, the same feeling I now had. "Hey you, I wondered where Bruno went, I was worried he got out" James piped up as he cracked a smile while pushing himself up from the post he leaned against. James had no idea how late I got home, he had no clue that when I got home I was so filled with Ben's spunk that I couldn't even take a sip of water and he had no clue that there might have been anything wrong with us, he was worried about the damned dog.

James grabbed his gym bag from behind the banister and as usual, I got a peck on the cheek and like that he was jumping into his truck to leave. My heart was racing nearly as hard as it was when I was fooling around with Ben, I was so close to having been caught that I couldn't stop smiling with relief as I packed the kids and sent them down the street to catch the bus. Once my children were out the door my knees went wobbly and I needed to lie down, my mind was racing all over the place but I liked it a little bit. James once knew every little nuance about me, he knew that I held my breath when I lied, (which I stopped doing long ago) he knew each little muscle twitch in my face or the tone in my voice, but now I felt like I was married to a stranger.

I never wanted to hide things from James before but in the last few years he became harder and harder to talk to. If I had some new thing I wanted to do he was not very receptive about trying it, from something as simple as tofu to dance classes, he grew more and more stubborn against it and it slowly evolved into it being my fault for wanting to try such things. I had the gumption earlier on to stand up for what I wanted, to voice my opinion but as time went on it became harder and harder to get my point across, or at least to get my point even heard, it just grew tiresome of even trying.

I didn't want to become a runaway train of chaos that could only result in divorce. I liked the comfort of my home life but I wanted a spark of real life to come back into me also, I wanted to feel alive. I didn't want to be a cliché, the bored housewife that has an affair and then loses everything. I never would have flushed away everything I had built up over the last sixteen years with James on a fling and I had to put a stop to it. I didn't get caught as I laid on Ben in my car as we were both basically naked and rubbing all over each other so for all intents and purposes I was free and clear, I just had to focus on finding my strength to stay with my boring marriage and not give in again.

I spent the weekend trying to rekindle my marriage; I needed to reignite my passion for my husband and I was bound and determined to make it permanent. My time at the cabin was pissed away but I had a three day weekend with James and the kids so I decided that I would go back to holding his hand, walking side by side with my husband and trying to show him I could be the wife I deserved to be. I found it odd that I wasn't stricken with paralyzing guilt when I held his hand but that was because I did my best to think about him and the life we've had rather than the slight small indiscretion that happened in my car, which was a mistake. My fingers fit better with James', my head felt comfortable for the first time in a long time as I leaned my head against his shoulder as we watched out children play soccer. I tried not to think of myself as some filthy cheater or scamp or anything, I tried to focus on being the good wife I vowed to be and I owed it to myself to let go of the guilt of what I had done.

I found that I liked being a whole family again, my husband by my side and my kids in my view, I was back to appreciating what I had and that it was what I wanted in life. James was less cold to me;

he helped me to make dinner at night and even became a little youthful in his grabbing and pinching at me. I felt myself falling in love with my husband again and I had to thank Ben for it. My fling was a little shameful for me but where it brought me back with my husband took the guilt away so it turned out to be more of a blessing than a burden. Over the weekend I felt more receptive to James, I felt his warmth towards me and I felt like this was where I wanted to be when we returned from the cabin.

On a scale of one to ten, ten being the sort of sex you'd pay to see, James and I started out around a five but as time progressed, we averaged about a three. I would have rated my time with Ben a six or seven, so of course I crave the wilder and hotter times; I wanted to experience a TEN. I wanted James and I to increase our average rating for our sex life, I wanted to get him revved up and try some of the things I thought about trying with Ben, maybe using Ben like a starting block I could run the distance with James and keep improving things. I thought about revisiting the list I spoke about. Maybe it was time to put on some steamy porn flick and encourage James to try some things with me. James didn't have the body Ben did, nor the hold over my sexuality that Ben did but Ben didn't have the longevity that James had with me so perhaps that might favor James.

On Sunday night I put the kids to bed and I decided that James should join me in the shower. James was changed and ready for bed before I caught up with him in our room. I wanted more passion and for the first time in a very long time; I wanted it to be with my husband. I thought about why I didn't feel any guilt, I definitely should have but the one time tryst with Ben helped me to clear away so much of my anguish about so many things that I had no choice but to look at it as therapeutic. James hadn't noticed me much in a long while, our bedroom romps were just quick bouts so he could get to bed and I could get to reading or any other thing to avoid him, we fizzled out and our fun had run dry and it was a sad way to just drift through life. I found that I was willing to want my husband and again and I wanted to build on the momentum that Ben started, and it was going to begin in the shower with my husband.

I know growing old is never really an option, one day a gray haired reflection appears in the mirror and then one day all you see is an old lady with wrinkled skin and great grand kids. No relationship has a happy ending for both people, one of you will pass on and the other has to experience life without their mate, it's sad really. I had the slight tinge in my gut that eventually my sin would come back to haunt me but I also thought about the thousands of soldiers that have had to kill people in their time and most seemed to be able to put it behind them, so I am going to do the same thing. I smirked thinking about long after James passes that maybe I'll be an old lady slowly being forgotten in some nursing home and I'll end up talking about Ben being the love of my life and all the nurses will keep thinking I'm going crazy because my husband's name was James.

James seemed elated that I was looking to have relations with him; he asked what had changed and why I had taken into consideration showering with him for some out of routine fun. It was hard to answer (not because I wanted to admit to the man that was supposed to be my best friend in life) because he couldn't just take my loving gesture as it was but rather he assumed there was some ulterior motive behind wanting to spend quality time with my husband. James stood behind me and held on tightly to my hips while the water trickled on our out bodies. James' hands were significantly smaller than Ben's but I tried to focus on the romance in the shower and not about whom I really wished it was with. I was excited to get to enjoy James but parts of me weren't as receptive as they should have been.

I leant a hand to get things started while James fumbled away to get himself ready. The shower lacked any of the passion I had hoped to find by taking us out of our bedroom, I had been a while without my husband and my lack of interest in him sort of depressed me, when I said "I do" I also meant that I would continue on to lust for him the way a good wife should. I tried to watch through the steamy glass shower doors at James thrusting at me in the mirror, I tried to pretend it was Ben and hoped that watching us might titillate me a little. Even in my own eyes I knew the difference between my aging husband and his little pooch belly standing and humping me from behind as I tried to hold on to keep from falling, and Ben, the larger more muscular man that I had pressed up against me three nights before, that was who I really wanted.

I offered a hand down below to make sure that my time spent with James wasn't a complete waste but I didn't really feel in the mood but I tried to be. I used to just go without orgasms for a long time, if I was real hard up for the release then I would go and hide in the bathroom (feeling like a freak that my own husband couldn't get me off during sex) and I would handle things myself. It took me years of faking the moaning and writhing before I was just sick and tired of it. James could get me off in other ways that were as much fun, but I have always felt that I was truly missing out on things and it makes me feel bad about myself. I just wish I worked like everyone else.

The whole growing old and drying really loomed over me for months before I turned forty, I'd be lying if I said those thoughts were behind me now, but maybe a little less. They say the brain has seven minutes of activity in which it replays all of your life's memories back like a movie until there is no more brain activity, I wonder if it's true. I wonder if your life plays backwards until finally, you see the light at the end of the tunnel, which would actually be your own birth, a memory hidden so deep in your brain that you can't even know it's there because it's the very first memory in your brain, like the first foundation brick that the pyramids are built on, it might be there somewhere. Would I have more good memories than not when it's my time to go?

What if your last thoughts are frozen in your mind the moment you die and that is what really determines heaven or hell? If you've lead a shitty life and have lived as an angry fool then your last thoughts would most likely be salty and you'd spent your last seven minutes replaying those memories and that would be your hell. What if the opposite was true also, what if I die surrounded by my kids and loved ones and that would be my heaven until all of the last neurons in my brain stopped firing and that was the last of me forever, only to return to the most basic atoms that make us all up. What if James passes long before me and I end up discarded into some senior center, rambling on about Ben being the love of my life, all the while the nurses and caretakers looking at me like I'm crazy because my husbands' name was James, would my one memory be enough to follow me forever or would time without James make me long for him in a way that I would hang onto the good memories until that was all I had left of my husband?

James slowed in his speed but increased in his intensity as he neared his finish, a similar routine I was all too familiar with. I just kept watching myself in the mirror, parts of me wiggled, parts of me jiggled and my tan lines looked awkward in the reflection. I knew why I wanted to have Ben, the close encounter in the car was exceedingly erotic and I had hoped it would quench my desires for him but it wasn't going to be enough. I have seen James and I have enough sex, we had our fun with mirrors and even with a video once when we were younger and full of vigor.

The sex tape James and I made was a disaster, two young idiots, a tripod, terrible lighting and no idea about how to *perform*. James wanted to watch us in a sex tape to be able to see me (his hot wife) long after kids ruined my body, I sort of wanted to see it just to see it. I was reluctant about filming at first because I was stricken with dread that somebody might find it, like a babysitter a few years later or something. James and I rolled around in the sheets and traded out a few positions and did our best to let the camera capture some of our youthful bodies and passion, what we got was a film with poor lighting, terrible zoom-ins on genitals (that had poor trim jobs) and other body parts that shouldn't have jiggled so much.

Once James and I finished out tape we of course wanted to see our grand work, rather than get as hot watching the tape as we were making the tape, we sat around on the couch and laughed at some of the grunting faces, the clumsy fumbling and squishing sounds that dominated the sound track. James was let down because "the camera adds ten pounds" didn't work in his favor, it all went to his stomach. Watching myself on film was horrid, I saw pimples in area that there shouldn't have been any, I saw the effects that gravity had already begun to cast onto my breasts and even before kids, my stomach looked awful. James and I agreed that we would try to watch that tape every fifth anniversary together, not so much to put us back in the mood but to get to laugh at how young and dumb in love we were.

Once I grew more comfortable with myself it took some time to delicately dance with James' ego about his inability to get me off during intercourse. James was willing to make up for it in other ways so we made do, as any married couple would, but it was frustrating getting right to that point and always faltering out. Looking at him in the mirror I saw that James didn't even bother to keep his eyes open to watch us, he was probably thinking about our taught little babysitter and her perfect little teen body, not my aged forty year old body that was just standing there, half bent over and taking it from him because I felt like I should. I'm pathetic. The mention of Ben gets me charged up and ready to lose my job but the safety and security of a man I have known for half my life can't even get me wet in a shower.

With a grunt and a huff James was holding still while his legs shook beneath him, I was wondering what Ben might have been up to and wondering if perhaps he was behind Lisa doing the same thing, except holding out longer of course. I wanted Ben to pin my against a counter in a bathroom so I could watch him behind me, his neck straining and his chest muscles flexing while he held on tightly to my waist and filled me with desire. My little romp in my car was amazing and I had to have more, here I am with my husband softening inside of me in the shower of the home I share with him and I'm thinking about Ben. I really was disappointed that I was letting my mind wander off to Ben, especially while I was trying to be passionate with my husband of sixteen years, I know for a long time I was insecure enough that I couldn't imagine James thinking about some other girl without going into a rage spiral but here I am, not just thinking about another man but actually recalling

I didn't get enough of Ben; I tasted him on my lips (even days later) and I wanted more. The few minutes of being with James didn't reignite any passion but rather echoed how little passion I had towards my husband anymore. I told myself that if I just had the one encounter with Ben that maybe it would be enough to breathe some life back into me and I could wash away some of the gloomy gray that filled me, and it seemed to, for a bit. I told myself that if Ben could jump start my battery then I'd drive home and stay there, except here I am at home and thinking about Ben again. My heart knew that I said my vows to James but my loins called for Ben and it was making me unhappy again.

The sneaking was just as hot as the actual time Ben and I had, it was a risk that one of the girls might catch me and it was also risky that James might find out but it set my blood on fire and it was exciting. The close call in my mind when I returned from my jog was breathtaking and even though I despise drama, I get it now. With a glass of wine when I got home after my fling with Ben I was able to sleep, I needed it to calm the fire racing through my body with the excitement that I brought home and it just capped off an amazing fling. As I slept I convinced myself that things had long fizzled out with James and by rubbing on Ben I was merely trying to see if there was that spark inside of me that could restore my love for my husband, but it was all a lie.

I wanted to be selfish. I wanted to have Ben before Lisa got him. I wanted to get the hot guy at work because I wanted to win against any of the other younger girls around. I wanted Ben because

I needed to know that I wasn't all old and washed up yet and I needed to know that I still mattered. Ben was more than a prize to be won, but winning him was going to be life changing, except here I am being mounted by my husband in our shower and the only thing I feel is the rail in my hand that is keeping me from slipping on the tile. James leaned down on me for a minute to catch his breath, he focused on him and didn't even bother to kneel down and take care of me in any way, I wanted to be that kind of selfish now.

James pulled back and I just held on to the handle in the shower, all I could do was let the water rinse off the little tinge of guilt I felt. I felt worse about not feeling bad than I did about having nearly slept with a man that wasn't my husband, was I a monster? Some women go and tan and hit the gym and hoist up their boobs in a sports bra to give them plenty of extra lift and then love it when guys whistle or stare. The confidence boost is often a cheap high and even though I often got them when I was out jogging in my extra tight pants; it wasn't enough. I didn't want to be one of the floozy girls that craved and did pathetic things for cheap attention, show some leg for a smile or whip out my boobies for hollers or beads, but I was getting naked with a man in my car to make myself feel better, am I just as bad as the sluts?

I wanted one life changing romp, I wanted to wrap my hands around Ben and take him into my mouth until he exploded, but and then I wanted him more and more. I knew that the odds of getting into major trouble were endless but for all I know, James is diddling the sitter so so what. I had to have Ben, if I made a good run of things and got some of my list crossed off then I could sit in the pews with my family and fake smile at all the other unhappy wives that fake smile while the husbands parade us around to boast about whose wife kept their looks the longest and so on. It was time for me, I put in my time being wife and mom, I wanted some time for me and for something I want. I slid my hand down my stomach and began to take care of business for myself as usual. I was focused on what I was doing, I had no idea if James stepped out or what, I just know his hands weren't on or in me so it didn't matter and I didn't care. Had James stuck around I would have gladly welcomed a hand or whatever from him, I want attention , I want roaming hands and fingers to explore my body and shake things up. I even wanted James to kneel down behind be and bury his face into my while I stayed bent over and enjoyed my own body, but sadly he was already long gone and probably in bed.

By the time I toweled off, inspected myself in the mirror and took the time to lotion, James was fast asleep. There was no kiss goodnight, no pause in the snoring when I climbed into bed with him, not even a moan to signify that my presence was noticed, there was nothing. I wondered how much I was depriving myself by holding back about Ben, was I cheating on James as much as I was cheating myself out of something? I didn't plan to leave James and there was a great chance nobody gets caught but I still knew the risk I was taking. Ben was worth the gamble. I don't know if it was even so much Ben himself as much as it was a matter of being romanced and pleasured like I had never gotten to experience.

I thought about that small list of things I'd be willing to try or things that might sound like an amazing opportunity had James been willing to try or even consider over the last few years while my appetite changed. The point I made earlier (about being starved for attention) was proved again in the shower, I just wanted to share an intimate moment with my husband in the shower and it was questioned, nothing makes you feel sexy and desired liked being second guessed when you make an effort. I was once again let down in the bedroom area, I wanted to be taken like I was a teenager again, I wanted James to want me so bad that he rips my panties off in a fit of rooting and grunting while face down in my crotch and that I'm so turned on by it that I don't care about ripping a high end pair if forty-dollar panties.

I tossed excuses and reasons around all night as to why I did what I did, my sleep took a hit because I tossed and turned but my mind would not stop churning. I wasn't losing sleep over what happened, I was losing sleep because I was giddy about what I wanted to happen . I validated every move I made with Ben and why I didn't want to pass on this chance, a fling or two with Ben wouldn't make me a total cheater, maybe just a small cheat, just one or two things to satisfy my desires and interests then I can settle into my old married life again with James and continue downhill with my husband while Ben goes and makes babies with Lisa.

Ben and I agreed that our fling was just that and that it wouldn't last long or put either of us in jeopardy of losing our jobs or romantic lives, it was just to satisfy one another for a bit so it seemed safe, overall. Ben and I had agreed upon short few sessions to get one another out of our systems and satisfied with our lives, I suspected he wanted to nail the hot older chick at work before going out with the more tame Lisa, which irked me a little but I would force myself to be ok with. I wanted the self-validating fling that I still had enough hots and looks that I could rile up the young stud of the office. I knew I was lying to myself but the degree of the lie was unclear. I found a way to sleep, I had the comfort of the home life with James and the kids but I also got the one or two chances to make some lifelong fantasies come true with Ben so I was going for it, having made the decision helped me to sleep.

I know I've heed and hawed back and forth but it was a heavy choice to risk my entire marriage for what I wanted. I know bitches that have done what I've done and then financially raped their husband of pensions or lifesaving because they wanted what they wanted and then blamed the spouse for causing them to run off. I'm not blaming James, I don't feel it's entirely his fault I felt the way I did, I just wish we were still as close as we once were so I could explain it all and have the closeness that he once gave me. I wanted attention on many levels, I got some from James but right now it seems Ben is giving me a majority of the attention I want and that is what's pulling me towards him. James' breathing at night is erratic and hard to understand his apnea makes sleep difficult, a breathing machine would ruin my sleep for the rest of my life and further stress me out. I know James and I have joked about apnea and how it sneaks up on you when you're older but listening to the Morse code like pauses in his breathing are making me think maybe he should really look into it.

The week days came as usual, up early to jog to get half an hour of quiet time before returning to get the kids up and off to school while James rushes out the door to hit the gym before his long work days and so on. Bruno still exploded with energy when I returned from my jogs but he was always a mess to contend with as I started laundry and house cleaning and so on. I went for second walks with Bruno to get more fresh air to help nurse my improving mood in the early morning once the kids were off and I had laundry started. The week was a much better one at work; I got along with the girls and felt I was returning back to my old self, a lot of my stress was lifting since I made my decision, I was still a little anxious but having made my choice took away a lot of my inner conflict.

Passing Ben in the warehouse was calm, I didn't feel the swell of my lady parts nor the uncontrollably urge to leap at him and rip his clothes from his body as usual, it was fun to have my head on straight and subtly flirt a little, he just gave a passing smile and it was as if nothing ever happened. I found my balance, I thought of Ben as just another coworker and it kept my pulse calm around him and we both behaved professionally. At home I tried to keep up with my family and all of the running and that was my focus. I thought I realized that the heaven or hell of life is a matter of conscience and mine was clear. I hadn't really done anything all that wrong, sure Ben felt me up but he was pretty innocent in things so I was guilt free and finding my understanding in my life.

I had two snot nosed kids show up at my door one day, they were knocking as I returned from my jog so I was trapped. One kid with scraggly reddish brown hair and one shorter mixed kid with a clean haircut and lighter tanned skin were both in dress pants and dress shirts, damn solicitors. "Are you secure in your afterlife" the taller white kid spoke up. These two shits were blocking me from getting into the safety and privacy of my home, I was stuck and I hated it. I was doing well at being the smiley happy housewife at home and the happy go lucky Ally at work so I was floating and doing well. The shorter mixed kid began to pipe up and raise his arm with a pamphlet in hand; "You should consider" was as far as the kid got before I began to speak over him. "What could you possible know about life, let alone some afterlife, you are out here willing to sell someone else delusion, come back when you've been to war, lost a child, lost an arm or a leg and are over fifty years old, if you can live a long life and go through real struggles, not just pissing in your huggies, then come bother me, I might even listen to your babble."

I berated both of the boys that blocked my door, I was calm and cool for the first few words, I don't know where the fury came from and once it started I found that I was getting louder and louder. Both kids grew wide eyes, they must have been barely eighteen and were out because some shaman swindled them to spend their perfectly good youth doing shit that would never benefit their lives. You pack a bunch of blank minded kids into school and force feed them anything and they'll be willing to die for what they think they believe; it's sad actually. If I had it all to do over again I would spend more time living my life and not letting people direct how to live it, I waited until I was almost forty to finally be brave enough to think for myself and looking back, I can honestly say I have let many opportunities to actually live, go by, and I certainly wasn't going to waste another minute listening to some magician in training blab on about shit they know nothing about so I stormed passed them and into my house mid-rant.

I only had a few weeks left before the kids would be out of school for the summer and my time would then be soaked up like a sponge and then there wouldn't be much left for me yet again. I love my kids and it was indeed a blessing when they arrived but it is full time work and for the rest of my life. I missed having some of the attention I needed, James was always long asleep when I arrived to my dark and lonely home and that was a familiar sad routine for me.

Over the next week or two I was holding my own against that surging desire for Ben and I was proud of myself. James was going through more than just his sleeveless workout shirts, I took notice of when I did the laundry each morning that there seemed to be more. It was normal for him to wear a pair of basketball shorts twice a week, he wasn't really much of a sweater but I started seeing more pairs every day and more clothes in general. I noticed that even in his sleep, his arms seemed a little more defined and I wondered if maybe James was returning to lifting weights. James was a strong man in his twenties and his attention to his body was definitely noticed when I first met him, he was ruggedly handsome and very polite, how could I miss it?

I curtailed my food intake a little to see if I could lose my pesky five pound to get in a little better shape, both for myself and for public viewing when I go back to taking the kids to the pool in the dog days of summer. On the weekend I mentioned cooking healthier and James was on board. I liked that my family was clicking better. James and I seemed to get along better, we worked around each other and he picked up on helping around the house more on the time we had together also, things were getting back to nice again. I did feel a tinge of guilt, was it because I convinced myself that I should go forward with an affair that my marriage improve, sort of like when you give up and get ready to drown that a boar arrives, or was it that deep down I did feel guilty and maybe I was looking really hard to find the good in my marriage rather than actually risk throwing it all away? I just didn't know.

On my way out to my second jog I crossed paths with Joy again. I am surprised the bitch isn't riding some old bike around trying to put Bruno in the basket and laughing with a cackle. Joy mentioned how nice it was to see James and I taking more time off to spend together and having passed him in town earlier in the week.

I smiled and did my best to escape from Joy, she was a harpy slag that just seemed to suck the life and happiness from people, I was feeling good and positive about myself and my husband again and I wasn't going to let her... Wait, the other day? Like during the day? As in he didn't go to work like he was supposed to? I prodded for a few more details about James under the excuse that he must have forgot to mention seeing her.

The spiraling began. It only made sense that James would give up basketball to start losing weight and toning up in the gym if he had someone on the side. If James was screwing someone it would explain why he was out during the day. Our babysitter Kaylie is a senior in high-school and she would have to be at school so it couldn't have been her, plus what would some popular seventeen year old want with a slightly overweight guy in his mid-forties? I couldn't help my mind from going out of control thinking about him with someone else. I felt my anxiety freak out, I finally convince myself not to get naked and crazy with Ben and I go back to focusing on my marriage and the bastard is diddling someone else, ugh the nerve.

It didn't make sense to me that I had partially been with Ben but yet I felt the rage in my chest thinking about James screwing somebody else. I had dibs on James, a long marriage and he was neglecting me for someone else. I didn't want my future with him ruined by some bimbo that spreads her legs for him but it looks like that is where the downward spiral with us began. I never would have thought of James as a cheater but two can play at that game. I returned home and sent Ben a text that I needed him and luckily he was quick to respond. I grabbed my work clothes and hopped into my car. Ben called me to guide me to his house, it was a little out of the way so I had time to run through dozens of scenarios in my head but all of them equaled James sleeping with someone else.

Once I got to Bens place I only had two hours before we were both due at work, I felt a little pressured and even though each stop sign I hit, I kept driving towards his house rather than turn around and go back to mine. When I saw Ben standing in his doorway without his shirt on there was no turning back. I parked in front of the neighbor's ranch style house and looked around to make sure there weren't any prying eyes before I let myself glide right on up to the door. Ben had a tanned body from working outdoors, he was rippled and strong and when he flexed while moving the creases between his muscles only deepened. I was taken aback, I knew better than to go eye for an eye, or an affair for an affair but I had to have him, I craved him. I was willing to submit to him and my knees quickly went weak. It was daylight, there was no hiding in the shadows and if he slid his jeans down I probably would have just passed out. "Shot" Ben offered as he pulled a bottle of Jack from the freezer.

I wouldn't advocate drinking before work but I had two hours and maybe one stiff drink would help to calm my nerves a little. I was wearing the same blue and white striped white sweater I was wearing the first time Ben and I kissed, it must have been lucky, or cursed, I am not sure. I rolled the shot glass off my lower lip and let it fall into my lower hand and then smiled through the burn in my throat. Ben tossed back his large shot and smiled at me. There was no going back now.

Ben stepped to me and wrapped his arms around me to grab my ass, his hands completely covered my butt and within his firm grip I was putty. Ben's kiss was so forceful and soft at the same time that I began to tingle all over. The kiss lasted minutes before Ben broke and asked "are you sure? We can just talk." The fact that he was a gentleman and offered to talk just made me want him even more. "Where is your bedroom?"

The wildness that ensued was a time that I will carry with me until I am long in the ground and years have gone by. It was right out of some cheesy steamy novel but actually happening. Ben whirled me around and I wrapped my legs around him as he carried me while we walked and kissed our way to the bedroom. Ben set me on the bed and eased his pants down while staring at me from the side. I crossed my arms over my stomach and pulled my shirt up over my head to reveal my skimpy tank top underneath, I hadn't even worn a bra. Ben slid down his boxers to stand and watch me further take off my clothes. I swept my eyes up and down his body, his was an amazing sight and everything about me wanted everything about him, his touch, his taste, his fingers and lips and tongue, I wanted all of it.

I was nervous but the shot kicked in well enough to slide my tank top off, letting the ribbed bottom hem hang up on my hardened and excited nipples before popping over them, causing Ben to expose his large beautiful smile. Ben was plenty excited for me and I wanted him in the worst possible way so I slowly slid my pants down my legs, trying to modestly keep them crossed a little in doing so. Ben had a beige comforter on the top and satin sheets underneath on top of his bed; it was all so warm and comfortable, and welcoming. The daylight shone through the drapes enough to light up the room but it didn't matter, as I slid my pants off I made sure to show more of myself to him to entice him more, I wanted him to crawl up the bed and run his tongue up my legs but he held firm.

Ben crept up onto the bed and began to kiss on my right knee; I ran my fingers through his hair and fought the urge to pull him to my face so we could kiss while he eased into me. Each gentle kiss made me tingle more and more, my breathing just spasmed as Ben neared my pelvis, hips lips were soft and the kisses on my skin he left behind felt the slight breeze between our bodies as his warmth heated me even more. My hands clasped his face and our eye met, I couldn't take it any longer so I pulled him on top of my and began kissing. Ben was amazing, his body strong and rippled and as he entered me, I completely lost my breath. I wasn't able to take Ben for long before I was gushing with him in me. My legs curled up as Ben held himself up above me, his eyes just made me that much more wet and having him stare at me with a tender kiss waiting on his lips for me brought me the orgasm during intercourse I had never experience.

Every nerve ending in my body seemed to fire at once, the pleasure was bordering pain, like that synesthesia that comes from the pins and needles feeling, both the insane tickling feeling mixed with the small pin pricks of pain that made you squirm. I clenched my finger nails into Ben's shoulders and I curled my head up to tighten my stomach muscles, as well as other muscles on him. I couldn't do anything but pause for a moment and begin to weep, feeling Ben in me was intense, all of the feelings I had been carrying around just left me and covered Ben and he just held there for me. Ben stopped with his easing back and forth when my eyes went misty, his gentle reassuring kept telling me that we could stop if I wanted to and that that it would all be ok. I didn't mean to cry, I honestly didn't and I began to freak out that I might be scaring him away but I also didn't want him to go, I was happy.

There wasn't anything that Ben could tell me I wouldn't believe, his soothing tone was all I ever wanted to hear for the rest of my life but that couldn't exist. I was already in a world of heartache no matter how my future transpired. If I left James to pursue happiness with Ben how long would it last; days, weeks, maybe even months before the reality of my now affair would come full circle and Ben not be able to trust that I wouldn't cheat on him, or the insecurity of my being a cheater would eat me alive and I shun what I've done and then I'd throw the rest of my life away? What if I found a way to exist and carry on like I had been the last week and pretend things never happened? I'd surely succumb to guilt, either for having cheated on James or for having passed up on experiencing Ben.

Here I am, curled up with Ben still very deep inside of me, he is motionless and waiting for me to talk to him to assure him that I am ok, he's so caring that he hasn't moved and he's still maintaining himself for me. My pelvic shutters aren't as rapid and they let me slowly begin to uncurl my legs a little. It took a few minutes to adjust to Ben but once I did, I was climaxing in an instant again. I wished I knew why I hadn't ever been able to reach this peak with Nick or especially my husband, I was ashamed that /might have been the reason, maybe I had some mental hang up from my mom that I should be a good girl and so on, never having been free enough to find myself might be why I have missed on so much.

Maybe the taboo of the illicit affair is what made it all hotter, it could have just been Ben and everything about him that I craved but I was smiling while tears still streamed down the sides of my head. Ben pulled back and laid down on his stomach to just talk with me, I wasn't ready to be down with him so I let my fingers run along his body while I caught my breath. Ben asked "why are you here with me, lying buck naked on my bed when you have a husband at home?" he was genuinely curious. I couldn't stop from weeping and I apologized for being a snotty sobbing mess but I couldn't help it. Ben's eyebrows were raised and his beautiful eyes softened as he looked concerned, I couldn't tell if he was genuinely concerned for me or worried that he had some man's naked wife crying in his bed, I would have been terrified of the husband thing if I were him.

I explained my turmoil, I didn't want either of us hurt but there was no simple way out of the situation between us, someone was going to get hurt it was now a matter of who and how much. I wanted everything I could get and for a long while, I spend too long focused on what everyone else wanted and it was my time, I need my high, my fix, and my fill. I couldn't resist myself around Ben, I just had to have him over and over and I didn't know what to do. I had no answers but lying there with Ben I had no problems or concerns either so I rolled onto him and began kissing him again while rubbing my hands along his glorious back. "Why are you with me" I asked, I had to know.

Ben rolled up and revealed again his nearly sculpted front side as he rolled me onto my back, I was bare and exposed but for the first time in a very long time, I didn't feel ashamed of myself. Ben stepped his fingers along my upper bent leg; "you're very sexy" he began to trace his fingers along the softer skin of my body. "You have an amazing ass that I could just run my tongue all over and kiss and grope with my hands and spread and kiss and rub against, *mmm* just all of it. Your body is firm and your slender sides make me want to kiss from your ankle bone up to your armpit, I want to make love to you entire body using only my tongue, and then start over with each finger one at a time. Your smile is so bright and beautiful that I want to kiss your neck to make you smile forever and I also want that smile wrapped around me like it was in your car." I smiled at how cute Ben was being, I sort of felt like he was being a player but I was getting what I wanted so it wasn't a matter of being played. I spent long enough being almost happy, it was time to *be* happy.

Ben continued to tell me things I had never been told before, things I had never considered and the more he spoke, the more I had to have him. I ran my hands along Ben, his stomach muscles gave way to that v-taper that makes a man endlessly irresistible. Ben was tan and has a very little tan line around his butt, a bathing suit tan I was sure but it was really sexy. I looked like I was wearing a white bikini still because I was much whiter where my suit usually covered but as Ben kissed my hip bones, he admired and told me how much of a turn on they were. I couldn't get enough of Ben, I had him over and over and with small breaks to keep talking in between but it still wasn't enough, I knew in my heart how much trouble I was in.

Ben and I agreed that we would be upfront and that there was nothing we couldn't be honest about. I had a husband at home so I couldn't judge Ben about anything and he knew that he didn't have to impress me or worry about the pressures associated with dating and keeping up appearances. Between lust filled bouts and moments of panic we worked out plenty regarding our arrangement and with less than an hour left of our tryst, we hurried to get in as much as we could before going to work.

Ben let himself enjoy me even more, I could feel it in his rhythm as well as the increase in intensity as he writhed with me, the contractions my body felt were intense as Ben outlasted any of James's times in the last sixteen years. Ben and I took turns being in control, it was exciting getting to take the reins on top and grind down on to him without worrying about whether or not he could hold up. Ben thrusted wildly below me, his large hands roamed my body while my hands slid along my stomach and thighs, my left hand felt up along my face and hair as I imagined there was a second Ben molesting me from behind. I leaned forward to thrust back onto Ben harder and harder until my legs once again began to shake and I jerked up and down in climax, Ben held on tightly and pulled me against him tightly.

There was no possible way I was on my fourth orgasm with Ben and he outlasted me, especially since I had never orgasmed by intercourse before, my mind felt like a million strobe lights were all flashing in my mind. I was lightheaded and hard to believe everything that was going on. There was no question I was a soiled dove now and yet, I wasn't ashamed of myself. Ben bumped his hips up and while holding my hips he lifted me up and back, pulling himself out of me. I sat on Ben's upper thighs and took him into my hands and helped to get him over the edge himself. Ben clenched onto the comforter with both hands and his stomach muscles came to life while I stroked up and down quickly.

I tried to catch most of the mess in my mouth but there was so much that came exploding out of Ben that it covered him in a layer of himself, his stomach nearly soaked and it streamed in the center crevice of his stomach, pooling in his belly button. I couldn't believe the amount that shot from him, it nearly shot up my nose from a good distance as he pulsated and throbbed in my hands. I really had no idea until that point in my life what I had missed and this afternoon was a life changing time for me.

I lost track of my life, my troubles were gone and now that I rode Ben until climax, it didn't matter if James was screwing somebody else. All of my troubles seemed to melt into a big gooey puddle on Ben's stomach. I told Ben he could never finish in me because James was fixed so I hadn't any need for birth control in like seven years so he had to be extra cautious. Ben told me that out of safe practice he never finished inside of a girl anyways. I was feeling brazen and curious so I continued to ask random questions while I traced my name in the mess. "What are other girls like, you know, down there." I don't know what I was really getting at but I wondered what sorts of feeling he had and what he could feel with it when inside of another girl, plus I sort of wanted more compliments (especially after two kids). "There is a different texture to the feel, different kinds of dampness and if you go in the back, it's a lot tighter and another completely different feeling."

I didn't think much before a lot of the words came out of my mouth when I asked, I was almost as surprised I was asking what I was asking as Ben was. I was strangely curious, sure I had seen plenty of naked girls in locker rooms, magazines and especially movies with James once I became comfortable with them but the thought of talking to my husband about other girls he had been with infuriated me, but with Ben it seemed to turn me on. Ben spoke about different techniques that girls used with their hands or their mouths while using his hands to work mine in example, it was all so new and I was growing proud of myself for not flying off the handle about any of it, it was strange to be excited and enticed talking to a man I just slept with (several times) about his past conquests.

I don't know why I hadn't ever really considered it but in the back was certainly different. I had listened to Reagan discuss one or two of her experiences with trying it and her neutral take on the subject but of course because it's such a taboo subject, all of us office girls squealed and "ewww'd" but I began to think a little more about it. "I want to try it" I said out loud before I gave it enough thought to back out. "Ok" was the simple response by Ben, his words were courted with raised eyebrows and a light smile. I was strangely turned on that Ben had tried it all before, maybe it was comforting that he knew what he was doing so he could teach me or go slow and gentle so that I wouldn't get hurt. The taboo of things was fun to toy with but I was willing to do much more than toy with it, I was in.

Ben explained that it's not easy at first because it's new and usually it takes a few times before it reaches a point of pleasure plus of course there is prep work but we'd deal with it later. I licked up some of Ben from his stomach; I wanted to turn him on again by reenacting some of the things I had seen in some of the dirty movies. I wanted to taste him plus it was dirty enough to be hot as I watched him watch me lick him up. I kept smiling as I ran my tongue up and down on Ben's stomach, he asked me what was so funny and I admitted that the dirty of what I was doing was keeping me hot for him. Ben explained that nothing is dirty except your perception of things, you should want to do anything to please your partner, it's that simple, go with what they like and build on it, just be careful to know your own limits so you don't get hurt in the process. It made plenty of sense to me so I began slurping him up.

I knew our time to get to work was drawing near so I slid my body up Bens to feel all of him against me before me got dressed, Ben let his eyes roll backwards and moan. I thought back to all of the times I shied away from letting myself loose with a man, the times I missed out on being scared rather than letting myself be free and having things my way. I wanted to stand up then squat down backwards on Ben's mouth and gyrate around more but the clock was ticking. Ben and I got into the shower together, it was a shame that there wasn't a mirror like in my bathroom but his bathroom was much smaller and we didn't have the time I would have liked, like eternity. Ben and I continued to kiss as the water sprinkled all around us, it was filled with energy and passion and it danced along our bodies as our tongues did just minutes before.

Ben hadn't entirely settled down after he got off, he was back in working form in a few seconds and I was completely willing to give myself to him again. Ben turned me and took me again in the shower, our need to hurry didn't stop either of us from reaching the peak once more before a fast towel off and then rush even faster to dress and then get to work. I couldn't get enough of Ben, he was my drug and I was addicted to him. Ben didn't hold back with me, his hands roamed and grabbed onto me, his tight grip on my sides made me feel safe in the slippery shower, not a comfort I've felt with James in a very long time.

I rushed to get my clothes back on, it was hard to feel like I was making any effort as I wisped my hair to one side and used my fingers to straighten out my bangs. I used minimal makeup and I was sure that it alone would be my downfall but I didn't have any other options. Ben took his time to put on deodorant in the mirror next to me, he remained stark naked standing next to me, letting himself sway left and right as I tried to focus on what I was doing with my hair for a few minutes. I don't know if James and I ever had fun getting ready at the same time like this, Ben made me feel like I was twenty again and his playfulness just filled me with good energy and a large smile. I sped off for work while Ben lingered a little so we didn't rush into the parking lot at the same time.

I forgot all about my worries that James was screwing someone else, it just wasn't my problem anymore to deal with. I had my time with Ben and as long as James was safe and being clean, he could have his once or twice and we'd be even. I thought long and hard about if I'd be ok with still fooling around with James still, would it be easy to stay fake and pretend that all was well and go on pretending that my family was all top notch or would that small seed of suspicion plant deep in my brain? The warm wind ravished my body as I drove, much like Ben's hands did and my mind cleared. I decided I would get mine, I would have Ben on the side and keep my family together like it has been, there was no reason to overthink everything, James could have his little girl and I would have my statuesque man with a body that looked hand sculpted.

I tried to picture James with Kaylie, I doubt he'd be able to handle that slim little seventeen year old and in all honesty I can't imagine what she'd want with the old man when she could have her run and stallions like Ben but I found some peace with things. I wondered what Kaylie looked like naked, she was a slender and young so I imagined perky, I bet her butt still had firm bounce and didn't sag at all when she slid her tight jeans off, I remember noticing the color of my nips darken more and more with each kid, I bet hers are still the new pink color and her body didn't have random strange wiry hairs spring up in places they didn't belong. I didn't want to sit and day dream about my babysitter's body so rather than grow jealous, I decided that I was going to get to know my body and be able to hold my head up because I was mature enough to know myself, I know what I like and I am ok with it all, there aren't any seventeen year olds that can boast this kind of self-confidence with themselves and *that* makes me superior.

Ch. 8

It was strange to have to pretend all afternoon that I wasn't walking funny, to be honest I could tell I was moving a little bowleggedly all shift but I tried to pretend it was perhaps from doing squats at the gym, not Ben nearly splitting me into two before work. It was hard to focus for the first little while when the girls talked, my mind was stuck in that bed, riding Ben and both of us gorging on one another. I tried my best to focus out the window and think about the trees or think back to home and think if I folded the last load of laundry or if I left it in the dryer or not but Ben kept coming into my mind over and over, and then each time I'd look out into the warehouse my eyes would find him instantly.

I had a million things running through my head and there were several occasions where one or the ladies had to say my name twice to get my attention before I realized it and I'd pop my head around and have to apologize. I was filled with awe, I was impressed I went through with something I knew would be so incredible but there was the fear that it was also something incredibly stupid. James and I both worked in different cities away from home so there was next to no chance of him catching me with Ben so there was some relief but that small sting of suspicion hit me that he just as easily could have been hiding things from me also. I couldn't figure out where Joy had crossed paths with James to think he was out running errands unless he truly was, except we were together all weekend so that wasn't the case, James must have been out and not told me, not that I had anything to be suspicious about then but that spark started a forest fire now.

It angered me to think James would do such a thing, it made me jealous that Ben still may sleep with Lisa and I was jealous that she had the opportunity to perhaps marry him and spend the rest of her life with such an amazing guy. I think I was more possessive of Ben than I was angry that my husband of sixteen years might have been fooling around on me, maybe I was still half full of lust for Ben that my brain had shifted or something. I felt lost and deflated that my strong marriage built on trust didn't mean anything to James and that he would even dare to sleep with the girl that watched our children in our house. I couldn't remember smelling her teeny bopper perfume on my bed but that doesn't mean that he didn't bend her over my kitchen table or drop her panties in my living room, of my home; what a prick.

Towards the end of the night I found that as my adrenaline from my discrete taboo session with Ben wore out, so did my resilience to being hurt by James. I tried to keep from weeping openly but with enough sniffles I felt I was starting to give away that I was upset. Lisa waited around for Ben so they could catch a beer and together they were off like a prom dress and in a hurry. Gretchen knew something was up and she was totally going to make me talk about it, I could totally sense it when I caught her glimpsing back at me on her way down the stairs making sure I was following everyone. I watched as Lisa scurried towards Ben in the parking lot, he was standing waiting for her with a big smile on his face and a big hug when she wrapped her arms around him. I felt my blood pressure rise; I wished I could be her and have him to myself all night.

Under my breath I could feel myself getting jealous, I wanted Ben waiting for me in the parking lot, I wanted to be Lisa and to have my future to do all over again and it wasn't fair. I was hurt that James might have been cheating on my for a long time and maybe that was one of the reasons my marriage was fizzling out, maybe it wasn't just me feeling left out but maybe he really was wasting his lust and sexual energy on someone else and that was why he no longer wanted much to do with me.

Gretchen pried, she cornered me because knew that something was up and that I hadn't really been myself so as my friend wanted me to confide in her. I came sort of clean to Gretchen as we sat on the curb between our cars, of course did hid plenty of truth regarding Ben and my afternoon but I wasn't ready to share that with anyone, that was just for me. Hannah wouldn't have wanted to hear about relationship problems, young married couples still in the throes of passion hardly do, but Gretchen had been married as long as I had so she would understand better anyways. I explained Joy's inquisition on us taking time for us, except that James was absent from the "us" and how badly it made me spiral out of control. I worried that I screwed up everything and was afraid that I might lose my family and life with it. I tiptoed through some of the real bulk of the emotion but it was way easier than coming completely clean and admitting the affair, there were too many people at stake.

"Text him, just check in and tell him you'll be running behind because you're talking to me, it's polite and maybe it'll help open up more conversation" Gretchen suggested, I was reluctant but I did. I sat and talked with Gretchen for twenty or so minutes, I revisited Charlie and how devastating it was to lose him so early in life and that barely mid-forties was way too young to go like he did. It was nice to vent to Gretchen even though it was edited, it was still nice. I didn't get any sort of response from James, I hadn't expected to anyways but it would have been nice. Gretchen suggested I check James' phone and see if there were any iffy texts or pictures, I had actually considered it but the moment you start down the path of being nosy suspicious, you lose your mind with paranoia and you become miserable and you somehow revert back to the high school sort of girl.

Being nosy investigative is daunting, you spend endless amounts of energy searching for ghosts only to find nothing, which doesn't satisfy your curiosity it just makes you feel that you missed something. When you begin snooping you aren't happy, you are dead certain there is something to find (even if there isn't) and you won't stop until you do. Once you find something that might be considered proof of something, you construe it until it fits exactly what you want to find and no matter what, you can't be happy. Being ignorant is a pleasant way to exist, not so much that you are ignorant but enough that you can let go of small things. Men look at other women, there is no secret and frankly, so what, any girl that thinks her guy only has eyes for her and all that middle school lovey dovy crap is just a fool, but when you marry you make an agreement that even if the eyes wander a little, the hands and genitals don't, or so I thought, maybe I'm a fool.

Gretchen helped me to my feet and gave me a giant reassuring hug. Gretchen was kind with her words in telling me that I was a true gift to James and I wouldn't be so dumb as to marry a fool and only a fool would cheat on me so I should be brave and just ask him what the deal was. I agreed that I would text him during the next day or even maybe ask him before he left for work, hoping that maybe if there was drama that he'd go to work rather than let it get ugly. I felt like a hypocrite all the way home, I could still taste Ben in my mouth and yet I was angry that my husband may have cheated on me.

My entire way home I relived each tantalizing moment with Ben, the way he smelled, the way his lips felt, the way he tasted as I licked his stomach and how his eyes were locked on me as I did it. I wondered if Lisa was going to ride him like I did, I wondered if she was going to get as many orgasms out of him as I did, I even wondered if she could blow him as well as I did. I found that thinking of them getting down was nearly as exciting as it was when I was with him. I don't think I would ever strike anyone as the type to have an affair but Lisa is very conservative and even as all of girls giggled and shared some stories of times passed, Lisa was always meek and quiet. I'm not judging Lisa for being a good girl, I'm simply thinking she wasn't using Ben in the right way and it was a shame, sort of like when the old guys with bad hips get Vetts and they putz around town doing five under the speed limit, it's a sad waste.

I had no claims to Ben and he and I agreed we'd have no connections or feelings other than erotic passion so I had to find a way to just let it go and be cool with everything so I kept trying to picture his sliding in and out of Lisa, I even imagined watching. There was nothing I could think of with Ben in it that kept me from getting hot and bothered, my lady bits had taken one good pounding this afternoon and were still pretty swollen but I was already ready for more. It was strange thinking about Ben and Lisa, she was much smaller than me and very cute but I had never had any notion of seeing her get down with a guy before, but now I couldn't stop. Most people watch the girl in adult flicks, guys like to watch the hot girl for the hot girl but girls usually like to watch things get done to the hot girl and imagine it is them being taken care of, I now wanted to direct how Ben treated and treated Lisa until she moaned out, something about directing all of it was making my blood hot again.

Lisa was a cute girl, fit body and good sized breasts, I hadn't actually seen her naked body but I can picture how well everything must look without any clothes on. For the sake of trying something new and also finding out how extremely hard it would make Ben, I think I'd be willing to fool around with her a little, maybe not taste between her legs but perhaps lend a hand if the two of them went at it. I would have never been so brazen with James and perhaps part of that lead to me Ben but I have also always been insecure about even thinking James was turned on by a girl we knew, it was just unsettling. My head was all a mess and I was without many friends that would understand any of it so I felt alone. I could talk to Ben about it all but not for a while until our next fun time together. I thought about many of the things that Gretchen spoke of, growing older, especially with someone, has its own demands and struggles but what makes it all beautiful is doing with the person you've loved the whole time, she sounded like Erin.

I nodded my head along pretending that I was entirely the victim even though that little voice in the back of my mind knew better. I wanted to drive right back over to Ben's house and climb into bed with him (whether Lisa was there or not). Ben was a sweet guy and I wanted all the best for him but I also wanted to be selfish and I wanted as much of him to myself as I could get. I felt a little bad that I was being selfish but it was also conflicting, I had given up so much because I couldn't be selfish for so long before and now it was my time to get mine for me so I didn't know how to feel. I was rightly disappointed in myself for breaking my vows but I also felt so alive when I was with Ben that I convinced myself that I owed it to *me* to have the experience. Deep down I knew that it wouldn't be long before I'd be in bed with a man that sounded like Darth Vader needing some snorkel respirator looking thing to help him breathe throughout the night. I knew I'd be the one helping to keep the spit covered nasty machine clean and working long into my future, all the while my needs would go un met.

I couldn't look myself in the mirror in my car, I was angry that I was letting my feelings get to me and it made me sick with myself. If I had stayed in bed one more day instead of gone to work I might have had some extra time and not have let Ben into my car. Had I had any self-respect I wouldn't have had let Ben into my body and if I had been a good wife, I sure wouldn't have snuck out to let Ben hump my brains out either. I didn't know what I was going to do but as I pulled into my dark drive way, I was assured that it could all wait until the morning.

I poured a hearty glass of wine when I got home, I wasn't tired with the turmoil running through my mind and once again, the house was as dark and quiet as my intimate life with my husband. I propped my feet up on the coffee table I keep adorned with magazines just in case we ever have company, even though we never did. My house was empty, even Bruno didn't bother to come greet me, I was just the maid, if I were just the babysitter then maybe my husband would throw me one more than once every other month. With each sip I thought more and more about Ben, I had my feet kicked up and my head relaxed back to unwind after work again, maybe just reliving a little would settle some of my nerves and I'd be able to relax.

I thought about some of the things Gretchen said, including checking James' phone for pictures or texts to see if he was in fact fooling around, the known is often worse than the unknown but I wasn't very sure of that. I let the warm buzz relax me, me bit of a headache might worsen in the morning but the relief I that came to me was worth it. Leaning back on the couch was a reminder that I was in fact very alone. How sad is it that even your loving family pet won't come down the stairs and greet you? I crossed my left hand over my stomach and let my fingertips twirl and swirl around my belly button and I thought back to Ben's stomach and tracing it with my tongue. I let my fingers wander and in no time at all I was leaned back on my couch and having fun with myself again. I can't recall a time where I enjoyed being a woman so much, I don't know if I had ever had so many orgasms in the same week let alone in a single day and I was beginning to realize what it must be like to be a fourteen year old boy discovering nudie mags for the first time.

I didn't bother to go on my jog; my ambition had waned and I knew I needed a slow lazy morning. I got up and started tea for both James and I and I sent Bruno out so he wouldn't be a bother. My nerves were wrecked, my hands shook and I could feel how puffy my face was from the uneven sleep. I sat at my kitchen table and waited for James to come around the corner and look me right in the face. "Good morning" James muttered with a slight cheer on his face. "No run this morning?" he quickly followed up. I swallowed hard and told him I needed to talk, my voice cracking through my words. I wasn't certain what I wanted to say, I needed something different and I even though I didn't know how I was going to go about it, it needed to happen.

I tried to grasp my coffee mug and keep it pressed against the table to keep from shaking hot tea all over the place. James saw the worry in my face and made his way to sit with me. It was never easy confronting James with things, often times he avoided some of the questions all together or turned many of the things around on me, all the while being kind of a crappy listener. "Joy said she saw you the other day, during the day." I began. My head spun and I braced myself for the punch in the stomach that was sure to come, I tried to take a deep enough breath in before James began to speak but it was just a gasp.

"Just a doctor's appointment, I got out early to go see the doc at Fourth and Main then I came home and let Kaylie off early, what's up?" I felt some light tears well up in my eyes and they threatened to drip down my cheeks as I believed him due to his cool demeanor. Relief sent my head spinning just as much as it would have if he told me he was going to leave me. I was so relieved that I wept as James reached forward to hug me, he could tell how troubled I was over the topic but I was more than troubled, I was *in* trouble. I explained that I hadn't really felt right since Charlie passed and there was just so much going on in my head and it was all a mess.

I should have apologized for not trusting him, I really should have come clean about having been with Ben but I was relieved and James was being supportive. I wanted to cry harder and harder but I was lacking the bodily fluids to really stream out the tears. I had pent up emotions swishing around in my mind and it was making me nauseous. I really should have told James everything, every painful detail no matter what the consequences but I felt like I was safe under my umbrella of James' not knowing. Had I owned up to James about all of my self-loving, he would have been jealous he missed out on a good show, but had I been honest and admitted that I did it all thinking about Ben, he would have been hurt, had I admitted to letting Ben screw me rightly, James would have been destroyed and I couldn't do that now that things might seem to be improving finally, I was scared and I didn't know what to do.

James told me that he could tell I was off for a few weeks now and that he did want to give us a week to reconnect at the cabin, until life got in the way. I tried to stop from crying but there were just so many emotions flooding from deep within me that there was nothing I could do. James asked if he could go and get going with his day but tried to assure that I'd be ok before he headed out the door for his work day while I began preparing for more of mine. I sniffled a lot while I cleared away tears before waking the kids, I felt for a moment that I had my bearings, that maybe I was given my purpose and this was supposed to be my reset point. I felt enlightened after my good hearty cry and I felt the lighter spring in my step.

I felt baptized by my tears, born again as I cried away my guilt and pain all the while coming through cleanly. I was going to keep my family, I was going to keep my husband and there was no sign that I had been intimate with Ben, other than a bit of tenderness in my downstairs (still the next morning) so I was safe from losing my family. I decided that I would keep my secret until I was dead a buried but I would do it while being happy to keep my family together, I had my burden to bear alone but my family was worth it. I scrambled through my usual morning routine and did my best to stay busy, I cleared out the kids' rooms of old toys and old clothes and the more I cleaned the more I felt clean.

The rest of the week went as I had hoped; I stayed busy enough during the day cleaning and trying to get the house ready for the twister that is two kids at home during the summer that I didn't let my mind wander a whole lot. I stayed busy enough to keep from feeling lonely and in need of Ben, my plan was working. I even stayed busy enough to keep from masturbating, even though those needs were through the roof, I even felt myself sitting on the arm of my couch and suddenly becoming aware of the sensation between my legs and then rubbing a little. I only had a few short weeks left before both kids would be dragging me all over the county to water parks and regular parks and Bruno to the dog park and then before I know it, it would be back to school shopping again and I would have made it all summer without another slip up with Ben.

My plan was flawless, on paper, except the real world application of my plan was shot and sunk before even leaving the harbor. During the first week it was pretty easy to cruise, I'd see Ben and I'd say hi to be polite but as fast as I saw him I'd picture him and Lisa holding hands, (nothing sexual to start my mind down that path) to keep it in my head that he wasn't for me. It was tough to think about trying to rekindle my old flame with James but I was still sort of convinced that some of the passion I had for, and with, Ben could be carried over and that might get the ball rolling to relight the passion I once had for him. It almost seemed that every half an hour my focus was blurring and it took a head shake to begin a mantra of chanting to myself that I loved James for a few quiet choruses before some of my stronger urges quieted back down.

The second week was another challenge. I wanted to spend half of my day in bed like I did after Charlie died but a knock on the door gave me a reason to do something. I was wearing a very worn-thin white tank top, one that I often slept in, no bra, and a short pair of thin running shorts. I grabbed one of James' work shirts to put on as I navigated my way through the house. The delivery guy at the front door was strapping guy with a wide chin so for the sake of just measly toying with him, and myself, I left the work shirt behind when I saw him standing on the other side of my door through the window. I flicked my nipples a little to fill them with blood. The idea of just getting a glance or a wink from the stranger was all I wanted, just a little reassurance that I was still attractive and lusted after, something almost harmless I thought.

Ok I felt a little like a floozy rolling the waist band down on my shorts to make them skimpier before I pulled the door open wearing as little as I did but it did in fact work. The delivery guy needed my signature for some package that James ordered but I pulled the door back to reveal all of me in my skimpy clothes and waited. The delivery guy was named "Oliver" and he let his eyes linger up and down my body as I took my time signing the electronic box for him while making sure my burgundy nipples pushed through my tank top. Oliver had darker tanned skin and dark eyes, the man didn't look like he would have been as much fun as Ben was in the sack but his lip licking and teeth sucking boosted my confidence like I had hoped. The box I dragged inside was fairly heavy but since it was for James I just left it next to the counter for him and went about my day.

My slight bit of excitement was enough to get my engine running, I wanted Ben immediately so I ran up the stairs to get started on satisfying myself while I had the privacy. I laid back on my bed and imagined that Ben was watching me. I pulled my shorts down and my shirt up and got busy pretending to put on a show for only him. I thought about how exciting it would have been to be playing with myself in my living room and the delivery guy walk up and look in to see me. I thought about Ben and Lisa both watching me or Lisa and I competing to get off first with Ben watching on, waiting to claim the victor. I have no idea why some of the things were in my head but each time I had a thought, it grew more and more wild, nearly bordering on depraved. I seemed to run hot and cold, one spark of being sexy sent me into a tail spin but yet, none of my fantasies included the husband that I wanted to want.

Each fantasy over the rest of the week left me hot and sweaty. My urges to have Ben deep in me were nearly out of control and I worried that he wasn't out of my system. Each time I saw Ben at work it was harder and harder not to want him, his smiles made me melt and each time I could feel myself craving him. Sitting at work was tough, my swollen parts lusted for Ben and parts of my ass went numb having to rock side to side to keep from sitting flat. It was difficult to keep smiling while listening to Lisa talk about how wonderful he was and how charming he was. I wanted to be romanced by him and seduced by him like she was and it flicked at my inner jealousy.

One pallet count I was waving my hand to Ben for his attention, I knew the girls couldn't see me and I let myself believe for a moment that I was just getting Bens help to count boxes. I needed just a fix and easily convinced him that I needed to taste his kiss behind the pallet as we worked, just a smooch to get me through the day, Ben had a large smile on his face as he ducked around with me. I felt like I was swaying between both sides of the world, I wanted so hard to be the great wife I once was but I also needed Ben to pound me so hard that I felt like I lost a title fight to Rhonda Rousey.

Ben gave me a small peck on the cheek, much to my disappointment but then I thought that maybe he was helping me to behave. I felt let down that all I got was the peck and I let my shoulders slump down as I returned to counting the boxes on the pallet. My bits trembled for Ben, I wanted to put my hands on the pallet and have him straddle up behind me right there at work. Ben waited until my back was to him when he scooped his left arm under my stomach, I tried not to chirp with the surprise but I let out a small squeak with the surprise embrace. I began to beg and plead: "what are you doing, stop, this can't happen, what're you doing" I panicked in my mind but I found that I couldn't make a sound with all of my muscles tensed and tight at the same time.

Ben slid his right hand down the front of my pants to begin to twirl them around inside of me; the force of intensity was so immense that all I could do was hang on and do my best to keep my mouth shut and my eyes clenched until it was over. I was terrified of getting caught but that also toyed on the excitement factor in the back of my mind. Ben was quick; he brought my excitement level up in a moment with a few flicks of his wrist I tightened all of my muscles while my feet kicked just above the floor while I was suspended up against Ben. Ben stopped just short of a minute which just made me want and crave him more. I tried to calm my heaving chest to recount the boxes in order to do my job diligently but I couldn't stop smiling or watching him while twitching in my panties. Ben walked away licking his finger while glancing at me, making sure I saw how naughty he was. Ben was something different, his unhinged personality was something new and I couldn't help myself around him.

I fought to hide my flush face and wobbly legs as I crept back from behind the pallet and headed back into the office. When I walked in I felt totally caught and it was almost embarrassing, I think Bens sole intent was to toy with me and let me go so that it was the only thing on my mind, or he really wanted to finger me at work and leave me soaking in my undies. For the rest of my day all that kept flashing through my mind was Ben slowly drawing his tongue up his fingers and smiling, if he had been some fat bum of course that would be a disgusting gesture but Ben was beautiful and it just made me mad with desire for him.

After work I thought about catching Ben so that he could finish what he started but as I exited the warehouse door, I watched his jeep pull away. I figured Lisa got to him before I did and I was once again jealous. I admired Lisa that she was young and hot and could easily get Ben but the fact that I already had him and could get him again left me wondering what he was really after. Ben didn't really flirt all that much so he wasn't a player, he was also very secretive about our indiscretion so he wasn't boasting or bragging so it kept me wondering what he was up to, but enjoying all of it.

My house was again dark, no porch light for my safety and no cute note from my husband on the counter that he missed me all day or anything to follow up our piece of morning conversation about me being down in the dumps, maybe he didn't care or even want to deal with it. I felt torn between wanting to be able to enjoy myself and a slaggy frumpy hypocrite that got fingered at work by a guy then to come home and feel bad that my husband isn't paying attention to me, I just knew I was unhappy.

I noticed some strange jugs on the counter in the kitchen that weren't there earlier in the day so I got a little nosy and investigated. I found a few jugs of protein powder and workout supplements, nothing I hadn't seen years back but it was a strange new twist. Maybe James was back to muscle building to feel better about himself, which was originally why I took up jogging (until I found the stress relief and better thinking that came with it also) and maybe the boost in muscle tone might lead to a boost in libido, which would be nice. I was proud of James, maybe he'd even build up some of his stamina with the weights and then we might have some fun. I looked through several huge jugs of protein and figured that was what was in the box I signed for when I was playing desperate lowly housewife in need of attention from the delivery guy.

I washed my face and as I opened the cabinet to pull out my dental floss I found another weird addition to my medicine cabinet, anabolic steroids! I was borderline pissed off with this discovery, I wanted to slap James awake and begin to chew his ass but it was late and my intimate parts were still tender from the touch of another man. It was hard to keep from getting angry all night. How could James be so reckless? At his age James risked a heart attack from pushing it too hard working out and steroids were only going to make it worse. I couldn't wrap my head around anything that was going on anymore, I truly was just lying in bed with a complete stranger.

As my anger surged through me all I could think to do was slide my hand down the front of my cotton sleeping boxers and finish what Ben had started, maybe the post orgasm let down would help me sleep. I moved my fingers into their familiar position and began thinking about Ben's hand sliding down my panties behind the pallet. James hardly budged even though I wasn't being very subtle lying next to him, part of me hoped that maybe he would wake up and join me. I never imagined I would be getting myself off in private, let alone out of spite while lying right next to my husband, I even wondered if it would be weird to use his hand either down there or to hold it on my chest to feel a touch that wasn't mine. I shook and clenched as I got myself off and as the flood of adrenaline and all the other feel good chemicals rushed through my body, James still didn't budge. I was no longer hurt or mad, I was just let down and sleepy.

Of course my sleep sucked so when I woke up it was hard to get moving but I had to drag my ass to go jog, but I needed to. Jogging cleared my mind and helped me to feel like I was staying in shape, or at least trying, not all that easy at forty. I shook off the pissy feeling that I cared that James was probably getting into good shape for some other girl, I was mostly worried that the retirement future I had built with him might be in peril but there wasn't all that much I could do about it until something major changed. I worried that because I was falling for Ben that I would get my heart broken when I finally came clean to him and told him about my feelings, which of course we agreed would be the end of us.

I wasn't ready to lose James, I wasn't ready to cut ties with Ben either, I wanted to be selfish a little longer and have more of it and still hang on to growing old with James once I got Ben out of my system. I cleared my mind with my jog, the fog slowly cleared and even after a choppy crappy night of sleep, I felt clear headed and able to think straighter. I decided to drop the subject about James and his side tramp, I convinced myself it didn't matter and that I didn't care. I could have my fun with Ben and James could have his little floozy and in a month or so when we had a solid weekend and perhaps a sitter, we'll sit down and have a brutal heart to heart and go from there, but I wasn't ready for it just yet.

Once I was in the door James was out like usual. He was looking slightly leaner already so whatever supplements he was using were working; "good for him' I muttered as I fought to untie my running shoes without falling over. I found some peace with where I was at, it was calming as I hurried the kids to the bus and Bruno out the door, it wasn't chaotic but felt more like I was in a choreographed dance among the goings on and it felt... not comfortable but maybe familiar? I had a peaceful balance for a few days, each jog kept me balanced and I held out and away from Ben at work. I wanted him in the worst ways but I'd scamper back to the office and return to listening Lisa talk about her dates, I did my best to picture them on their dates and not myself involved, it took some practice but I grew proud of myself for holding out, even if it meant tightly crossing my legs.

I listened intently when the girls in the office spoke, they each jabbered on and I tried my best to be a good friend by listening. Lisa was still trying to pin Ben down but he was adamant about not being exclusive just yet, he wanted to take thing slow because of work and all. The thought of Ben not willing to commit to her upset her a little of course but I smiled on the inside hoping that he was leaving the door open for me longer. Hannah was all happy and go lovey blah blah; she was hardly thirty so what did she know. Reagan was still a wild child but things were slowly getting back into their normal groove. I was able to pass Ben in the warehouse without having that yearning desire in me that sent me on a brainless mission to get Ben in me that I had felt before; I had some control back in my life.

I watched as the levels of James's steroids slowly dropped over time and I wanted so badly to ask him about it but I wasn't finding any needles and he seemed to keep it away from the kids so I let it slide. I felt like James and I were at a stalemate, neither of us wanted to blurt out the truth or light the fuse on what would be a marriage ending fight but we both seemed to know that there was some major tension right below the surface. I guess I wanted to stay oblivious to James' steroids because if I didn't call him out on it then maybe he wouldn't call me out on my affair.

I felt like James and I still enjoyed the look and appeal of being a happily married couple on the weekends when we strolled the parks together with the kids. James and I put on a great show on how happy we were and after a week passed we seemed to find a mutually agreeable lifestyle. James was beginning to seem a little more active, I assumed the steroids were helping to boost his energy and one weekend I was impressed to find that James was getting some of his lust back for me. James hugged up behind me in the kitchen, both kids weren't paying a whole lot of attention to us and he took the time to rub himself up against me as he held me from behind. I liked that James was still trying to keep hold of his husbandly role but it was hard to see him and not Ben as I was pinned against the sink with a hardened man leaning against me.

I wasn't sure how I felt about being intimate with James, he was my husband but he was also a stranger. James and I occasionally partook in some whiskey or wine depending on what we felt like drinking and we were both responsible adults but it shook me to discover he was injecting steroids for some reason and I still didn't like it. By the end of the second week James' changes were noticeable and his attention on the weekends was actually quite flattering, I wished it was like this at the cabin. I had tried some newer things with Ben that I craved, I tried to initiate James to take me from behind, I only wanted Ben in me from behind but I hoped that James would still play with things he never did before, just to spice things up and be playful.

One night James and I got an unhinged opportunity to revisit our youth. I let James and his new found youthful passion have his way with me and it was much to my liking. James started off by going down on me, not a priority of his in what seemed like years but a fun way to start any evening nonetheless. In my mind most of what James did I pictured Ben but I did my best to keep my attention on James if I was going to retrain myself to lust for my husband once again. James was much wilder than he had been, his leaner body seemed years younger and for the first time in a long time, I was able to actually get into the mood with my husband.

The increased action only started a craving in me, I wasn't bound to just waiting for James to be in the mood when I had Ben on the side, Ben was good to go any time I wanted him. James' increased desires for me over the weekends only made my urges frequent during the week when I was without him, it was a struggle wait but I did try. I found that I was hoping to find James awake when I got home or even up early so we could have some pre-work fun but I was let down each time. I tried my best for the first two days to jog off the aches and needs I had in me but there wasn't much luck. I took to taking care of myself rather often and more boldly each time during the days, to the point where I was getting myself off like an addict while driving to and from work.

I reviewed my diet, I checked my temperature and even researched things like thyroid problems or hormones pills that might help to stabilize me better because I felt the manic highs and lows in my lusts. I had been more intimate with James but I craved more and more, I just couldn't get enough. The few times I enjoyed James it was comforting because he was indeed my husband but each time he rolled over I found myself immediately ready for another go even though he was done for the night. I loved Ben's youth and energy and wished that the steroids would have given James more staying power but I also began to question why I was rearing to go all the time; I chalked it up to changing hormones and I kept fighting it.

There was no satisfying me, I was insatiable and there was nothing I could do to curb my hunger for sex. Midweek I couldn't wait any longer so I decided to signal Ben that I was meeting him at his place. I waved my fingers to Ben as I passed him on one little walk around between all the pallets, he flashed a big smile that he understood and like that; I was giddy. I wanted another go with Ben and even though it meant turning away from my husbands' new found desires for me, I wanted both men that wanted me. I wanted the love I have had and will have with James but and also the lust from Ben I was getting. I wanted wings and roots and I want to be free from the guilt that might catch up with me someday.

I listened to the girls all make their plans for the upcoming weekend while I was making plans for after my shift with Ben. I wanted to have the wildest night I could think of with Ben in hopes that this night of bliss would satisfy my every last naughty desire. My feet tapped and my fingers wouldn't stop moving all afternoon as the clock dragged on. I was impatient and could not stop clock watching until it was time for the shift to end. I felt like a kid again, that last hour of the last school day before summer vacation, the wait was killing me.

I tried not to bowl the girls over on my way down the stairs and then across the warehouse floor towards the parking lot with them. Everyone but Reagan was shuffling along and ready for bed and I grew anxious. Reagan was always headed to some bar or another after work, the local hotel lounges were her hunting ground because you can get plenty of travelers that you'll never see again, plus if you stay with them in their room you can get in on the complimentary breakfast when you leave in the morning. I tried to avoid some of the idle chit chat and scurried into my car, some of the ladies were still talking a little in the parking lot so it was annoying to have to wait for their milling around to stop before I could navigate out of the parking lot.

Ch. 9

I pulled up to Ben's house, the neighborhood was as dark as mine usually is and just as quiet. I wasn't even trying to be sneaky when I strolled up to the porch where Ben was already sitting. I had been pushing the limits to get stronger and stronger orgasms, I wanted to find the most intense way to get off and maybe that would cure my urges once and for all. I didn't know what was going on but I had needs that needed to be met. Once I climbed out of my car each step I took towards Ben grew faster and faster till the point I was almost jogging by the time I got to him. I loved that Ben was a younger guy that actually wore his hat forward, not some scrubby high school drop out that kicked is to one side or the other, it was a relief that there were still guys that actually knew how to wear a ball cap.

Ben was sitting on his porch, his hands crossed and holding onto his knee, he also had a big smile on his face. "I hope you're ready" I warned him. I began to unfasten my slacks and before I gave Ben a chance to stand up, I dropped my pants and pulled his face into me. I felt my ass clinch as his tongue met me, his hands slid up the back of my thighs as I spread my legs further to take Ben into me. The neighborhood was dark but the risk that someone might have been watching and masturbating to me getting eaten out was intensely erotic. I rubbed against Ben as he shook his head back and forth and once I was good and warmed up, it was time to head inside.

Ben took me by one hand while the other tried to keep my pants up enough to keep from tripping as we hustled through his house. By the way Ben gripped my hand I knew I was in for a whole new sort of night and I wanted all of it. Ben led me through the house so we could start in the bedroom. I didn't even get to lay on the bed Ben just bent me over and pulled my panties back down and thrust into me with climactic force, once he was all of the way in to me I couldn't even close my mouth. My eyes fought to stay open through Ben's starter thrusts and then with a single swoop he swung both of his arms under my legs and lifted me to the bed and onto my knees.

I was on all fours when Ben reached up between my legs and pulled down on my lower back, encouraging me to be face deep into his duvet as he buried his face into my exposed backside. I was familiar with where he started licking at me but his tongue slid higher up between my legs and the gushing pleasure mixed in with a weird tickle. I wasn't entirely sure when Ben's plans were back there but I enjoyed all of it. As I felt a slight breeze beneath me as my legs were spread wide open Ben played and explored me like I was the ocean and he was Magellan mixed with some Jacque Cousteau. My body was Ben's playground and I never wanted it to stop.

Ben flipped me around and spun me so that my head hung off the side of the bed. I did my best as best slid into my mouth and then returned to kissing me along my body on his way to burying his face between my legs again. Ben thrusted and pumped in my mouth, my jaw was open so widely that I had a bit of jaw pain and each time he pushed too deeply I'd begin to gag and I'd have to push him away from me until I caught my breath again, but I loved taking more and more of him than I thought I could.

I felt dirty, I felt evil and vile and wrong, but I felt alive. Ben whipped me around like ragdoll and in an instant I was back on my stomach with him climbing up on top of me. Ben eased up between my legs and warned me that he would be gentle. I relaxed knowing that I was in safe hands with Ben and I wasn't afraid of anything anymore. Ben and I spoke about trying some newer things, I had been aware of Ben's experience in the matter and I was curious to try it with him, it turned me on.

There was a slight burning pain in me, I was beginning to feel my anxiety and with it my chest began to tighten. Ben started to whisper in my ear to keep breathing and on each exhale Ben slowly inched in further, his large hands held mine as I gripped handfuls of his comforter. Ben bit on the back of my neck, it had a slight sting but it was mixed with enough pleasure to raise the intensity level of everything. Ben used his left hand to keep my legs spread and once he was all the in me, the burning stopped. The burning wasn't that bad after a minute and once I was adjusted to his size, Ben began to ease in and out. Once Ben had some rhythm in his pelvis he reached one hand underneath me and played with me from the front.

James once ignited a flame in me in the form of a love that could have lasted a lifetime, or so I thought when I stood across from him and vowed my love to him. When I began my fun with Ben I had hoped that maybe just being flirted with by the hot guy at work would boost my confidence, it was kind of stupid and very dangerous to teeter on the edge of such a taboo but I wanted to live. My eternal flame for my husband James, was there I thought and I thought maybe getting a kiss from Ben would fan that ember and reignite my fire for James, I had no idea it would take me to doing what I was doing with Ben.

Things with Ben raged out of control several times and my mind and body were opened up to all sorts of new things. I wouldn't go back and change anything I did with Ben; I might just change a lot of things with myself; like hesitation. Ben took his time and introduced me to a whole new kind of sex, one at I had heard Reagan talk about a few times in the office. The first time wasn't all that great but trying it more later on was intensely more erotic once I let go and stopped fighting. Ben crawled off of me when he was done, he made plenty sure that I was not hurt; it was so sweet that he truly did care for me and it made the experience all the better

The passion of the night wasn't done because he was, I wanted so much more and I wasn't taking no for any form of an answer. James had been slimming down and getting into shape so I knew my time was limited and before my life imploded, I wanted to burn through my list of things I wanted to do with Ben as best as I could before I was surprised with a manila envelope of divorce papers or something from James.

Longevity with Ben wasn't in my future, I knew that I would love him forever but he couldn't have children or a future with me so I was a lost cause for him. I knew that I couldn't be the adulterer any longer and my conscience would catch up with me (with a vengeance). Had I been twenty years younger I could have been an amazing wife for Ben, he was everything I could have ever hoped for but that isn't the case now. I was done having kids and because he wanted them, that was a big divider between us, plus our entire relationship was clouded in taboo and temporary so all we could do was make the best of it and only have memories to hold when it was all over with.

I wondered what all I had done and part of me wanted to go back to being just James' wife and the mother to my children that I wanted to be when I first got pregnant but there was no going back. I gambled enough and even though a clean break wasn't fathomable, if I found the courage to be honest with Ben I could at least get away with minimal mess. Ben was standing up against the bathroom sink brushing his teeth, a good idea after all of the places his mouth had been, so I stepped up behind him. There was nothing about his body that I couldn't lust for, his back rippled with muscles, his torso gave way to a tight v-taper that lead down to his manliness, and even after he got off, he was still partially ready for more.

Seeing Ben in the bathroom lighting was awe inspiring, he was lean from head to toe and even just brushing his teeth his arms bulged and rippled while shimmering in the light, once again I felt the warm tingling that told me I had to have him again. I stepped up to Ben and began kissing along his shoulders again, we had been all over each other's bodies and it just wasn't enough for me. I reached my right hand around to begin to fondle him again, I just couldn't get enough of him and I didn't care if he wasn't ready for me, I wasn't ready to be done with him yet. I ran my left hand up his back and began to tug more feeling into him; Ben just dropped his head and took a deep breath while widening his stance.

As I ran my hand down Ben's back and neared his waist, Ben widened his stance even more. I was hot and flush and still dripping wet from him so I went for it. I ran my hand between my legs to get my fingers plenty wet before inserting them into him. My fingers slid down his backside until they found their intended target. I don't know what possessed me to try this but Ben's willingness and submission was a major turn on. I had complete control over Ben, he submitted to me and completely trusted me with his very guarded parts of himself

I was gentle at first with the in and out but I worked both of my hands while watching his eyes clench and his eyebrows wriggle. Working both of my hands had Ben breathing heavily and his excite only excited me more. I let Ben finish inside of me in the back, it was a strange warming feeling when he let his cream fill me up and now I had two fingers massaging the inside of him. Ben's muscles danced under his skin, his arms flexed as he fought the urge to rip the sink from the wall and I couldn't help but to watch both of us in the mirror.

Ben let me into him, I had complete control and the power was enticing to have. Ben let me try what I wanted to, he let me have my fun little fantasies and thanks to him, I wasn't ashamed of them. I let Nick explore me a little and James too but Ben was the one that really opened me up. There was safety with Ben and for that I knew that he would forever be in my heart, he made it ok to be me. Growing up my normal sexual thoughts and urges were just that; normal. In my late thirties my mind began to wander further than I had ever expected, thinking about things like Lisa and Ben having their fun or she and I maybe even trying some things together while Ben watches on or instructs us. My need for more and more to get myself off was taking some work, putting two fingers in Ben while wrapping my other hand around him as he seesawed between my hands.

The visions of me working Ben while he flexed and fought the urges to finish will forever be some of my favorites. With hardly much time having passed Ben was quickly turning me and pushing me to kneel. Once I was on the floor Ben released all over me, the warmth of him felt amazing and to watch as he throbbed and urged while grimacing with pleasure confirmed that it was all because of me. Looking up at Ben I knew that I loved him, I knew that I could reenact this every night for the rest of my life but looking up at Ben, I knew I couldn't ever be enough for him, I would be plagued that I was the whore that cheated on my husband and that would slowly eat away at both of us as a real couple.

Ben standing up and over my while I knelt down was a sight that could have been from a roman statue, the nude petite lady succumbing to the muscular man and taking him in every possible way that he can give it to her. I craved Ben more and more, even before I began to slurp more of him down I wanted him to mount up behind me and to use a toy down the front, I wanted to be completely filled with him, I wanted to know what Reagan felt like when she got to enjoy two men at the same time, I wanted to roll around with Ben and Lisa and maybe even James. The thought of going down on a girl used to disgust me but I also had to urge to taste Lisa on Ben, both out of curiosity as well as the excitement to see Ben's face while I did.

I wanted to lay Ben down and trace my tongue from the tip of his tongue down his neck, down between his firm chest muscles and over the ridges of his ab muscles. I wanted to continue to lick down Ben until I began to lick under him and then roll him up onto his shoulders so his knees were next to his head and put my tongue in him like he had done to me and return the favor of licking and wiggling my tongue in him until he was on the verge of crying from pleasure. I surprised myself with such vivid imagery. I wanted to kiss and suck every spot of Ben and I wanted to gobble at him every single night for the rest of my life, but I knew that was sheer fantasy; I could only borrow him a few times, never own him.

I knew I was beyond unrealistic and as I stared up at Ben, I knew I had to tell him how I felt. Ben was standing over me, he might as well have been carved in marble, his face in intense pleasure while his eyes were closed and his mouth wide open in awe, much like mine was. I couldn't think of anything I could have wanted more at that moment except for Ben to take me into the shower and have his way with me again, over and over, but I knew that once I left his house it had to be for the last time. I pushed myself as far as I could, I had done more than I ever imagined and had peaks of an adrenaline rush I couldn't have described but it was all temporary, it had to be and it was getting close to time to say goodbye.

I was in the limbo of my own doing and I was trying to find a way to back out of it. I knew I would regret making any move with Ben, but I also knew I would regret not taking the chance so for the first time in my life I took a huge risk and went for it. Each time I touched Ben, or let him touch me wasn't just cheating on my husband; it was taking me away from myself and my vows. I immensely enjoyed the pleasure of being with Ben but like an addict searching for a better high, I was sure that in no time I would need more and more to keep getting my fix. I went from safe and boring to wild and mentally planning orgies for the thrill of things in just a short time, there was still a slim chance at returning to my role as wife in my home and even though it meant spending the rest of my life without at more thrills in my life, it meant keeping my family together for my children.

I had truly come to grips that I had backed myself into a corner where the only person that was guaranteed to lose was me. I knew if I continued on that Ben might get hung up on me (I hoped anyway) and then he would get hurt. If I carried on then it was a matter of time before James found out and then he'd be hurt and if I got caught and James and I did split then my children's lives would be forever changed and I couldn't be the monster that did that to them. If I backed away now then I was the only one that was going to really be hurt over everything. I was the one that started everything, I was the one that instigated and toyed with the line morality and I am also the one that was guilty of crossing it so it was on me to pay for it all.

Maybe James was trying to get into shape so that he'd appeal to me again. Maybe James just missed being in good shape or even disliked being middle aged and was trying to turn back the clock a little, just like I do with my expensive ass skin creams or maybe I was so lonely and realizing that it was too late to go back and make changes in my life but that James knew that his physical appearance was within his power to change. Maybe I just over thought every moment in the last few months because I was lonely or burned out or maybe even starting to notice some of the effects of menopause. Oh god, what is going to happen if I just dry up and stop getting my period? It sucks dealing with all the hassle once a month but my visitor *Doug* assures me that I'm not that old and there was something comforting with that. Maybe I was fighting turning forty so hard that I was willing to throw everything away, only to end up forty anyways, except now my marriage could be in jeopardy.

Did I know what I was doing when I started playing with myself that night in my kitchen; was I lighting a fuse that would eventually blow up in my face, like Ben just did? I stayed there for a minute, covered in warm Ben and kneeling in front of him in his house: "I love you" I muttered as I looked up. Ben's closed eyes shot open, his face of pleasure dropped to look at me with concern. There could be years and endless pleasure between Ben and I but I didn't like who I was slowly becoming, I liked what I was doing and I was enjoying every sensual kiss and touch but it wasn't who I sent out to be when I said my vows to my husband.

"I am falling in love with you" I rebutted with more force in my voice. I knew that what I was doing was like throwing a stick of dynamite in a pot-hole but I had to make everything terrible before there was a chance of fixing it to make it better. I can't imagine what I looked like, knelt down on the floor with *Ben* running all over my chest but it was now or never to pull the pin. I wanted to go on forever but I know that the longer time goes on in life the more the heartache, the only difference is that there was comfort in the history I had with James and only distress and pain if I stayed with Ben.

Ben reached his hand down to lift me up. There weren't any words said between us, just solemn looks. The shower was quiet and soothing, I helped to run the soap over Ben's body as he did with mine, neither of us wanted to let go. As Ben scrubbed my back I looked up at him over my shoulder and flashed him a smile, I wanted him one last time before it was entirely over. Ben eased up between my legs while I reached down to guide him into the right place this time. Ben was rearing to go for a third time in a short while, I can't recall the last time James even had three erections for me in the same week and here Ben is heaving himself into me yet again, the man was an animal, but one that I couldn't tame.

With every thrust from Ben I felt a big part of me regret what I did, but equally I was feeling terrible for what I had been doing. My conscience wasn't poison in my mind like I figured it would be and once I passed the first "oh my god" of everything I was able to find the joy and pleasure in it all. I opened myself up to new experiences, some of that in as literal a way as possible but above it all, looking down at what I was willing to become was what began to weigh on me. I dreaded being that cliché, a lot of guys cheat because their slaggy wives cut them off, whatever. Some guys cheat because there are so many hot girls out there that staying with one once her looks go and she stops taking care of her body weighs on their marriage, eh, but the few women that seek out pleasure outside of their own marriage often do it for power. I didn't realize that I liked having some power until I had fingers inside of Ben and a firm grip on him while telling him what to do, I was also lonely.

You never see any of the druggies on TV talk about how they liked the feeling of their very first high, they always defend that it wasn't this drug or that drug that was the gateway to the harder stuff but it often was. Everyone has that little moment of fun that might be taboo or naughty but then they keep pushing it more and more and in no time, the limits are all shattered and there is no turning back. I had to call it all quits before my needs grew stronger and stronger and then I was arranging more sultry trysts and spending more energy hiding my addiction. It was hard not to cry in the shower as Ben plowed into me for one last time of extramarital sensual skin slapping. I wanted to focus on feeling him in me, I wanted to take the time to run my hands all over him and let his over me, but I could only try not to openly cry.

I couldn't believe what I had done. I wondered if my spur of the moment was actually just another surge of action, a not so thought out jolt of having to do something that I also would end up regretting just like a lot of other things lately. I was more disappointed in myself than anything else, I was hurt that I would be willing to let myself be so irrational and careless, but this is what I deserved. I just wanted Ben to hold me as I cried, I wanted him as a friend to hold me and help me through this, but I had to be completely done with him. I thought about what it would be like in thirty four years, would I be able to confidently stand up at my fiftieth wedding anniversary and toast my husband and not think back to my time with Ben. Would my children and grand-children toast me and my long marriage and not know about any of this.

Would I be haunted by what I had done at each anniversary to come? I felt bad that I betrayed James and his trust and it all boiled over as I knelt down in front of Ben on his bathroom floor as he was still oozing out on me. I felt guilty that I used a small insecurity to give myself permission to be with Ben and to be able to deny that I was forty and growing older by the day. There was no real reason to suspect James was cheating, I think I just hoped he did in order to even the playing field and absolve myself of feeling bad about what I have done. Ben herked and jerked in me and before I caught on that he hadn't pulled out he was done. I didn't care about the "oops" I just wanted him to stay in me for some last few moments so I pulled him close to me and wrapped his arms around me one last time.

The water trickled down on us as Ben stood tall and firm behind me; I refused to let him out. I knew that this moment would have to be enough because it could never happen again. Ben began to whisper, "why" as he dropped his head onto my shoulder and kissing along my neck. I couldn't come up with an excuse so I just went back to our original deal, honesty. "I like this too much, I like you too much, I want to have a life with you but you've mentioned wanting children and what kind of life would we really have? I can't be a wife to you, not with a start like we've had and I have a husband I need to relearn to love, I hope you understand." Ben just kept kissing on me and running his hands along my stomach and chest.

Ben reached his hands down my front and spread my legs apart before running his hands back up the front of my body while his mouth slid down the back of me. I gripped as best as I could on the wall as my back arched to him. Ben let his face wander down my while I felt fingers insert everywhere imaginable. The swollen parts of me were tender and sensitive but the rest craved each touch from him. Ben eased up on his kisses and I set my feet flat against the floor again, my heart sank knowing it was over. I turned to face Ben for some last kisses, he was still firm and pressing against me but I knew that the temptations would only make things harder to leave. Ben didn't have to be as heart broken, he seemed pretty secure knowing that it was all just a fling. I guess I just let myself love the lust, love the attention, and love the man I was finishing my shower with.

I finally pulled the pin, I told Ben the truth and all that was left was to finally say goodbye. I felt sick as I got dressed. I had to ask Ben to put a towel on because if he stood around naked much longer I would have never left. Ben told me that his next door neighbor lady saw me the one night and watched us through the window and expressed her interest in watching us again, in person. Ben was trying to excite me and it was tempting to stay but I just couldn't. Ben pulled a long sleeve shirt on over his head and finished watching me pull my clothes on as well. The flashes of his cute neighbor girl watching us began to turn me on, the notion of being watched while Ben took me like a large dog made me smile but the notion that I was liking it all over again gave me more reason to get going home.

Ben walked me to the door and we shared one last strong passionate kiss before I just turned around and left. If I would have tried to speak my voice would have cracked and the tears would have drowned me. The air was cool on my still damp skin and I could still taste Ben in my mouth as I climbed into my car. Ben stood at the door to watch me leave because he was a gentleman but I also think he might have been waiting for me to turn around and come running back to him and his arms, which I wanted to do so badly that my hands shook as they fumbled my keys.

The drive home was nearly impossible, each stop sign I came too seemed to be a godly sign to turn back around but I fought it. Each struggle to keep driving away from Ben had mixed feelings; I was proud of myself for going but angry that I couldn't stay. If I would have never started I would have never had to experience having to stop. If I had never given in to a momentary failure of my own self-control I wouldn't have to feel ashamed that I gave in but then again I wouldn't have the memories of Ben inside of me and the moments of pure bliss that came with what I did.

My street was dim, as if anything would have changed; I guess it better reflected me than I thought. My driveway was dark and devoid of any porch light for my safety, probably a sign from the universe to show me my husband's love for me, another reassuring sign that would change in my life. I was familiar with the routine, I was aware that it was going to remain the same as it had been but at least the brief fling with Ben gave me a sense of life once again, except I wanted to hold onto to it too hard and that was why I had to let it go. Maybe Ben and Lisa would get married and have their babies. Maybe Lisa would be enough to convince Ben to me monogamous and maybe he'd be enough for her to finally let herself fall in love with.

I could hardly sleep and was not even a little tired when I got home. I poured a drink and sat on my couch, even Bruno had no interest in being my company. The living room was dark and as I sat on the couch I just wanted James to come down the stairs and sit quietly with me as I sipped my drink and stared at some of the faint lights down the street, not to talk but for the company, the kindness, and for the reassurance that he did in fact still have a place in his heart for me. This was the moment I was going to set myself on the right track. I was either going to go upstairs or out the front door. I sat with misty eyes over everything I had let go of and continued sipping my drink. I wanted that long happy life, and I had it until I forgot how to be happy.

I wish I could call Erin and go and lay in bed with her for another week until I figured things out. I think one of the points where many things began to go wrong was at the cabin. A small crush to masturbate to is harmless, if someone gets your engine going you might as well give it a spin but to let someone else drive, that was definitely a big no-no. If I had just sat with James at the cabin and kept my head like I used to then maybe the crazy steamy hot self-session in the woods might not have enflamed my lust for Ben and maybe James and I would have gotten into our rhythm again, which may have been enough to fall back in love with him and then perhaps all of my heartache and sadness may have been prevented.

I felt comfortable in the darkness, I couldn't look at myself in the mirror, I didn't have to face up and responsible for risking my marriage and my home and my kids, I had the dark to comfort me and it covered over any reminder that I was me. If James had woken up and come down to sit with me I could have fallen in love with him all over again, I needed him and I wanted him, but he was not where I needed him; beside me. When James and I married we made our vows, and for sixteen years I held those vows as tightly as I held my baby children but in the last few months I began to slip. As I slipped James wasn't there to take my hand and guide me back to him but rather Ben was there to make me feel safe and okay and I was angry at him for that.

I had to touch Ben, I had to taste him, and I had to have him. I wanted to be loved and I needed to know that there was someone that could lust after me. I felt alone for a long time and even with James' quick hookups once or twice a month; there was no passion or romance. I hated that I became so needy for someone, I became pathetic. I used to rely on my independence and was secure in my marriage that I would never even glance outside the home, and yet I shared a bed with another man, and a shower, and his living room, my car, his front porch, his kitchen his bathroom, in fact I shared a lot with Ben, probably more than with any other person in my life.

I grew tired of feeling ignored, I may have been subtly angry that I felt unnoticed for a long time and perhaps somewhere in all of my thinking was the real answer why I sought Ben's company. Even Bruno was being a bum, I used to come home and he would be excited to see me, now he just stays sleeping somewhere up stairs and doesn't even care to come and greet me, why should he? I originally liked the idea of getting Bruno for myself and for the kids. Bruno kept me company during the light hours while the kids were transitioning to school and it was nice to have him as a jogging buddy before he learned how to fake being hurt or tired so I would go back home sooner.

Here comes the shame; my eyes began watering, the fuzzy dim lights down the road blurred to the point that just a glimpse of horizontal line streaked in my vision before a tear seeped out. When Ben touched me I felt eternity, I felt intensity and passion like I never knew had been missing from me. I was sad for myself that I had my eyes opened to what I could have had once and now all I could ever do was dream about what once was. I know I will forever miss Ben and everything I could have had in my life. Animals born into cages never remember having been free, wild animals only remember being free once and will always yearn to go back there. I felt like I was freed and now I'm trying to put myself back in my cage and my head and heart are trying to rip me into different directions.

Looking back to before I made the choice to fool around with Ben I'd say I felt like a caged animal for sure, sort of pacing because I had a feeling there could be more out there for me but I hadn't experienced it so I wasn't all that sure, but that was before I experienced Ben and all his beauty. Maybe this drink might make me too mushy soft and emotional, which isn't going to help me either but the numbing aspects kept me drinking. I need to cry out my issues, and I need to put my head back into my marriage again. I liked that James was trying for me, I guess he does work hard and does take plenty good care of me but I was still missing so much I didn't know about in my life.

I decided that after slowly sipping one good sized drink that chasing it with another (faster) was a necessary requirement to help me to reset my head and to rest overnight. The room was still dark as I returned with my glass to my big plush couch but after I adjusted I could just as easily navigate around the coffee table without bashing a toe or spilling. I could hardly make out any of the decorations or furniture I nested with but what was on my mind was Ben sliding down his pants the first night. I swallowed my drink rather quickly and decided that I was going to sit on the couch until the streetlights down the block blurred and forced my eyes shut for good. My head was heavy with both burden and drink, my skin began to feel warm and my eyelids slowly grew too heavy to hold open, and like that everything was completely dark.

The next morning came as early as usual but without my normal alarm to wake me. Bruno was nose to nose to wake me up and with a long lash of his rough tongue from my chin to my nose; I was greeted for the day. My head was groggy and now my mouth tasted like Bruno's, not an ideal start but it was the next day. My right eye felt permanently crossed as I pushed myself up from the couch, it took some vigorous rubbing to try to attempt to make sense of my surroundings. I have a blanket on me; I didn't have a blanket last night, why do I have a blanket on me?

I felt my own bedhead, I felt my head begin to pound as gravity pulled the blood back from my brain and the edges of my vision were cloudy. I buried my head in my hands and thought back over to the promises I made to myself, especially to do what I had to do to rebuild my marriage with James, whatever it takes. I looked up to the stairs to see James coming down, of course Bruno left me to go and get loving from him. Trying to wipe dog slobber from my dried mouth was enough to pull on my chapped lips, the small cracks stung and the dry skin to dry skin tugged on my lips a little.

James was pulling a shirt over his head as he slowly stepped down the stairs, his tones calves flexed with each step. James was looking muscular and he's been making good progress at firming up his tummy. I'll admit James was looking pretty good. I was still sad about my heart break but I tried to turn my attention on what I needed to do rather than on what I had done. "Late night?" James actually had interest in me and my night. I was shocked to find out that James noticed in the night that I wasn't in my place in the bed next to him and he came to find me. Usually I am in bed after him and gone from the bed before him so I was exceptionally impressed he even noticed my absence.

James found me lying on the couch, he missed me but rather than wake me, he covered me and let me continue sleeping before going back to bed. James and I really hadn't connected in weeks, not even much in the months, I knew why but I didn't know what James knew so I tried to just shy away. James sat next to me and began to ask how I was doing since Charlie passed and what else was going on at work. My guilt began to build up in my throat but I was also feeling extremely flattered that James was taking the notice in me again. James held out his hand for me to place my hand in his palm, my hand fit comfortably again and images of Ben were slowly crowded out by long years of marriage to James. James guided my up the stairs and tucked me into bed while assuring me that he had the kids covered so I could just bum in bed for the day if I needed some me time to figure things out.

I was bewildered, I couldn't recall the last time I had the warm feeling of love or affection toward my own husband. I felt terrible. I had been a horrible wife for weeks and barely even cared about it and here he is, getting the kids off to school so I could cuddle with my depression in my bed. I was in fact sad for losing Ben but I convinced myself that maybe returning to James as a rebound might indeed refill me with the love and passion I wished I had never lost for him. I heard the door shut as the kids headed off to catch the bus, the last few days of school were upon me and then I would have to shake off the ugliness and go back to full time mommy during the day, maybe that was what I needed.

I knew that no matter how my future was going to go it all mattered that I accepted everything behind me and put my best foot forward from here on out. My bedroom door opened to startle me, it wasn't Bruno but James, and he didn't go to work. "What are you doing?" I was confused and couldn't figure out why he was home. James neared the bed then swatted my rear; "scoot" he suggested as he lifted the covers to climb in with me. "It's been a very long time and I have missed you. The last few weeks have been a blur and we only have a few days left before the kids are out of school and then we're scrambling for months till they go back." James made plenty of sense and told me that he called in after he got the kids out the door to help around the house, or around under the covers with me.

James was wearing his basketball shorts and a t-shirt, he didn't make any efforts to cop a feel or grind against me as we cuddled. I missed his arms wrapped around me, they weren't Ben's large arms but his increase in strength was noticeable. I began to weep, I had spun so wildly out of control and was on the verge of destroying so much and then here I am, safely where I should have been the whole time. I sniffled and curled my head down to kiss the forearms that were wrapped around my chest, the arms I felt safe in once again. I let go of a lot of the aggression, a lot of the pain and hurt and regret that hung heavy in my head since Charlie passed away and I attributed it all to that one moment where I hit the ground in the cabin and then my weeks turned to an emotional blur.

I fell asleep in James' arms that morning. I don't know how he didn't lose feeling in his arm beneath me but his warm body held up against mine and his arms wrapped around me were an old familiarity that I had truly missed. I jerked awake sometime in the later morning to find that James had fallen asleep with me, something that hadn't happened in I don't know how long. I was filled with relief that James still seemed to love me, his breath on the back of my neck made the small hairs stick up and then my skin speckled with goose bumps but it was soothing.

To my surprise I was feeling turned on to James, I was aware of his body against mine and I could feel that I was letting go of some of my sadness about things. I wanted the comfort of intimacy from my husband so I began to rub my butt on James to arouse him. I was sad about Charlie passing and that should have made me seek comfort in the company of James but I sought refuge with Ben instead, sadly. I was craving the physical intimacy that is should be an unlimited blessing in a marriage and I was feeling playful enough to initiate things with James now. It hadn't even been twelve hours since I was engaged in extremely taboo and risqué things with Ben but I was feeling James' warmth against me and my desires turned me to him.

I was trying to keep the thoughts of Ben out of my head, all of the things he made me feel and things we did together will always be fodder to get myself over that hump to get off if I get stuck but for now I wanted to want my husband. It took me a few minutes of trying to awaken James before his warm breath on my neck was accompanied by a slight moaning. James began to rustle lightly behind me while I waited for him to take the hint of what I was doing to get him going but there was no feeling of *him* against me. I kissed on his arms while he began to kiss against the back of my neck while beginning to shuffle a little behind me. I worried that James might not be able to get going now that I was ready, I was even ready to go down on him to start things, even if there was a significant difference in equipment compared to Bens.

I felt my face smiling as I was anticipating special time with James in our bed, I half expected some disappointment but now that I had actually orgasmed with Ben, maybe James might actually be able to get me to the same peak. After a few minutes I still didn't feel James against me, I slowed my grinding since he wasn't getting aroused for me. "Give me one sec" James spoke up while he slid back out of the bed to duck into the bathroom for a minute. As James exited the bathroom there was no telltale toilet flush so I wondered if he ducked into his stash of steroids he kept in our medicine cabinet. I felt my face get warm with anger that he would shoot that shit up and then climb into bed with me. I tried to fight my urges to call him out, I wanted to just have him want me and be plenty glad about that but my anger raged inside of me.

It was hard to ignore what I knew, even though I was plenty guilty enough of adultery, he was still lying and hiding stuff from me also. "I know about your drugs" I couldn't help but blurt out as he slid under the covers with me. "It's prescribed" James assured me. According to James he went to see his doctor to get some help combating fatigue associated with his age and also wanted to be able to shed some weight and perform better with his wife, according to him. I was still angry but as I began to feel James against my leg I did my best to ignore my anger and focus on the man I married. For too long James just kissed my neck a bit, my mouth some and jarred against my with a finger to prepare me enough for him, it was a miserable routine and perhaps the biggest reason I detested having sex with my own husband, now James was kissing me passionately. I felt James rubbing against me through his shorts and my panties and rather than just run into things he seemed to be taking his time and enjoying me, it was a pleasant surprise.

James was performing like he was twenty-four again. I rode James for a short while and we wrestled back and forth for who was in control and making what moves. From the top view James was more tone, I watched as some of his stomach muscles flexed as he pumped away at me from lying down and he didn't all short of breath every two pumps either. James had a youthful energy and lust for me as he snarled and growled playfully while rooting his kissing lips against my neck, his newer strength was impressive (as was his stamina). I was impressed that James was once again a talented and gifted lover; things I thought were lost to the waves of time. I enjoyed James for the better part of the midday, his muscles flexed when he was on top of me and it was exciting for the first time in a long time.

James and I huffed and puffed from exhaustion as we lay in bed together like a husband and wife are supposed to. I was greatly relieved to feel normal towards him again even though I couldn't admit it or admit why. James felt in love with me, I was intrigued that his stamina had come back in spades and his ability to last through a few different positions for the benefit of both of us was eye opening. I brought up the steroids topic again and asked why he hadn't mentioned it at all before. James told me that after the blow up at the cabin and how much I expressed what I had hoped it would have been he gave in and made the doctor's appointment. I was relieved that he wasn't having affair and I put it from my mind that / did.

The kids came home shortly after James and I got done with our shower and I soaked up the fact that I got to have romantic time with my husband and then a long lovely weekend with my kids. The school year was days from ending so there was of course plenty of preparation, but I had my husband to help with that over the weekend, we were back.

The last week of school for the kids was a busy one, as it always each year. Things were normal at work, like good normal, like before I even met Ben kind of normal. It didn't move me to listen to Lisa describe more dates with Ben, I was broken hearted over him for the night and rebounding with my husband the next day so I was at peace with everything and I was feeling like I was right again in my life. I knew I should have probably talked to someone but who? Hannah was too stuck on herself to be bothered being a confidant while Lisa and Reagan were obvious no's and Gretchen would have understood but I didn't feel all that comfortable talking about this with her because it would have been way too ugly for the work place, I had no one to talk to. I thought about talking to Ben because there wasn't anything I couldn't have said to him, we even spoke about my husband not having the staying power to get the job done while we made love.

Ben understood, that was what drew me to him, that and a rippling body and a hypnotizing bulge between his legs that seemed to attract my eyes like a magnet. Ben listened to me whenever I spoke, I told him about why I called my period Doug and he didn't shutter like most men do when you mention sloughing off bloody clots and so on. Ben listened when I told him about missing Nick and his ambitious tongue between my legs or feeling free enough to ride around topless with him in the car. Ben even listened when I griped about James and his quick to bend me over for our date night romps and him being done in two minutes. Ben didn't get jealous that I spoke about being naked or kinky with another man, he liked me for me and even though I had to go home to my *HUSBAND* afterwards, he understood.

The day before the kids' last day of school Joy asked me again why James was around town so much, she wondered if he had perhaps lost his job but she didn't see him at home any more than usual, she just casually passed him in town here and thee. I was pestered to no end by Joy and her investigative reporting but there was that tiny insecurity in the back of my mind also. Of course since I cheated on my husband I knew exactly how easy it was to become a cheater and the notion of James cheating on my made my blood boil in my veins. I understood the irony of me cheating because James not giving me the attention I needed and yet I was profoundly furious at the notion that he was out sneaking around and slipping it into some floozy tart, I didn't care, I was pissed off.

I decided to hire a private investigator, I heed and hawed for a few minutes when I was looking up a number in my cellphone but as soon as I found a local guy, I was dialing before I realized it. It was petty and childish and I knew that my insecurity was purely based on my own indiscretion but I wanted to be sure in order to fully let go and move on in my marriage. I wanted to fully trust James, I really did. I wanted to go back to putting all of my faith in my husband especially since he wasn't the one with the dalliance that I knew of but I had to be sure. Joy was a nosy wretch and her little snipping at my trust in James was eating away at me. James came clean and admitted that he saw the doctor to get the steroids in order to be a better husband but I still couldn't help but to think that because he didn't bother to communicate with me about any of it that maybe there was indeed some tramp he was throwing it too on the side.

I hired a younger guy I looked up online, I wasn't entirely sure of what I needed so I went with what I found the cheapest and fastest. I couldn't own up or admit that I had anything to do with anything but it was worth three hundred bucks for the week. I met "Roger Boone" at a fast food restaurant where the kids could play and not pay much attention to my conversation. Roger was a lighter skinned man with short trimmed hair and he spoke eloquently with a deep voice. Roger introduced himself and we negotiated what exactly I was looking for. I wanted to know what James' day entailed for the course of a week and half way through we'd meet up to determine how the rest of the week would go; I had to know if he was in fact cheating or going to work when he said he was.

I was a nervous wreck when the kids were out of school for their first week. I had to know that James truly loved me and was faithful; I had to know that the foundation I built with him was solid and that I could let myself love him again. The first night to work after dropping the kids to a neighbor until James picked them up I pulled into work to notice Ben's jeep wasn't anywhere to be seen, I shouldn't have cared but I was saddened a little. It was tough not asking Lisa where he was because I didn't want to show that I had any interest but my mind was racing on the inside.

Lisa finally mentioned that Ben took another job somewhere and it brought a huge relief to me. I had that shadow of guilt follow me that I had let Ben completely hump my brains out but if James was in fact missing as much work as Joy had implied then why wasn't he either saying something or even coming home to surprise me? Oh shit, what if James had tried to come home and surprise me on the day I was out letting Ben use me in very vile (and fun) ways the day before work. My mind began to race to come up with excuses as to why I hadn't been home; I decided that I would use the excuse of my boss's wife's baby shower or something.

I felt a little conflicted, I hoped that Ben didn't leave the warehouse because of me but I also spent spared because I wouldn't have to see him each and every day and be reminded of what I had done. After a day I realized I was going to miss seeing Ben, sure the burden of guilt would be there but just like seeing a picture and remembering all of the details of that day, seeing Ben would take me back to us again and again.

Things started looking up, I was nervous to go and meet Roger but I also wanted to know everything there was to know about what he found over his few days. On a Wednesday Roger met me at the fast food restaurant again; he had a thick folder with him and it made me very nervous. I wanted to know how Roger was so stealthy to get the info he was getting and I will admit that the man was stunningly intelligent. The kids played and strangers passed on through as I prepared myself for what I was going to be hearing. Panic hit me as thoughts of divorce lawyers or other shady meetings filled my head, I even began to worry that maybe James hired a private detective of his own and already had photos of me and Ben and was making plans to end me.

"There is a redhead" was the first thing that Roger said. My eyes tried to roll into the back of my head and I immediately felt sick. My eyes welled up and my stomach began to churn as I grabbed onto the table for dear life. I thought about having been with Ben so there was absolutely no reason I should be hurt or upset, but I was. Words blurred and hummed in the background like busy traffic noise until my whitened vision came back too. Roger followed James to work after he left the gym and then hung out around the parking lot each day to see how the days went.

Roger would do plenty of walking and with no less than three different changes of clothes he posed as a student, a ragged guy just moseying around and on every other day, in his wife's car, he'd wear either a suit or different hats to better blend in to just being another person in the traffic. Roger spent one day panhandling by a door that lead to some offices, one of them was a lawyers building.

how to tell me but as he planned one last get away to the cabin then Charlie passed away. James tried several times to tell me but I was so beaten up and distant about Charlie that I didn't give him the opening so he decided to just tell me after our seventeenth wedding anniversary.

James was trying an experimental trial of using steroids to keep his strength up while the cancer took away his strength and libido. James didn't want to have his prostrate removed due to the risks involved, and besides, it was already in his pelvis. James bought the workout supplements to keep his energy up to spend a few hours a day learning to dance to the slow song I fell in love with that just came out where the guy serenades his girl on a stage. James wanted to have one big anniversary party and then one last night in a hotel room with me, using the side benefit of the steroids to keep up his ability to get an erection. James didn't want his prostate removed because he knew what it meant in regards to us having our married fun on our anniversary night, the doctor told him that the surgery wasn't worth the pain because the cancer had already made it into his pelvis bone and some other soft tissue so it was too late.

I thought my world was going to crash down around me before I found out everything, it turns out that because I was so busy focused on myself I became closed off and withdrawn. James found out about the progression and because the cancer was in his pelvis near his spine and major veins, it was truly only a matter of weeks before he was no longer with us. James took a medical leave from work to do everything he could to make sure that once he was gone, that myself and the kids were well taken care of. James wrote me a letter that he left with the estate lawyer he hired, apologizing that he didn't force himself to tell me sooner, that my unhappy withdrawn status might have meant that I already suspected something or that perhaps I was considering moving on, in which case he would understand and hope for all the best for me and my new life after him.

James told Erin earlier in the week but wanted her to help to get me to the hotel where he planned to have everyone we loved to spend our last anniversary with us. In the room was a brand new gorgeous red dress for me as well as plenty of make up to get dolled up for one last evening with the man I married nearly seventeen years ago. James knew that it was only a matter of days before his spine was attacked by the cancer and he wouldn't even be able to walk, let alone dance so he pushed up the date of our anniversary.

Erin loaned me some of her fun happy anti-depression pills to try to get through the evening as she helped to do my hair in my hotel room. Erin didn't leave my side and even though I seemed to float through the night and the rest of the weekend I couldn't really function. I died inside, I had nothing left and with everything hitting me with the force of an extinction causing asteroid, I just did my best to go with the flow. Erin made sure I didn't drink too much that I started sloppily blurting out what I had done after mixing alcohol and some medications. The numb feeling was welcomed after all of the stress I carried with me, I had been miserable and now it seemed better for the night.

James died three days after our early anniversary. The cancer weakened the lining of his femoral artery and he bled out in minutes as he slept, I found him with a large purple bruise on his lower back and abdomen when he wouldn't wake in bed. In his letter James spoke about moving on and being thankful that he had the life he had with me and how perfect it was from the very beginning. James took the time to make sure lawyers and funeral arrangements were squared away to save me the hassle. James spent hours reading books to the kids in front of a video camera so that after he passed away he could still read them stories and if the tapes survived they could play them for their own children.

I can't recall most of the week after James passed away because it was a blur, his parents helped significantly in keeping the kids in order and making sure that we were all taken care of. The magnitude of everything was like getting hit by an entire planet, the brutal force that came with the sudden death and my seeking comfort with Ben and the suspicion and hiring a detective, it all hit me over and over again, for months.

James was diligent to make sure that the house would be paid off and that his pension would pay enough that I could become a full time stay at home mom to raise our kids if that was the way I wanted to go for them. James made hours and hours of videos with the kids in the afternoons and also had some parents from the kids' soccer teams take lots of pictures of the two of us over the last few weeks when we were together as a family strolling in the parks. Some of the large wooden framed pictures slowly arrived to the house, beautiful oak framed gallery sized photos of us, many from past anniversaries but also new ones from us walking in the park, and each one made me relive everything over and over.

I spent weeks suffering over everything and the way it all happened. Tom and Laura were instrumental in helping to make arrangements for James and after the third week of being completely devastated, I decided it was time to begin counseling to figure out how the rest of my life was going to go from here.